How to Get into Our House and Where We Keep The Money

Also by Panio Gianopoulos

A Familiar Beast

How to Get into Our House and Where We Keep The Money

Stories

Panio Gianopoulos

Four Way Books
Tribeca

Please direct all inquiries to:
Editorial Office
Four Way Books
POB 535, Village Station
New York, NY 10014
www.fourwaybooks.com

Library of Congress Cataloging-in-Publication Data

Names: Gianopoulos, Panio, author.
Title: How to get into our house and where we keep the money / Panio Gianopoulos.
Description: New York, NY : Four Way Books, [2017]
Identifiers: LCCN 2017000678 | ISBN 9781945588020 (pbk. : alk. paper)
Classification: LCC PS3607.I2245 A6 2017 | DDC 813/.6--dc23
LC record available at https://lccn.loc.gov/2017000678

2nd printing, 2017
This book is manufactured in the United States of America and printed on acid-free paper.

Four Way Books is a not-for-profit literary press. We are grateful for the assistance we receive from individual donors, public arts agencies, and private foundations.

This publication is made possible with public funds from the New York State Council on the Arts, a state agency.

We are a proud member of the Community of Literary Magazines and Presses.

Distributed by University Press of New England
One Court Street, Lebanon, NH 03766

For Molly

Contents

Another Life

"So tell me," Hayden asked the detective, leaning across the table. "How do you know when someone is lying to you?"

Except for an initial flash of unease, visible in the brief widening of her eyes, Deena was careful not to react.

"I don't do interrogations anymore," the detective said. He separated a leaf of baby gem lettuce with a smooth, heavy-handled knife. "I went private a few years ago."

"But you still talk to people," Hayden said.

"Most of what I do is online. Things like insurance fraud, background checks. It's not as glamorous as—"

"Listen to him being modest," Rachel interrupted. "He's not telling you that they ask him to consult on television shows." Since her husband had left her a year earlier, Rachel had paraded a series of impressive and exotic suitors by her friends. And while Deena understood the instinct, particularly at a dinner hosted by Hayden and his wife and attended by their long-married couple friends, she wished she'd been warned of the detective's attendance that evening. It was irrational, she knew, but she felt exposed sitting beside him, with her husband, Stephen, only a few seats away.

Hayden's persistent line of questioning wasn't helping either. "How about before you switched over to the private sector," he asked the detective. "Come on, let's hear some tricks of the trade. Human nature hasn't changed in a few years."

The detective blinked his narrow-set eyes. He was tall and lean and capable looking, but there was something vaguely off-balance about him, like a chair you don't know is broken until you sit on it.

"Come on," Hayden prodded. "What are the tells?"

"Let the man enjoy himself," Hayden's wife said. "I apologize for my husband's enthusiasm," she told the detective with a warm practiced smile that dimmed as her eyes briefly met Hayden's.

"It's fine, I don't mind talking about it," the detective said. "Thing is, it's all over the place. Some people stare you in the eyes when they lie to you. Some people look away. Some make up crazy details. Others keep it simple."

"Like me," Rachel said. She raised her arm up and then quickly withdrew it, giggling. The women all laughed.

"The really good ones, though, the *great* liars," the detective said, "all have one thing in common."

Deena gestured to one of the young catering staff to bring more wine. The girl's outfit was messy, her white button-down shirt escaping in the back, as if she'd been dressed for church by a parent and untucked it again once out of sight. She refilled Deena's glass, then pivoted to refill the detective's. On impulse, Deena reached up and, keeping her hand out of sight, intentionally jostled the girl's elbow. The girl pitched forward, losing control of the bottle. Red wine gushed over the detective's hand and sleeve.

"Be careful!" Hayden's wife shouted.

"Oh my God, I'm so sorry," the girl said.

As the rest of the catering staff hurried to clean up the spill, the girl darted out of the dining room, her face crumpling, tears in the corners of her eyes.

"Excuse me," Hayden's wife said to the table before she turned and stalked into the kitchen to deal with the staff. Deena picked up her glass and sipped her wine. A moment later, muffled scolding could be heard through the walls. Hayden nodded along to the piano concerto tinkling out of tastefully inconspicuous speakers. Then his wife reemerged, looking refreshed, her lips pursed with satisfaction. She had the posture of a new, triumphant skyscraper. She was one of those happily embattled people for whom conflict is a vivifying agent. Deena had always envied this capacity for strife in people. She was the type that preferred tranquility—until three months ago.

"So what is it?" Hayden asked the detective.

"What's what?" the detective said.

"The thing all great liars have in common."

"Oh," the detective said. He glanced down at his stained right shirt cuff. It looked like a birthmark someone was tired of hiding. With his left hand, he slipped free the button and rolled up the cuff. "They can't help themselves."

Halfway through dessert, Deena's phone began to vibrate. She discreetly removed it from her clutch and read the message under the table.

Call me

She glanced to her right. Her husband, Stephen, was talking with the detective. She typed her response in a flurry of thumbs.

Can't at a dinner

There's a car here that reminds me of u

Car?

**cat*

What r u doing with a cat? Deena typed.

Admiring it

Grinning, Deena switched off her phone and slipped it back into her small purse. When she looked up, she saw Hayden watching her.

"Everything all right with the babysitter?" he said pointedly. When he smiled, his upper lip exposed his crooked canine.

"Yes, yes," Deena said. "All good."

Her phone buzzed again. Deena commanded herself not to answer it. But as her phone continued buzzing, the urge to check grew stronger, almost irresistible, like the cry of a baby in another room.

"I just have to make a quick call to the sitter," she said.

Stephen looked over from his conversation with the detective. "You should tell her not to bother us unless it's an emergency," he said.

"She's new," Deena reminded her husband pleasantly, pushing back her chair and reaching for her purse. "Excuse me, I'll be right back."

With a fake smile affixed to her face, she strolled down a long hallway flanked by black-and-white portraits of Hayden and his blond family. She passed a meticulously organized media room, a salon choked with marble, an exercise room, the locked door to a supplementary pantry, until at last she found the second guest bathroom and ducked inside.

"I told you I can't talk," she said into her phone, flush with happiness. The wallpaper and the towels were the color of pink coral, the fixtures delicate and off-white. It looked like the inside of a giant's mouth.

"This would be a lot more fun if you were here," Alec said. At the sound of his voice, she felt her cheeks grow hot. His lilting British accent was no less appealing for its predictability.

"Hang on," Deena whispered and opened the bathroom door to be sure she was alone. She had sensed correctly—there was a sound coming from the laundry room across the hall. Deena peered inside, past the half-open door, and saw the girl who had spilled the wine. She was hunched on a foldout chair, sorting cloth napkins. "Are you all right?" Deena asked. The girl shrugged. Her eyes were red from crying. She was even younger than Deena had first thought, almost a teenager, and her relationship with embarrassment possessed the intensity of new love.

"Deena?" Alec said.

"I'm sorry," Deena mouthed to the girl and hurried back to the guest bathroom. She locked the door behind her and, leaning her hip against the deep sink, raised the phone to her ear. "I'm here."

"That's the problem, love, isn't it. How long until you're free?"

"This might go really late."

"I don't care. No more no-shows."

"Don't you have the cat to keep you company?" She caught herself smiling in the mirror.

"Kitty ran off when the place filled up with shrieking women. How is this Malibu? Is it always tipsy mums in yoga pants?"

Deena laughed loudly, eager to confirm that she wasn't one of those sad women—unaware, embarrassing, irrelevant. "Shit, I have to go," she whispered. "I'm taking too long. I'll call you after the dinner gets out."

"I believe we were talking about a visit."

"One of us was."

She opened her clutch, dropped her phone in, and snapped it shut. Then she ran the faucet for a few seconds, needlessly rubbing her hands beneath the cold stream of water. She was glad she had been the one to end the call. After drying her hands with one of the pink towels, she bared her teeth in the mirror, turning her head left and right to check her molars. Satisfied, she exhaled and reached for the door handle: back to normal. But then, just as she was about to open the door, she impulsively snatched her phone back out of her purse and texted Alec to meet her at 11 p.m.

When she stepped outside, she was surprised to find Hayden there. He was standing in the middle of the hallway. He held a tumbler loosely in front of him, as if searching for a surface to set it upon.

"Hey," Deena said.

"Next time run the water *while* you're talking," Hayden said.

"I'm sorry, what . . ."

He pressed the glass to his mouth, his tongue blocking the ice. "Deena," he said, after swallowing, "It's me."

She stared at him as blankly as she could. A week before, Hayden had run into her and Alec in a café on Abbott Kinney. She'd invented something about a nonprofit project, but it was obvious Hayden had been unconvinced: he'd called her an hour later, which she ignored, along with all of the subsequent texts.

Now he finally had her cornered, and she thought she saw a flash of predatory delight in his eyes. For a moment, Hayden resembled the lean, handsome youth he'd been when they had met as fresh new assistants at the talent agency and struck up a friendship based on a mutual dread of their horrible bosses. It had been a corporate culture of cruelty, exploitation, and betrayal, and though they only lasted two years before leaving—first the agency, later the industry—the experience had forged a bond between them that a decade and a half of irregular friendship had failed to erode.

Now, Hayden was no longer an excitable boy but a shrewd, hollow-eyed man, with gray streaks in his hair and a perpetually bemused gaze. He lifted the tumbler again to his fleshy lips. "Keep it face to face," he warned. "Texts, emails, posts—it's the digital trail that gets people in trouble these days."

"I don't know what you're talking about."

He reached past Deena and flicked off the bathroom light. This close to him, she could smell the bourbon on his breath, wooden and opaque, like a flower made of smoke. "I'm trying to help you," he said. "You're giving yourself away left and right. If you were any more revealing you'd be a thong."

"I have to get back to dinner."

He leaned his hand against the wall blocking her exit. "Deena. I'm not your husband's friend. I'm yours."

She ducked under his arm and quickly headed down the hall. She heard him murmur something under his breath and then laugh, for her benefit, she supposed. She hurried on without turning around and closed the heavy wooden hallway door deliberately behind her.

During the drive home, while Stephen silently steadied the car along the black curves of the Pacific Coast Highway, Deena wondered if she ought to have come clean to Hayden. Despite his smirk and his insolence, she did trust him. He would never expose her. But as desperately as she wanted to unburden herself, it seemed an additional betrayal to tell a man about it. What she needed was a girlfriend, someone to whom she could open up without risk of judgment. But her friends had all moved away over the years, to New York, to Seattle, to Austin and Vancouver and even Hong Kong. The exodus had happened gradually, and it wasn't until these three frenzied, disorienting months of seeing Alec that Deena realized just how isolated she had become. Even with Lucy, her closest friend, who still came back from Chicago once a year to visit, things between them were not like they had been. Nor did it help that Lucy's husband had cheated on her with his assistant and almost left Lucy for the girl. They'd gotten through it with couples counseling and were ostensibly stronger now, but Deena couldn't bear to bring all that up again—worse, to play the role of the ruthless home-wrecker that Lucy had once railed against. Of course, her own situation was very different, Deena reasoned. Alec was in his midthirties, far from the impressionable twenty-something girl that Lucy's husband had deceived Lucy with; there'd be no pregnancy scare to turn the whole thing inside out (Deena was vigilant about birth control); and most of all, she wasn't seriously flirting with escape, the way Lucy's husband had—this was diversionary, not destructive. Deena had a handful of other arguments on hand to defend what she was doing, but ultimately they all relied on the same fundamental premise, which is that she was a good person doing a bad thing.

But what if that were untrue?, Deena wondered What if, instead, she was a bad person who had spent her life doing good things?

Of the three children in her family, Deena had always been the good one. She took pride in this assignment from a young age—there is a home movie where she's standing in the background, shaking her head with four-year-old disapproval, while her older brothers wrestle over, then break, a giant candy cane—and the familial designation of virtue carried itself to school and out into the world at large. There were minor lapses, naturally, as she got older, and a predictable swerving toward relationships with men who were anything but good. But her defiance was only by proxy, and short lived. When it came time to settle down, she married a man as sensible, prudent, and respectable as his antecedents had been impractical, wild, and disreputable. Her brothers, meanwhile, continued to thrive on self-interested provocations she gradually learned to conflate with masculinity. That old tired division of virtue, with women as the civilizing, enlightening influence, was slowly pushed into her heart like a thick, stupid needle.

Not that Deena blamed her husband for the affair. An unusually decent man, he responded with sympathy when, barely a year into their marriage, Deena lost all interest in sex. Deena's mother had abruptly passed away, and so Deena let Stephen assume it was grief that had shut her off, but the truth was she had been faking it for months already. Now, at last, she had an incontestable excuse that let her put sex entirely on hold.

After six months, however, Stephen's patience began to fray. He pushed her to find a solution ("It's for your sake, too, Deena—don't you want to be happy?") but nothing could banish the sexual listlessness. Medication, meditation, massage, therapy, pornography, masturbation, marijuana . . . she tried them all, and while something might work a couple times, inevitably things would return to the way they had always been. With each failure, Stephen grew increasingly irritated, until his sulky frustration became more unbearable than the act itself, and depleted by guilt, Deena relented. Pretending that her problem had miraculously vanished, she gave up on being sexually excited, let alone fulfilled, and faked a renewed interest. She was a mediocre actress but her husband didn't care; if it was authentic chastity versus inauthentic sex, he was decidedly for the latter, and once a week he would eagerly climb on top of her and kiss her neck and squeeze her breasts with routine attentiveness and then, shifting his weight onto his left forearm—always the left side—he would reach down and put himself inside her, while she feigned pleasure.

It was a disheartening surrender, gloomy in its banality. Before Stephen, sex had been an escape from tedium, the one place where she could divert herself from obedient practicality, but now it had been recruited as just another tool of the obligatory and the dull. Viva marriage! Soon enough, at least, she would get pregnant with their first child and have the pregnancy to hide behind. After that, there was a year and a half of postpregnancy recovery, then young parent fatigue, followed by a second pregnancy, more parenting exhaustion, a cycle of unobjectionable concealment and withholding that went on for almost nine years.

And then, while attending an art show with Lucy during her annual LA visit, Deena met Alec. He was from London, and had a foreigner's easy amiability, that dreamlike distance, as if nothing happening in this country was too real. He asked Deena a question about a painting, and she confessed that she didn't know much about art.

"I thought I was the only one," he said. "I just came here tonight to try something different." They drank themed cocktails from clear cups while she plied him with a series of questions, to avoid talking about herself. He had recently embarked on a year of experimentation, he told her, inspired by his father's death last May. "He never did anything but work. Travel, hobbies, all of it saved for later. There was no later." After the funeral, an old friend who had moved to LA offered to put him up for a few months. Among other pursuits, Alec was trying to develop senderball, a beach sport he'd invented one summer with friends. "It's like volleyball, but the net's on the outside, like a boxing ring. And it's one against one."

"How is it going?" Deena asked.

She was surprised to hear that it was a struggle. He seemed capable of just about anything, but then a single man untethered by responsibility and in pursuit of his passions has a confidence that can easily be mistaken for achievement. She was confusing freedom with success.

"Attendance will pick up," Alec said. "I started an email list for announcing exhibition matches."

"Nothing excites sports fans more than getting an email."

He grinned. "Fair enough. Still, what's the alternative? Not doing it?"

"Yes," said Deena, laughing. "That's *precisely* the alternative. Not doing it is the mantra of every married person I know."

Lucy came back from circling the room and took them on a guided tour of the exhibit. "To be honest, her last show was stronger," Lucy whispered, as the three of them drifted past giant red gouache scrawls. "This all feels a bit recycled. You know? Like I've been here before."

"You're crazy. It's amazing," Deena said. She was halfway through her third cocktail, that ideal moment of intoxication when happiness and hopefulness rattle in the glass like ice cubes. In truth, the art on the walls was simple and obvious, but drunkenly flanked by her lost best friend and this cute, earnest foreigner, she found the boldness of the paintings charming. For a moment, it seemed that perhaps life wasn't about restraint—that it could be more than not yelling at the children, not buying the dress, not going back to bed in the morning, not drinking a fourth glass of wine, not skipping the gym, not eating pasta, or pizza, or a cheeseburger (*always* it was the salmon, she ate more salmon than a fucking bear), not honking at the stopped car ahead of her, not ignoring the obnoxious parent at the school meeting: for a moment it seemed that life could *be* something instead of the avoidance of a thing.

Hardly a surprise, then, that just before leaving the party, she handed Alec her email address, scrawled on a cocktail napkin. "For your superball group," she explained. He didn't correct her, just smiled and slipped the folded napkin into his pocket. A week later, she received a group email about an introductory senderball match slated for the dead hours between drop-off and pick-up at her children's school. After managing to get her stylist to squeeze her in for a highlight, she drove to the beach. When she arrived at the volleyball courts, however, Alec wasn't there. Deena shifted her feet in the sand and raised a hand to shield her eyes against the noonday light. Scanning the terrain beyond the empty nets, she saw only strolling couples, tourist families, and twenty-year-old girls tanning in caramel batches. She checked her watch: 12:47 p.m. Maybe the game was quick and she'd missed it.

When she turned to head back to the footpath, she spotted Alec stepping out of the ocean. Deena almost didn't recognize him as he emerged onto land. His hair was redder than she remembered, and his bare shoulders were wide, his chest broad and muscled. He moved across the sand with an easy agility. As he came closer, she was perversely relieved to see he had a small belly, like a soccer player who had gone slightly to seed.

She apologized for missing the game, and he told her that she hadn't, that he had rescheduled it for tomorrow.

"I would have sent an update but no one's ever shown up to watch before," Alec said.

Her embarrassment and unease at having come, the foolish solicitousness of it, made her blush. She quickly accepted his offer to take her to lunch, before she could change her mind.

They walked to the nearby beach café. It was the middle of the week, and the café was full of tourists in brightly colored shorts and tee shirts. Deena ordered a chicken Caesar salad without the croutons.

"But those are the best bits," Alec said.

"They're just bread."

"They're the crunch."

"The lettuce crunches."

"Bring the croutons," Alec told the waitress. "She's going to change her mind."

After a few minutes, their drinks arrived. Deena swapped her iced tea for white sangria.

"I'm taking a page out of your book," she said. "Trying something different."

"Have you never had sangria?"

"Oh sure," she said. "Just not at lunch."

When he laughed, deep curved lines appeared in his cheeks, like parentheses, enclosing his smile. Deena fished out a segment of peach with her fingers and bit it in half.

"May I?" Alec asked.

Deena slid her drink forward. He pushed aside the straw to drink directly from the lip of the glass.

"Too sweet," he said.

"You love it. Don't pretend."

"Am I that obvious?"

She smiled and raised the glass to her mouth to stop herself from saying more.

It was the first of a series of lunch dates, what playing hooky from high school must have felt like, had she been the type, and though they talked for hours about their lives and texted when apart, by some unspoken agreement they never discussed what they were doing together. It was important that they feign ignorance about where they were headed, and one Sunday afternoon, while Stephen was away on another of his work trips and after she dropped off both children at birthday parties, Deena stopped by Alec's house in Venice. It was her first time seeing the tiny guest cottage he rented on the back of another British expat's property. He offered to give her a tour. This meant standing in the center of the living room and turning around in a slow circle while saying kind things about furniture that didn't belong to him. The wireless radio in the kitchen was playing music she liked but hadn't heard in years, and when the DJ interrupted the song to announce it was a nineties station, she realized her youth was now a genre.

They went back outside, past a fruitful eruption of lemon and fig trees. Alec unlatched the gate that led to the pool.

"It's salt water, which makes you more buoyant, so it takes greater effort to stay under," Alec told her. His newest passion was free diving, swimming underwater without a scuba tank or snorkel, just the power of a single held breath. He had trained himself to last up to three minutes. After enduring weeks of Alec's evangelizing, Deena had agreed to try it, but before she headed out into open waters, Alec told her she would have to practice in a swimming pool first. He waded into the water up to his hips and reiterated the safety protocols. He would keep time and tap her on the shoulder periodically to ensure that she was still conscious. If she failed to respond with the okay signal, he would pull her out.

“Not that that’s going to happen,” he said. “It’s quite safe.” He glanced over at her standing at the edge of the water in a striped blue maxi dress, a pair of leather and rope sandals threading her feet. “Where’s your bathing suit?”

“Inside.”

She turned and walked toward the cottage.

With her back to him, she heard him pull himself out of the pool. Then came the sound of his feet padding along the grass behind her. She slipped out of her dress and dropped it on the ground under the bougainvillea growing wild over the doorway.

Stephen switched off the ignition and stepped out of the car, careful to apply the emergency brake before locking the doors. As they walked up the driveway to the house, Deena loomed over him in her heels. On impulse, she reached over and ruffled the thinning hair on the back of his head. The prospect of seeing Alec had imbued her with a secondhand, indiscriminate affection, one that her husband, of course, misinterpreted as arousal. He paid the babysitter and, after the kitchen door had swung shut, reached for Deena’s hand, tugging her toward the bedroom.

“I have to go to the supermarket,” Deena said, twisting in his grip.

“Now?”

“The kids don’t have anything for school lunch tomorrow.”

“So go in the morning.” He leaned in and wrapped his arms tight around her waist, trapping her.

“There won’t be time.”

“Don’t they sell lunch at school?” he asked, biting at her neck. She felt like an apple being nibbled by a deer. “Dee-na . . .” he sang. Through the screen windows, she could smell the white evening primrose in the flowerbeds, beautiful and funereal.

“I’ll be right back,” she said, slipping free of his embrace.

Holding her heels in one hand, she barely suppressed the urge to sprint to the car. She forced herself to slowly exit the driveway though what she wanted was to stomp on the accelerator, to press the rubber and metal pedal flush against the floor and hear the tires shriek in excited submission. But there was only so much indulgence she could allow herself. Flicking on the headlights, she nosed the car onto the dark, quiet street, sliding past the dimmed faces of the neighborhood homes. The once-modest houses had been rising in value year after year—the most recent lot had gone for 2.2 million, a teardown at that—and the older couples were all selling, moving away, replaced by younger, more ambitious version of themselves.

At the intersection with the main road, Deena turned left and began to climb the mile-long hill that led, eventually, to the strip of stores that made up the local shopping center. Boutiques mingled among upscale hair salons, Pilates studios, and organic juice bars. At this hour they were all shuttered. She spotted Alec standing outside the pharmacy. He was wearing a blue-striped Ben Sherman windbreaker with sleeves half an inch too short for him. She pulled up next to the curb.

The tallow-colored light inside the car flashed when Alec opened the door. Deena hastily reached up to switch it off.

"Keep the light on, darling," Alec said, "I don't believe I've ever seen you dressed up before."

"Funny." Deena motioned for him to hurry up and get in. She didn't want a neighbor to drive past and recognize her.

"I mean it—you look stunning." He fell awkwardly into the seat, his body turned to face her. He reached out and batted at her earring. "Like a very expensive cocktail."

"You're drunk," she said.

"Doesn't discredit the observation," he said and twisted the hair at the nape of her neck, sending a shiver down her back. He ran his other hand flat along her ribcage, slipping the tips of his fingers under her bra. She could hear his breathing speed up, could almost feel him expanding to fill the space.

"There's not enough time to go to your place," Deena warned him, subtly raising her shoulder.

"Are you certain?"

She nodded. "Let's just drive around for a few minutes."

They advanced slowly down the avenue. Imported palm trees lined the modest roadside park, a skinny strip of grass where affluent housewives met with their personal trainers. Some mornings, there were so many assembled that passersby had to cross the street, and the city had begun threatening to levy a tax.

After a mile and a half, Deena made a U-turn and headed back the way they had come.

"You can just leave me on the corner," he said and gestured for her to pull over.

"Here? Don't you want me to drop you off at your car?"

Alec shook his head. "I sold it a few days ago."

"Why?"

"I'm broke." He laughed. "Doesn't matter, darling. I can walk to the beach."

She pulled onto a side street and let the car drift to a stop along the curb. There were no streetlights lit, and the trees further concealed them. The engine idled softly as they sat in silence. She knew she should go home, but she also knew that as soon as she did, she would regret leaving. What she had wanted all night was this feeling, the two of them together in the dark, in the insulated containment of the vehicle, untethered from her ordinary life. It was the root of ecstasy, as Deena recalled from a Latin class she took in college, to exist out of time, *ex stasis.*

She switched off the ignition.

"I thought you had to go home," Alec said.

"Shut up," she said, and reached for him.

*

Deena turned her body sideways to slip through the half-closed bedroom door. Stephen was asleep in bed, snoring, the open laptop glowing on his lap like a magical oyster in a children's fable. Delicately, Deena lifted the computer from him and placed it on the bedside table. As she went to shut it down, she noticed the perilous white pearl of text nestled in the search bar:

How do I find someone?

Oh God, she thought. Was Stephen tracking her? Her stomach spasmed at the thought of him knowing she'd spent the last half hour in her window-fogged car with Alec. Seized by dread, she stood paralyzed on the carpet, staring at her sleeping husband, waiting for the moment when he would spring awake and let loose his rage and indignation, a furious bedside reckoning part exorcism, part damnation.

Only it didn't come. Stephen simply slept, as stolid as ever, and after a few long minutes of queasy observation, Deena retreated to the shower. Closing her eyes, she ducked her head under the stream of hot water. Southern California had been in a drought for years now, signs urging conservation littered the roads, but she let the water pour over her without end. She was afraid to get out. She felt marked, as if every touch of Alec's had left a secret incandescent print on her skin.

In the morning, she woke early and prepared the kids for school, hoping to hide in domesticity. Just as they were about to leave, Stephen came downstairs, his laptop tucked under his arm, the way men of other generations had carried a newspaper or toolbox. He spooned himself a bowl of steel-cut oatmeal and stared at his phone while the children hugged his legs.

"The kids have a karate belt test this afternoon!" Deena announced, trying to sound lighthearted and upbeat and innocently maternal, forgetting that every mother she knew spent half of her waking hours annoyed by her family. Glazed cheerfulness was far more suspicious than weariness.

"Can you come watch us?" their daughter asked.

Stephen shook his head. "Sorry."

"You *never* come," she snapped.

"Your mother'll be there," Stephen said.

"Mommy's always there," their son said.

Stephen looked up from his phone, an inscrutable expression on his face. "That's because your mother gets to have all the fun."

Stephen wasn't above the occasional dig about being the sole breadwinner—even though he was the one who had urged her to quit her job to raise the children—but coming on the heels of last night's online search, his comment seemed more than just a reflexive jab.

All day, Deena brooded over whether or not he knew. Her anxiety ratcheted itself to such heights that by the time of the children's karate practice, she gave in and turned to Hayden for help. He attended his son's classes unfailingly—real estate development and a wealthy wife allowed for flexible work hours—and after the children had scampered into the wood-paneled dojo, Deena pulled him aside. She told him everything with feverish speed. "Don't worry," he whispered, ushering her over to the corner of the viewing area, so that they could talk while watching the children perform their silly, sincere rituals of bowing and punching and kicking. "If Stephen knew anything for sure, he'd have said something."

"What if he's biding his time?" Deena said. "Gathering evidence? I saw him talking to that detective at dinner."

"So don't give him any evidence," Hayden said. "End things now and there'll be nothing for him to find. You're home free."

"You're telling me to stop?" The last thing she had expected, when reaching out to Hayden, was prudence. "I don't know if I can. I mean, yes, it's reckless and selfish," she said, "but what if it's . . . the real thing?"

"Deena, you know better than that."

"I don't know what I know. From the start we've had this connection that's only grown stronger."

"That's called sex."

"It's more than that."

"Don't underestimate the power of intrigue, either."

"But what if I'm in *love*?"

"Love is great," Hayden said and rubbed her shoulder. "As excuses go, love is unbeatable. But that's not what this is."

"I shouldn't have brought it up," Deena said with irritation. "Forget I said anything."

"I know what you're going through. You're at the point where you want to hide. Pretend it never happened." His gaunt eyes grew big and bright. "But you're better now, not worse. The way ice cream tastes better after it's melted a little, lost some of its hardness. Men are the same way."

"You mean women."

Hayden smiled. "Isn't that what I said?"

Deena jerked back when she heard the loud slap. Then she saw the boy, Hayden's son, smacking the glass separating the parents from the children. Beside him were her two children, mimicking him as they battered the divider. She waved at them, and then all three children hurried away in muted delight. Once class recommenced, Hayden urged her, again, to put an end to things with Alec. "The only reason you've gotten away with it is because Stephen hasn't suspected. As soon as he starts looking . . ."

"It's not that easy to end it," Deena said, staring out at the children as they punched the air with joyful insignificance. "I can't just stop feeling what I'm feeling."

"Well you're going to caught if you don't. You're making every mistake in the book. You probably haven't even deactivated remote location in your phone."

"What's that?"

Hayden took out his cell phone and navigated to a Web browser. "If Stephen has your log-in info, he can find you by searching for your phone online. Watch." He called up a website and prompted Deena to enter her ID and password. Once she did, a map of Southern California materialized. A blinking blue dot scrolled across the screen, gradually settling to a stop among a series of local streets. When she clicked on the dot, "Family Dragon Dojo" appeared in a box, appended with contact information and hours of operation.

Deena gasped. She pulled the phone out of his hands. "Does it record my history?"

"No, it's only a current reading. But your car does. So that's another thing you have to be careful about—never use GPS if you're going somewhere you don't want recorded." Hayden raised an eyebrow for effect. "The subterfuge required for infidelity these days is unbelievable. Between browser histories, email, GPS, online banking and social media, it's easier to sell state secrets than to get away with an affair."

"Where is this?" Deena said.

"Where's what?"

Deena pointed to the screen. Out of curiosity, she had logged out of her account and reentered with Stephen's credentials. Only instead of showing her husband's downtown LA office, the blinking blue dot had surfaced in Culver City.

"I think that's near the Sony lot," Hayden said. "Just off the 405."

She pressed the blue dot. A box popped up. Inside it, in tiny white letters, were the words: *Detective Owen Stevens, Private Investigations.*

The next day, Deena deactivated the GPS in all of her devices, scrubbed her online search history, and switched phone carriers to wipe out the call logs. To further minimize the risk of exposure, she told Alec they shouldn't see each other until the detective had completed his investigation.

"That's bollocks," Alec said.

"I don't like it either but—"

"You can't be serious."

"Assuming he just started today, it'll take a couple weeks and then he'll—"

"A couple what?"

"Weeks," she repeated, louder this time. She had called Alec from what looked like the last remaining pay phone in the world, a vandalized half booth in a 7-Eleven parking lot on Lincoln Avenue. "He'll give up after he doesn't find anything."

"Find what?" Alec said.

"Anything!" she shouted into the cracked black handset.

It was a sensible plan, and though she was the one who had initiated it, within a week, Deena was miserable, barking at the children for trivial infractions. Even Stephen remarked upon it.

"You're sure you're okay?" he asked again, on Sunday night, after the kids had fallen asleep. "Because you seem—"

"I'm fine," she hissed, angry at herself for her irritability but angrier still at her husband for his interference. Why hadn't he realized that their marriage had been better off when she was still seeing Alec? She was a better wife after she spent time with him, the happiness made her kinder and the guilt made her patient. But now she was a mess: cranky, impulsive, quick to take offense. While on the phone with Lucy the night before, Deena had snapped at her friend for calling her a bad mother.

"Relax, it was a joke," Lucy said.

"It's not funny."

"Everybody knows *I'm* the one who's a terrible mom. Jack's first word was iPhone, that's how often I gave him the damn thing."

Deena let out a laugh, but the sound caught in her throat.

"Are you okay?"

"I'm fine," Deena said, though suddenly she found herself crying.

"What's wrong?"

"Nothing."

"Nothing nothing? Or nothing you want to talk about nothing?"

"I don't know." Deena blew the air out of her mouth deliberately as though she were blowing out a candle. It was a trick that she had learned as a child to stop herself from crying.

"Does this by any chance involve that British guy we met at the art show?"

Deena didn't say anything for a moment. "What . . . British guy?"

"Let's see: the guy you recently friended on Facebook, followed on Twitter, and liked every picture of on Instagram?"

Deena sighed. "I fucking hate social media."

"How serious is this?" Lucy said. "And does Stephen know?"

"I think he suspects. But before you tell me I have to come clean—"

"Do *not* come clean," Lucy said. "It's a terrible idea."

"But shouldn't . . ." Deena trailed off, confused. "When you guys were going through it—"

"I know, I wanted to know everything. But that was then. Now? I'd take ignorance. Because the knowing never goes away."

Deena pressed her thumb into the base of her jaw, massaging the tight, knotted muscles. Most nights, she was so unhappy she could barely sleep. "I wish you didn't live so far away," she said.

"Me too."

"I miss when we were little," Deena said. "Don't you miss that?" She felt her eyes burn again with tears. This time she didn't try to stop them and just let them fall, darkening the front of her blouse. "Remember the time you rolled the watermelon into the ocean to see if it would float?"

"Yeah," Lucy said. "It was supposed to!"

"It must have cracked before it reached the water," Deena said.

The next day, Deena burst through Alec's front door, nearly knocking him over.

"Close the blinds!"

He watched her blinking and confused as she darted around the cottage lowering the dusty window treatments. "Can I ask why you're—"

"The *detective,*" Deena said. "He's driving the same black Prius I saw parked outside the post office yesterday." She twisted the spindly wooden rod that angled shut the blinds on the bathroom window. "When I spotted him behind me on Lincoln, I cut across two lanes of traffic, stranding him at the light. Then I came down the back way and parked in the alley. But we have to block off all the windows in case he's canvassing the area."

"The cottage is behind the house," Alec said. "It's completely out of sight."

"This guy's a professional. He can find it. Does that have your name on it?" she asked, peering through the slats at a handful of mail-order catalogs left forgotten on a patio chair.

"Deena," he said, shaking his head, "you don't have to do this."

"Oh, I do. The smallest mistake—a mailing label—can give me away."

"There's no one outside."

"Hopefully not. I did a good job losing him."

"There's no one outside because *there's no detective.*"

"What are you talking about?"

"This LA noir story you're spinning, it's a fabrication."

"What?" She laughed. "I saw his car at the post office. It's the same black Prius—"

"Half the cars in Venice are a black Prius. They practically hand them out with a new apartment lease. If you want to end things, have the decency to tell me, instead of inventing these ridiculous stories."

"I'm not making this up!"

"It's just a coincidence, is it?" Alec said. "Such odd timing: right after I tell you I'm broke, a mysterious yet unseen detective arrives so we can't see each other."

Deena stared at him, incredulous. "You really think this is about *money?*"

Alec ran his thumb along a cutting board suspended on a nail above the counter.

"I can't believe you think I'm lying," Deena said.

Alec shrugged. "Darling, what else have you done since we met?"

She walked out of the cottage in a daze, past the borrowed pool and the borrowed lawn, into the contested affluence of a gentrifying neighborhood. It was hot, even in the shade, and by the time Deena reached her car, she was clammy with sweat. A shirtless man walked past with his arm around the shoulder of his tattooed girlfriend. The name on the tattoo etched along the back of her neck had been changed into a lion, but "Ken" was still faintly visible within its body. Deena unlocked the door and slid into the front seat, and with the ignition and the air-conditioning humming a cool mechanical duet, she put her face in her hands and sobbed.

After a while, she reached into the door's side pocket and pulled out one of her son's bundled, forgotten tee shirts. She used it to blot the corners of her eyes. The mild little-boy stink of him soothed her, and at last the tears stopped. Balling up the shirt in her hand, she flipped down the visor mirror to inspect the damage. The crying and the heat had made her eyes red, and the delicate skin just above her cheekbones was swollen.

It didn't matter. No one would notice now.

After picking up the children from school, Deena took them to the park and the bookstore and then out to an early dinner at the greasy Chinese restaurant that she ordinarily denied them. They wolfed down spring rolls and spare ribs and mounds of noodles while she poked at her soup with a blue ceramic spoon, pretending to eat. Squished up against their mother on either side in the booth, their feet dangling under the table, they reached over every few minutes to touch her hand, or her shoulder, or the side of her face, as if to check that she was still there, still in love with them, and then resumed coloring the paper placemat or playing tic-tac-toe poorly, happiness radiating off them like the heat from the sidewalks outside.

That night, when it was time for bed, her son ran into her room and dove beneath the white duvet. Deena came in and circled the concealed, giggling lump. Without warning, she snatched at his exposed left foot and yanked him free. He shrieked with the joy of being caught. His body, still warm from the bath, thrashed against the sheets as he scrambled to hide again. "Mine!" Deena cried and kissed his belly. "Mine, mine, mine! " He continued writhing against her in delight, his dark, wet hair leaving slashes on the sheets like the strokes of a paintbrush.

From the doorway, Deena's daughter, three years older, watched in circumspect silence. She had changed since starting second grade. It had taken some of the fight out of her. "Hey," Deena told her. "Get over here." Her daughter shrugged and did as she was told, but Deena could see in her face an expression of sly gratitude.

Once the children had fallen asleep, Deena went to the kitchen to open a bottle of wine. She poured a glass, thought better of it, and carried the bottle upstairs. In bed, she sipped the wine while scrolling for new documentaries on her tablet. The Gavi tasted sour. She drank it anyway. She watched the first half of a film about the ama pearl divers, Japanese women in their fifties and sixties who would free dive to gather abalone, seaweed, and shellfish, a tradition that had lasted thousands of years but was now on the precipice of extinction. Why did annihilation seem to threaten everything these days? Deena wondered. Or maybe oblivion was always around the corner, and we were just now pointing our cameras at it, entertained by our panic.

As the women sank again and again into the cold, dark sea, their bodies covered in only a loincloth, Deena reconsidered Hayden's argument. Was it just sex and intrigue that she wanted? Had she deceived herself about falling in love with Alec? Or was she allowing Hayden's cynicism to make her question a true thing? The problem with living a second life was that you began to mistrust your own motivations.

After the ama film ended, she clicked on a documentary about a famous female jazz singer. Deena abandoned it for one about a sushi chef. But this, too, failed to hold her interest for long, as did subsequent documentaries, about a tightrope walker, backup singers, an art forgery ring, a Chinese dissident, a winning Little League team, and a gay Columbian drug lord. It was now almost midnight and yet she remained wide awake. She didn't like to take Ambien when she was the only one home with the children, so she compromised on half a Xanax. Stephen would be home soon, anyway; his return flight from Chicago was scheduled to land at LAX in half an hour.

She swallowed the half pill with the remains of her third glass of wine and switched to a documentary about quantum theory, sure that the scientific jargon would deal the desired knockout blow. With an anticipatory yawn, she listened to a series of bespectacled researchers drone on in obscure, increasingly confounding language. A man with an unfortunate goatee explained that a Level 3 parallel universe arose from the many-worlds interpretation, just as Athena had sprung forth from Zeus's head. "Every quantum possibility inherent in the quantum wave function exists in a reality," he said. A white board appeared next, upon which was animated a series of divergent decisions and outcomes. "Every choice you make," the man narrated, "creates a rupture, splitting your current self into an infinite number of future selves, all with slightly to radically different fates." Deena nodded along dully but lost the thread when the discussion turned to how the superpositions of different universes coexisted simultaneously in the same infinite-dimensional Hilbert space. Letting her eyes drift shut, she imagined leaving Stephen. What would a universe in which she lived with Alec actually look like? She pictured them holed up in the tiny cottage, with the strangers' furniture and a shared swimming pool, making love whenever they felt like it, reading weathered paperbacks in bed. It felt oddly innocent and completely unreal—like the opening credits for a sitcom, all conflict and sadness stripped away. Where were her children? Where was the rest of her life?

By the time Stephen came home, the half tab of Xanax and the partially metabolized alcohol from the wine had combined to put Deena into a state that was, if not quite bliss, then a passable approximation. With her eyes closed, she happily listened to him remove his shoes and shrug out of his suit coat and unzip his pants, the concerto of familiar husband sounds continuing into the bathroom, the creak of the toilet seat lifting, the splashy tumble of urine, the clatter of the hot water pipe, the whine of the electric toothbrush, then the click of the light and the almost imperceptible breeze of the door swinging shut.

On the other side of the bed, Stephen sat with his back to her. His weight pulled the sheet taut beneath the duvet, pinning her legs and hips in place.

"Are you awake?" he said.

"Yes."

The mattress sank slightly as he climbed into bed. "Are you really tired?"

Every marriage invents its own language, and in theirs, this phrase was the idiom of sexual solicitation.

Deena opened her eyes. Stephen was on one elbow, watching her. His eyelashes were long like their son's. Why did boys always get the best eyelashes? she wondered.

"Hey, I think I missed you," she said.

It felt unexpected and good to kiss him. Rather than feeling beholden by his desire, she felt grateful. He tugged down the bed sheet so that he could get to her. The stubble on his cheeks scratched against her breasts. She twisted onto her side and pushed him onto his back. Lifting her nightgown up over her head, she climbed on top of him. As she moved her hips, circling slowly, she whispered, "I know about the detective."

His hands dropped away from her hips. Deena smiled, pressing against him still. She hadn't intended to say it, but mixed up in the pleasurable physical sensation was an equally visceral desire to discharge her anxiety, like electricity looking to ground itself.

"You shouldn't have gone to see him," she said.

"I didn't—"

"I know you went," Deena said.

"But I—"

"I *know.*"

"I'm sorry," Stephen said, abandoning dissent and astonishment at the same time. He pressed his lips together. "I should've told you. But I really . . . I didn't think he'd actually find her."

Deena felt a queasy rumble in her stomach. She slid off of her husband and stepped away from the bed.

"Her?"

They had gone to prep school together, Stephen explained, confessing in a rush that sounded almost giddy. She was pretty and inattentive, with a smile that stretched too wide, as if someone had taken a knife and slit the corners of her mouth half an inch. For the winter of his sophomore year, she was his girlfriend, and he couldn't believe his luck. Then one day she asked him to break her leg.

Behind the dormitory was a stack of cinderblocks and she told him to drop one on her knee and send her home. When he refused, she wouldn't talk to him. A week later she ran away from campus and never returned. For years, he'd felt responsible for her disappearance, worried that his softness had doomed her to a life as a drug-addicted runaway or prostitute. When he met the detective at the dinner party, it reignited his uncertainty and curiosity. He tried to locate her first himself, online, and when that failed, he hired the detective, who tracked her to a suburb of Chicago.

"Your trip," Deena interrupted. "You went to see her."

"That's not why I went. We have a client in Chicago."

"But you saw her while you were there."

It wasn't a question. He just stared at her.

"Did you sleep with her?"

"No, no. Absolutely not. I just wanted to talk to her, tell her I was sorry. She told me to forget it. It all worked out. She has two kids, a boy and girl, the son plays concert piano . . ."

As he recounted more of his covert trip, she thought of all the ways he could be lying to her. The details he offered gave the story an air of authenticity, but it was also a technique that she had found herself using to get away with deception these last few months.

She crossed her arms across her bare chest, suddenly aware that she was cold. The door to the veranda was open. Had she opened it? She couldn't remember doing it.

Maybe another parallel version of herself had done it, she mused, and she had switched places with that Deena. Wrapping herself in a robe that hung from the back of the closet, she went over to shut the veranda door. So which one was she, Deena wondered, the instigator or the inheritor of the act? Or was there a third version of her, a fourth, even a fifth? How would she know the difference?

Whoever she was, she was safe now. No one had been keeping tabs on her. She was as anonymous and unobserved as ever. It ought to have comforted her, Deena reflected, as she stepped outside onto the veranda, the dew-licked tile cold against her bare soles.

"Deena?" her husband called nervously from the bedroom.

Above the low railing, thin white clouds moved against the moon. The sky was full of stars and airplanes pretending to be stars. The sweet, familiar scent of jasmine came rising up from her garden. Suddenly, something caused the neighbors' dogs to begin to bark. An animal had either gotten loose or come too close.

"Deena?"

It was time to go back.

"Was she happy?" Deena asked, as she reentered their bedroom.

"Hmm," Stephen said, squinting at her in the dark. "I didn't think to ask."

Venus in Fur

He recognized her instantly as his adversary. Despite the thin black lips bared in a replica of a smile, there was no mistaking Millicent for a friend. She circled George's ankles, sniffing and rooting, and then in a gesture at once defiant, indulgent, and confirmatory, urinated on his shin.

"Millicent!" Helen chided. "Bad girl! Naughty Millie!"

Millie lowered her tiny head, revealing a white vertical stripe that slid through the toffee-colored fur with the ease of a loosed arrow. Helen scooped up Millie and rubbed their faces together. "She's berry berry sorry," Helen said.

Millie glanced up at George. She blinked her bulging, unapologetic eyes. The absence of remorse stemmed from insight as much as imperiousness: Helen's version of scolding involved a half dozen kisses on her lavender nose.

"It's okay," George said, shaking his pant leg.

"I hope it doesn't stain."

"A little scrub and they'll be fine." He plucked a sponge from the kitchen sink and waved it under the faucet. He was not put off by Millie's attack. Since the day children had cheered him on, at seven years old, while he dangled a shiny green cricket on his tongue, George had understood that being liked involved enduring some unpleasantness. Scooping up spiders, licking frogs, nibbling worms—these early adolescent acts later had given way to more complicated but equally undesirable social concessions.

"What's that?" Helen asked and went over to the fire escape. She gazed out beyond the collection of plants that expired on a semiannual basis. "There's a big truck coming to get you!"

"Where?" George asked.

"I was talking to Millie." Helen pointed out the window at a dumpster—without her glasses, which she didn't wear around men, she had trouble identifying distant objects. "See that truck? See that truck?" Millie licked her neck. "She hates trucks," Helen whispered to George. "Oh no, is that nasty old truck coming for you?" Helen asked, crushing Millie to her chest.

Except for the species disparity and a hundred and thirty pounds, they could have been sisters: Helen, a petite, big-eyed strawberry blonde, and Millie, a runty Pomeranian with freckles on the tips of her glamorous white paws, and eyes as glassy and spherical as soap bubbles. Helen kissed the top of Millie's head, assuring her that she was safe. "Don't worry, everyone wubs you, Millie!" It was a performance resonant with the immoderate pride of the maternal, but in this case it was correct. Everyone *did* wub Millie. The dry cleaner and the hardware store owner fawned over her. The florist and the pharmacist yelped when they saw her. The pizza delivery boy danced with her. The cobbler crooned to her in Italian. The barber, bald and widowed, put down his scissors and sighed whenever Millie trotted past. Strangers on the street gawked at Millie, the bolder ones whistled or waved, children followed until called off by their embarrassed parents, who blushed with delighted apologies. Even the cranky hipster bookstore cashier and the stern Israeli locksmith adored Millie.

Only George did not love Millie. To be precise, he hated her. It was an antipathy that steadily grew over the next six months as he continued to see Helen—and, by necessity, Millie. His animosity had little to do with the reasons he normally disliked dogs: their territorialism, their explosive and pointless vitality, the way they breathed hotly out of their mouths, as if a dirty sneaker were being repetitively squeezed. It was simple jealousy: watching the way Helen clutched Millie to her chest, the way she dotted Millie's small furry skull with kisses . . . all that misguided, unconditional tenderness outraged him.

A few days before he left for a two-week vacation with Helen, George confessed this private hatred to the Greek Orthodox priest on East Thirteenth Street. Elias was far from nonpartisan—he had often slipped Millie slivers of Cretan sausage—but George admired Elias enough to overlook it.

Thin and hollow-cheeked, with an ecstatic dark beard and long black robes that seemed the attainment of stylish severity, Elias would surely understand the awkwardness of the imposition Millie made on George, the ethical confusion, all the troublesome etceteras of a man struggling to secure love for himself in a skeptical, closed-hearted city. And if that failed, George could point out the way Helen cradled Millie in her arms as she walked the streets, like the Virgin Mary with baby Jesus, and, in condemning this pagan perversion, George could win an ally.

"You'd like to know how to ask Miss Carver not to bring Millie along?" Elias asked, after George had finished his plea. They were seated in the unventilated study in the rear of the church. The backs of George's knees were sweating.

"Not . . . quite. I want to know how to tell Helen that Millie isn't coming."

"I don't understand. Didn't you just say she plans on bringing her?"

"Well she *plans* on it . . . but she can't. I never went to the Greek consulate to have Millie's travel paperwork approved. And we leave Saturday morning. It's too late."

Elias flipped a loop of red worry beads tucked into his palm. He looked bored with human nature.

"We all make mistakes, George. Just tell her the truth. Our lives can be overwhelming at times, but people understand."

George hesitated. "It wasn't a mistake. I had plenty of time to get the papers."

"Well my advice remains the same. Tell her the truth. You'd be pleasantly surprised by how forgiving—"

"Yes, of course," George interrupted. "I think I should have been clearer about what I'm looking for. I need *practical* advice. I'm only half-Greek but you're the real thing. You know the Greek consulate. You've got to have some idea about its bureaucratic workings and what a credible excuse might sound like."

"Are you asking me to lie for you?"

"No, of course not," George said and smiled. "I'm asking you to come up with a lie. *I'll* tell it."

Elias ushered George out of the study. Beneath a bright golden dome as extravagantly decorated as the tattooed back of a prisoner, the wooden pews sat empty. It was an early Friday afternoon in July and too beautiful outside, it seemed, for piety. At the doorway, Elias pulled George aside. "Please remember that I'm always available."

"I don't think I'll be needing any more advice."

"For Millicent, I mean." Elias cleared his throat. "Since you won't be taking her along on vacation, you're going to need a reliable dog sitter. It would be no trouble at all to find room for her in my home."

George returned to the post office and sullenly finished his afternoon shift. After work, he skipped the crosstown bus and walked to Helen's apartment. He was in no rush to give her the news. The sun was setting, sinking behind the river with the disarming and sudden acceleration of the end of things. When George arrived at her building, the doorman waved him past the front desk with indifferent recognition. George entered the empty elevator. Impulsively, he pressed all the buttons. The elevator stopped at every floor, announcing each arrival with a joyful, irrelevant ding. Then he was standing outside Helen's door, stripped of deferrals.

"Guess what we're doing?" she cooed, answering his knock. She was dressed in a cream-colored waffle robe that had been loosely tied. Her hair, pulled back into a ponytail, accentuated the size of her eyes. He could hear water splashing into the tub.

"Taking a bath?"

"Hurry!" she said, and raced off toward the bathroom.

He would tell her afterward, he decided, as he rushed through the apartment, undressing. He kicked off his black rubber-soled shoes and undid his belt, nearly tripping over his pants as he shed them in midrun. He flung his shirt on the kitchen counter and tossed his socks over his shoulder like spilt salt. Ahead of him, at the end of the hallway, the bathroom door was swinging to a close. He hurried, excited by the thought of what awaited him. He imagined Helen sliding out of her robe and stepping into the water, her eyes drifting shut as she reclined against the supple curvature of the tub. She would lean her head back, the ends of her hair growing wet and dark. Hearing his footfalls, she would slyly acknowledge his arrival by raising her bare knees up out of the water, twin islands parting in invitation.

He stepped out of his last remaining article of clothing, dangling his boxers from his upturned index finger as he swaggered into the bathroom.

"Why are you *naked*?" Helen said. Still dressed in her waffle knit robe, she was kneeling beside the tub, inside of which sat a shivering Millie. Her caramel fur was matted to her bony ribs. With her dour, pointy face and pronounced whiskers, she resembled a satirical cartoon of a Beat poet, missing only the beret and cigarette.

"I thought we were . . . the bath . . . that it was . . . " But he gave up as Helen ignored him to further drench a scrawny, waterlogged Millie with the showerhead. George pulled his boxers back on, one of the more disappointing activities known to man, and sat dejectedly on the toilet lid. Citrus-scented steam gusted against his face. He swatted at the fog with an annoyed wave of his hand.

"No, no," Helen chided when the dog sneezed. "No getting sickies before we leave for vacation!"

"She's not coming anyway," George snapped.

"What?"

"The consulate was closed," he said, deliberately softening his tone. "Every time I tried it was the same thing. Sorry. There's a reason Greece has the worst economy in Europe—no work ethic."

Helen switched off the tap. She reached for a freshly warmed towel and wrapped it around Millie. "I already took care of Millie's paperwork," she said.

"What? When?"

"Last Friday. You kept saying how hard it was. So I stopped by. Didn't I tell you?"

But that wasn't the important question. The important question was "Who took a bath?!" Helen screamed it twice, then segued into the equally urgent "Who smells like oranges!"

Millie barked, raising her head excitedly into the air.

"You do! You do!" Helen said, her face exploding into rapture. She rubbed her nose against Millie's soaked neck. The dog squirmed free of Helen's embrace and head-butted George's legs. Then she ran out of the bathroom, trailed by Helen.

George caught up to them both in the living room. Millie had found George's hastily discarded pants in a pile on the floor and was rubbing her soaked hindquarters against them.

"She hates the hairdryer," Helen explained.

Millie sat up and rammed her head into George's bare shins again. Then she hopped up onto the couch and shimmied against a cushion. She barked at George with defiance, triumph, joy. All the world was her towel.

They arrived in Athens late in the afternoon and, after clearing customs and picking up Helen's many suitcases, went to retrieve Millie. The man at the cargo area, smitten, had illegally removed her from her carrier. Helen was surprised to see Millie happily lounging on the cool concrete floor after nine hours in the cargo hold, gnawing on a lamb rib, as Millie was ordinarily an anxious traveler. George was surprised to see Millie at all. He had slipped the man at the loading dock fifty dollars to send her to Rome.

Jet lag consumed their first and only night in Athens, and the next morning they boarded a ferryboat for the Cyclades. Drifting toward the small, uncrowded port of their destination, an overlooked island east of Naxos, George strained for a glimpse of the staggering beauty that he had imagined would greet them. His mother, a first-generation Greek American, had often described her parents' homeland as a landscape of lush olive groves and luminous beaches. What George saw, however, was a craggy mountainside, dotted with bleached white homes like teeth set in an excavated jawbone. He had anticipated beauty so luscious and poignant that it would annihilate any distance between him and Helen. It was a childish wish in its disregard for the subtleties of engagement, stemming from the same impulse for acceptance that had had him eating worms decades earlier, but it was no less potent for either its simplicity or familiarity, and as he climbed into the taxi beside Helen, he worried that the clamorous, lonely hunger that had dominated his life would never depart him.

He gazed out the window as the taxi ascended the cliff, and then, a few coiled kilometers later, the road unfurled into the greater of the two towns on the island. It was a hopscotch of homes and shops, with the greenish-blue Mediterranean peeking through the gaps between houses like a jealous gaze. Helen cleaned Millie's irritated eyes with a puppy-wipe pad.

The Hotel Sunshine was a meandering, three-story gathering of white rooms and blue shutters. Architecturally, the hotel seemed to have no definite plan but instead to have expanded the way a coral reef grows, with new rooms arriving beside and above the old ones in eruptions of calcified necessity. George followed a confusing pair of hand-painted signs to reception, wiping the sweat from his forehead as he stooped to enter. A pretty black-haired girl sat at a table, folding towels. Behind her hung a collection of painted icons and framed black-and-white portraits of a family. In the corner, a television was softly gossiping.

"Hello?" George whispered, worried that he had stumbled into someone's living room.

The girl paused from smoothing flat a towel and looked up. Her face broke into a grin.

"Hello! How old are you?"

George smiled. "Forty-two."

"Tsoo-tsoo!" the girl said and clicked her tongue.

"Tsoo-tsoo," George replied.

I like this hotel, he thought, and then Helen appeared in the entranceway, calling out for Millie, who, George realized with embarrassment, had been hiding between his legs, the real object of welcome.

"How long has she been with you?" Helen demanded. "I almost stepped on a cactus looking for her."

The girl came around from behind the table and, crouching, gestured for Millie to approach. Before she could, however, Helen scooped up Millie. The problem, Helen explained, was that she was a bad Millie. A berry berry bad Millie. Such a bad dog she should be squishy-wished.

Ah, but the real problem, as it turned out, was not Millie's cheerfully exonerated badness but that the hotel did not allow dogs. "This is the way here," said the girl's mother, who had been called from the kitchen after Helen had insisted on speaking with an adult. She was balding and weary looking. She smelled of cinnamon. "I am sorry," she said, wiping her hands on her spotless apron.

"But we made a reservation," Helen said. "Check the book."

"We no dog reservations allow," the mother said.

"But why?"

"They have the hairs. Also the noisy."

The girl said something to her mother in Greek that, though only faintly intelligible to George, he identified from tone as an appeal.

"I just saw a cat on the stairway," Helen added.

"Cat is wild," the mother said. "They goes."

"You can't do this," Helen said, placing a squirming Millie on the ground. The dog trotted over to the girl and turned around to allow the backs of her ears to be scratched. "It's discrimination."

"Maybe we should leave Millie somewhere for the week," George said. "I'm sure we can find a good kennel for her. We'd visit every day."

Helen pressed her palms together with a pained, prayerful expression. For a brief moment, George entertained the hope that Helen would agree to be separated from Millie. Their seclusion seemed suddenly, almost unbearably achievable. Then, with a puppyish huff, Millie rolled onto her back. Baring her tender belly, she wriggled against the tile floor, her slim furry paws bent at the wrists. Her caramel tail fluffed up and down. She glanced coquettishly out of the corner of her huge, watery eyes. All the women sighed. How could they not? She was cotton candy. She was makeup. She was new shoes. She was strawberry lip balm. She was a girl's first phone. She was everything pink, everything soft, everything small that fit inside a purse.

They threw their suitcases on the bed, changed into bathing suits, and hid their jewelry in obvious places. As George gathered beach towels and sunscreen, Helen called for Millie.

"Should I take her travel bag or let her walk on leash?" she asked.

"I hate to leave her in the hotel room," George said, petting Millie with the sole of his shoe, "but sanitation codes don't allow dogs on the beach."

Although she wore flip-flops in her own shower, wiped down silverware in restaurants with her napkin, and referred to street hot dog vendors as bacterialists, Helen readily dismissed the local health statute. "Oh please. Millie's cleaner than our cab driver," she said, and snatched up the leather leash with the cry "Who's coming to the beach! Who's coming to the beach!"

It was a long blazing walk from the hotel. Millie trotted in the shade when she could, and when this became impossible—the homes were sporadically built up at the far edge of town—she veered in and out of their legs in a dignified panic. George frequently tripped over the agitated butterscotch blur at his ankles and pretended, with less success each time, to find it endearing. Despite Helen's bewitchment with Millie, or perhaps because of it, she hadn't introduced George to Millie until a month into their courtship. And now, only half a year later, George already recalled those early companionless days with nostalgia. The sprawling, leisurely dinners, the unescorted strolls along the Williamsburg Bridge, the scent of Helen's perfume on his skin after a night of lovemaking, freesia and labdanum unsullied by Millie's citrus-scented dog shampoo. Yes, there had been doggie bags and check-in calls to the dog sitter, but they were afterthoughts, incidental gestures. During those heady, blissful first weeks, Helen had been exclusively his.

They arrived at the beach and chose a section down the shore, away from the tourists. George laid their towels on the rocks while Helen looked for a tree to secure Millie's leash. The only significant vegetation was some forbidding Y-shaped succulents, so she gave up and pinned the leash beneath a cairn of heavier stones.

"Rub some more lotion on my back?" she asked, unfastening her bikini top.

George poured the sunscreen into his hands both to warm it and to prolong the anticipation. Helen's body was dizzying, with generous curves. That she invited his touch still seemed to him a bewildering generosity. His ex-wife's adultery had done much to banish the meager sensual confidence he'd accumulated over the years, and while rubbing the lotion into Helen's skin, he felt his disbelief hardening into a carapace of need. He reached around and massaged sunscreen onto her ribs, grazing with just the tips of his fingers the underswell of her full breasts. She pressed down on his shoulder with her chin.

"Who's a bad boy?" she said.

"I am?"

"Yes you are. A berry bad boy."

He leaned forward and kissed her warm freckled shoulder.

"Do you want to swim?"

"Race you to the water," she said.

They sprinted from their towels, scattering stones with their wild strides. George dove in and felt the slick undersea rocks skim his thighs as he quickened toward the deep. He arched his back, arms elongated, and kicking hard, sped toward the surface. Erupting out of the water, he heard Millie's yelp puncturing the air—high pitched, indignant, hysterical. He wiped the salt water from his eyes, blinking until he could see again. He was alone. Helen had stayed behind, pinned to the coast by Millie, who was hopping and snapping at her ankles.

"Come on in!" George shouted, waving while treading water with his legs.

"She won't let me! She's never seen the ocean!" Helen shouted back. She turned to Millie and said, "It's just water, honey. It's just water."

But to Millie the sea was enormous and menacing, and no words would calm her. Helen was vanishing! Life was departing! However sluggish Millie grew from the heat, with Helen's first steps into the ocean she stirred, racing to the water's edge and barking until Helen reemerged. George said nothing as he watched this operetta. The past two days had been a wearying series of obstacles and irritations; all he wanted was the simple reward of seaside languor with a handsome body. That this should be obstructed by a dog's fear seemed an absurdity bordering on injustice.

They left the beach at dusk. The walk back through town in the changing light confused them, and soon they were lost. George asked directions from an old woman sitting on a porch, snapping the ends off green beans.

"Barack Obama!" she said.

The street they were following split into two nameless tributaries. They took a left and later a right. "This seems a little familiar," Helen said. "I think I remember the bougainvillea on that terrace."

"Which terrace?"

"Forget it—it's a dead end." Helen whistled for Millie to turn around. Released from her leash for the walk home, she was trotting twenty feet ahead of them, rooting through roadside piles of trash.

George saw the cat first. It was a husky gray tomcat with broad paws hosting an extra toe. The whiskers on one side of its face had gone missing, and this deformity leant it the air of a gangster. Turning its back on George and Helen, it stalked up the narrow street toward Millie.

"Where did that cat come from?" Helen said.

"Someone's house probably," George said.

"It's not wearing a collar."

The cat crept closer, its ears rotating backward.

"That's not a housecat. Millie honey, turn around," Helen called out.

Millie ignored Helen, tugging free an ice cream wrapper from the torn bottom of a trash bag. She placed a paw on the wrapper to hold it in place and licked at it with her head turned sideways. From behind, her fanned, white-bottomed tail resembled the lacey bloom of a ballerina's tutu.

"Millie," Helen said, carefully stepping toward the converging animals. "I want you to come back here right now."

The tomcat paused. It sank down until its belly touched the ground. Its thick tail twitched back and forth.

"Millie!" Helen shouted and broke into a run.

Startled by the clatter of Helen's sandals, Millie looked up from the ice cream wrapper, but it was too late. The tomcat had covered too much distance. He lunged and sprang onto Millie's back. She yelped. Her giant eyes bulged in terror. The cat swiped at Millie's side with its massive six-clawed paw and Millie jerked sideways in a futile attempt to dislodge her attacker. She let out a series of panicky cries as the cat continued to batter her, and then Helen was there, wrenching the yowling beast off Millie's back and flinging it aside. It landed in a collapsible run, sprinting behind a dumpster. Helen scooped up Millie in her arms, cradling her as she mewled. It was a pathetic sound, a wail of misery and betrayal, the disbelieving breach of adulation. They were three streets away when her crying finally stopped, and George, at last, could unplug his ears.

Despite her lurid protests, Mille was unhurt, and within an hour she was padding around the hotel room performing her regular endearments: balancing on her hind legs, raising a paw, defending her knitted stuffed monkey with a *tewwifying* growl. Every few minutes Helen would scoop up Millie in her arms and dot kisses along her snout. Then she would release the dog, and Millie would scamper back and forth, sniffing various objects, including George, before returning to Helen's embrace.

In light of the attack, George suggested that they leave Millie in their hotel room when they went out for dinner. Helen, however, wanted to keep Millie as close to her as possible. From now on, she explained, Millie would accompany them everywhere, at all times.

It was a disheartening development for George. Gone were the few luxurious moments of independence when Millie would remain behind napping. Millie came with them to meals and to marketplaces, to monasteries and museums; and as irritating as George found Millie's constant presence, he found the frenzied reception she met a hundred times worse. Even on an isolated Greek island, Millie inspired giddiness, infatuation, and largesse at every turn. While strays cats lurked under tables in search of trampled French fries, enamored taverna owners placed Millie on her own chair and offered her lamb bones. As scrawny wild dogs sprawled neglected in the shade, another toast was raised to Millie's health. "If only Millie could drink her wine," Helen reflected one evening, as a tour group of besotted Swedes sent over yet another glass. If Millie *could* have partaken of her offerings, she would have been perpetually drunk.

Yet just as in Greek myths, where the movement from glory to suffering is inevitable, Millie's heightened attention gradually became an ordeal for Helen. A picturesque stroll down a residential side street would be transformed, after a glimpse of Millie's divinity, into a flurry of housewives scrambling for a closer look. Scooters followed behind them when they walked to the beach, manned by dark-skinned boys without shirts, their girlfriends seated behind them and pleading into their ears, *Parte mou ena* —"Get me one." Shopping grew impossible: shopkeepers would crowd Millie against a rack of leather sandals, and though Helen would eventually escape with her, by the time they arrived at the next store, a phone call had been made and a new batch of disciples awaited. Helen began carrying Millie in her mesh travelling bag, concealed from her fans.

On their eighth night on the island, after George returned from the mini-market—he did all the shopping now, alone, to avoid the Millie crowd—Helen handed him the leash.

"What's this for?" he said.

"You mind taking her out tonight? I'm really tired." She removed a royal-blue tube of moisturizer from one of the shopping bags and went into the bathroom. "I think maybe I got too much sun," she called out.

Sensing release, Millie rose up on her hind legs. She hopped against George's leg. He flung the leash under the couch with annoyance. "She just went out a couple hours ago," he said. "She'll be fine until the morning."

Helen didn't answer him. He peeked through the crack in the bathroom door and saw her positioned before the mirror, rubbing moisturizer in circles on her cheeks. She wore a thin white nightgown that reached to the middle of her thighs. As she leaned in to closer examine her reflection, the nightgown rode up, exposing her peach-colored underwear.

He shrugged into the bathroom and came up behind her. "I have an idea," he said, kissing the nape of her neck.

"After you walk her . . ."

George and Millie were a quarter mile from the hotel when he realized he'd forgotten the leash under the couch. He considered turning back, but the prospect of revealing his mistake to Helen dissuaded him. He wanted to be heralded as a hero, not a screwup. Besides, no matter how far ahead Millie ventured, invariably she would pause to investigate a potential scrap of food, giving him time to catch up.

They wandered along the outskirts of town, away from the foot traffic of the main streets. This close to the sea, the air smelled sharp and briny. Except for the occasional radio, the houses were silent. Dark-purple wildflowers burst out of the stone walls like children fleeing the yard on the last day of school.

A few feet ahead of George, Millie sniffed at a garbage bag propped beside the entrance of a vineyard. It was a modest well-kept space, staked with wooden trellises upon which grapevines clung. George picked a handful of grapes but they were small and unripe and he let them fall to the ground untasted. Then the moon appeared, sliding out from behind the clouds like a woman slipping out of a dress. George watched in awe as moonlight illuminated the vineyard. He wished that Helen were with him to share in the vision. It was the kind of beauty that induced transcendence, a disarming splendor that could, if he were lucky, tip affection toward love.

Instead he had Millie snuffling the trash. Angrily, he called out to her that they were leaving. She ignored him. She had detected a salami skin and was snapping at the plastic garbage bag.

He opened his mouth to chastise the dog but then, impulsively, stopped. Some instinct inside George, as yet unacknowledged by him, urged otherwise. In deliberate silence, he watched the animal wrestle in the dirt with the bag. He took a step back. Millie dug her rear paws into the ground, a growl issuing from between her ensnared teeth. George took another step back. Her neck tightened and her head jerked side to side as she devoted the entirety of her small body to obtainment. George took a third step back. Then he spun on the heel of his left foot and ran.

At the intersection, he veered off the path from which they had come and diverted toward the harbor. After ten seconds, he glanced over his shoulder. Millie wasn't following him. He hadn't intended to leave her. He hadn't known what he was doing until he had done it. Then it was done.

When he reached the harbor at last, he stopped to rest. There was nowhere to sit except for a bronze sculpture honoring World War II veterans. George limped over and took a seat on the enormous anchor. His legs felt weak and stringy. His chest ached with exertion. He leaned back against the cold bronze and listened to the lapping of the surf. It was gentle but steady. It sounded like the beat of a child's heart. Or was it his heart? Or Millie's, untended for the first time?

*

George had heard "Who's a Millie?" "Who's a Millie-Dillie" and "Who's the Milliest Millie?" with such regularity that when he awoke to Helen demanding "Where's Millie?" he at first misinterpreted it as just another of her affectionate mock queries. This time, however, it wasn't followed by a jubilant cry of "You are!" but by tears.

"I can't find her. You have to help me find her," Helen pleaded as George staggered out of bed. With her swollen eyes and disheveled strawberry hair, Helen's resemblance to Millie was even more striking that morning.

"Yeah, of course." He yawned. "Did you check the bathroom?"

"I've looked *everywhere,*" she moaned, haunting the living room in her white nightgown. She flung aside throw pillows and got down on her knees to peer beneath the couch. The night before, after returning alone to find Helen asleep, George had zipped the leash into the side pocket of his suitcase until he could safely dispose of it. Yet even with the evidence out of sight, Helen's ceaseless searching made him nervous.

"Maybe she got out when the maid came by this morning. Slipped through the door," George said, wrapping his arms around Helen.

"I didn't hear a maid."

"You're a heavy sleeper."

"Millie wouldn't do that. She's never run off." She blinked her red, puffy eyes up at George. "Unless someone took her . . ."

Helen shrugged free of his embrace and rushed out of the room. She sprinted barefoot toward the reception office, a streak of pale American melancholy. When George caught up to her, she was interrogating the receptionist's mother.

"I *need* to talk to the maid."

"Miss, no one clean your room today," the girl's mother said.

"Then how did Millie disappear? She can't open doors by herself."

"She doesn't have a thumb," George explained helpfully, sidling up beside Helen.

"The maid stole her," Helen said. "She snuck in while I was asleep and took Millie."

The woman asked her daughter something in rapid, agitated Greek. The girl lifted up her head with that peculiar Greek nod of negation. They spoke briefly, heatedly, and then the manager waved her hands in quick little circles of acceptance. The girl turned to address Helen.

"I am sorry," she said. "We understand you are upset. But the maid has not come yet today. She could not have taken your Millie."

George had never heard the girl speak more than a few words of English, and her unexpected command of the language unsettled him.

"Maybe you left the door open and she escaped?" the girl asked.

"She doesn't want to *escape* me," Helen said. "She loves me."

"Yes, of course. I mean maybe she does this by accident. What time did you return with her last night?"

"Around ten," George said.

"No, at ten you were alone," the girl said. "You must have walked her later."

"Did you take her out again?" Helen said.

"I walked her once. We came back at ten, like I said."

"Maybe you are confusing nights," the girl suggested.

"You're the one who's confused," George said.

The girl shook her head. "At ten, the news begins and interrupts my music show. This is a disappointing time for me. But then I saw you pass by the window and I became excited to greet Miss Millie. I thought she would make me happy. But when I opened the door, you were alone."

"This is ridiculous," George said. "I'm not about to be told by Generation Omega here what I did or didn't do last night."

"Why didn't she bark?" Helen said.

"Exactly. Why didn't she bark?" George repeated, unsure of the relevance but grateful for Helen's diversion.

"I don't understand," the girl said.

"Because you're wrong," George said.

"Millie barks at everything unfamiliar," Helen said.

"Everything," George said.

"If a person comes within two feet of the door, she barks."

"Two feet," George echoed.

"So this morning," Helen said coldly, turning to face him, "If the maid had opened the door, Millie would have barked at her."

Helen spent the day searching the island for Millie. She went alone, refusing George's offer of help. His revised account of the night's events had failed to placate her. Yes, he came back without Millie, he'd confessed, but only because he'd accidentally forgotten the leash and she'd run off too quick to catch. And sure that she would return on her own, he'd refrained from waking Helen and needlessly worrying her—it was not that George wanted to continue lying to Helen, it was just that he found the truth intolerable in what it revealed about his desperation.

Helen returned at dusk without Millie. Her face and shoulders were sunburnt, her lips blistered, and her feet had swollen a full shoe size. As she lay down on the couch, she exhaled a sorrowful sigh that descended the musical scale. George ran a bath for her. It was an undesired kindness, permeated with anxiety and servility, but she accepted it out of exhaustion. All day, hope had been bleeding out of her. That morning, the thought of Millie's permanent disappearance had seemed impossible, but now that night was falling, it had become gruesomely possible. She could no longer put off the empty future that awaited her. A life without Millie was a life without enchantment. Gone were the brash baby growls and the bunny hops, the limpid eyes and the fuzzy ears, the soft belly and the delicate nose . . . Closing the bathroom door, Helen sank into the contours of the tub with another decrescendo lament.

The next day, she searched the far side of the island while George holed up in the hotel room. At lunchtime, he left to buy a toasted sandwich from a beach vendor, and while coming back to the hotel, he heard movement in the bushes beside the outdoor staircase. He froze. The rustling continued. What if it was Millie ferreting through the undergrowth, trying to find her way back to them? Giddiness overtook him at the thought of the reward Helen would grant him for Millie's return. Gratitude? Forgiveness? Possibly even love?

He drew closer to the bushes. Pushing away his fear of snakes, he parted the spiny leaves and reached blindly inside.

He felt something soft and slight beneath his hands. As he picked it up, he realized what it was: a kitten. Its fur was black except for a flash of white on its belly, and its young body, no more than eight weeks old, was skinny to the point of emaciation. It blinked up at George, its mouth jawing open silently.

That night Helen came back to the hotel empty handed again. She dropped her purse by the door and lay on the couch. George waited for her eyes to close, then he snuck into the bedroom where the kitten was dozing in the closet, George's contact lens case serving as a water dish. The animal mewed when he picked it up, emboldened by familiarity. He shushed it and crept out to Helen.

"Helen," he whispered. "I have a surprise for you."

"What?" she murmured, her eyes still closed.

Gingerly, he placed the kitten on her chest. It stretched its front paws, kneading its claws into her collarbones.

Helen's eyes fluttered half-open.

"What the hell is—"

"Cute, right?"

"Get it off me!" she cried, sitting up with such haste that the kitten tumbled onto her lap. She parted her legs as if to avoid a burning ember.

"Watch out, you're scaring her," George said and scooped up the kitten.

The animal rested its petite chin on his finger.

"Get it out of here," Helen said. "It's feral. It's full of diseases."

"Her eyes are a little goopy but otherwise she seems healthy."

"Just get rid of it."

"I thought you'd like her," George said. "She might cheer you up."

"That's not Millie."

"I know. I was only—"

"I don't want it. I don't want anything else. Please," she said, beginning to cry. "That's not what I want."

George apologized and carried the animal outside.

Helen woke the following morning with a fever. Her nose was stuffy and her throat raw. George brought her orange juice and a damp washcloth for her forehead. She sipped weakly at the juice, wincing with each swallow, then handed it back to him and shut her eyes. Soon she was asleep again. He wet a second washcloth and dabbed at the pulp on her chapped lips. Her face was flushed with heat. He pulled the curtains tight, drenching the room in darkness, and went out to get medicine.

The pharmacy was situated between a butcher shop and a newsstand. The pharmacist was an old man with liver spots on his hands. He stared over the top of his square-lensed metal glasses at George, who employed pantomime and his limited Greek vocabulary to relay Helen's symptoms. The pharmacist made a clucking sound when he'd heard enough.

"You like basket?" he asked George, bagging a clear liquid.

"I don't need a basket."

"*Basket,*" the man said, and dribbled an imaginary basketball.

"Oh. Sure. Basketball."

The man shook his head. "Football—better."

When George came back to the hotel, the black kitten was waiting for him. It faced the door politely, like an encyclopedia salesman. George scooped it up and returned it to the bushes. The kitten mewed in defiance. George poked it in its tender white belly and it fell over, quiet and awed.

Helen gagged as she drank the medicine but it brought the fever down. She ate some crackers George had picked up at the mini-market and then laid her head on the pillow without speaking. Soon, her eyes drifted shut. George sat on the edge of the bed and watched her sleep. He had never been allowed to gaze at her with such forthrightness. Despite his admiration, Helen was self-conscious about her appearance. He had twice overheard her on the phone telling a friend that Helen's eyebrows were too blond, that if she failed to darken them, her forehead looked titanic. There were other insecurities voiced: her wide hips, her flat feet, wrinkles at the corners of her mouth. Her dissatisfaction bewildered George, who thought her beautiful. But he understood, too, the injury that still disoriented her. Her ex-husband had left her to marry his pregnant assistant, twelve years younger than Helen, a grievance that she had only mentioned once, on their first date, after George had come clean about his own failed marriage. "She gets my husband and a baby girl; I get Millie." Then she rolled her eyes, as if to discredit the pain for its egregiousness, its obviousness, and spoke of it no more.

But she was no longer that deserted woman, George assured her while she slept, and though he had defrauded her, too, that had only been out of a longing for more of her. "I just wanted all of you. I'm sorry," he whispered, as her shallow breath rustled the coarse hotel sheet. "I shouldn't have let Millie go."

Helen's eyelids twitched. Overhead, the fan bullied hot air around the room. George leaned over the bed and kissed her clammy forehead.

Her eyes opened.

"You're awake," he said.

She tightened her mouth, deepening the unwelcome wrinkles at the corners.

"You're going to be okay," he said, and stroked the side of her face.

She watched his hand touch her cheek.

"By tomorrow you'll be back to normal," he said.

"She's all I had left of him," Helen said, rolling over and closing her eyes again.

George walked to the harbor. It looked smaller during the day, like a grammar-school classroom we revisit as adults, marveling at the tininess of our past. Calling out Millie's name, he backtracked along the path that led out of town until he reached the vineyard. He continued shouting her name while moving among the green vines and their hard, unripe fruit. There was no reply—and there would be no reply, George understood. Millie's high-pitched, pampered bark had been silenced for good. She was gone. Killed by alley cats. Swooped upon by a hawk. Flattened by a truck. She would never survive alone.

Yet what George had failed to recognize was that the world is a different place when everyone loves you. A quarter mile from the vineyard, where a lemon grove opened up into a succession of small, sunlit homes, George glimpsed Millie sitting on a veranda. An array of bones of various sizes lay before her. As George approached the yard, she sniffed a short rib with the delicacy of a sommelier.

"Psst! Millie!"

She sank back onto her haunches and growled.

Hastily, he unlatched the outer gate. Dusk was approaching, saturating the air with a deep orange light, but the twilit radiance did nothing to obscure him from view, and he ducked his head as he hurried across the lawn.

When he reached the veranda, Millie began to bark. "Shh, it's me, George," he whispered, flinging one leg over the banister and levering himself onto the other side. Millie backed away from him, snarling and yipping. "Come on, let's go," he hissed, and grabbed for her. She skittered to the side, barking louder. George heard the rumble of an upstairs sliding door as it skidded along a track. He lunged for Millie. She ducked away and circled behind a wicker chair. The thump of approaching footsteps shook the inside staircase.

"Please," George whispered, kneeling. "Helen needs you. You have to come back. For Helen."

Millie paused. She raised a single paw. Then she lowered it and trotted up to George, her feathery tail wagging. He stretched out his hands and she hopped into his arms. It was a trick he had seen Millie do only with Helen, and it so astonished him that he barely got the head start he needed to outrun the elderly couple and their two tearful grandchildren.

"She looks different," Helen remarked, as Millie lay newly cradled in her arms, nuzzling the skin between her thumb and forefinger. "They did something to her. I know it."

Before returning Millie, George had checked her carefully for injury—an examination that took less than thirty seconds, since Millie possessed the surface area of a grapefruit—and concluded that no harm had come to her. Helen, however, was unconvinced.

"Her ID tag!" she cried in triumph, seizing Millie's leather collar. "They switched it out. I *knew* something was wrong. The monsters *renamed* her."

"To what?"

"Doesn't matter," Helen said, removing the new tag and flinging it away.

George retrieved the tag from the floor. "Aphrodite," he read aloud. "A little hairy for a goddess."

"Oh no, that's not you, you're my *Millie,*" Helen said. "My Millie-Dillie. Yes you are. Yes you *are.* Who's my Millie-Dillie?" Millie's four-pound body trembled in affirmation.

George sat on the end of the bed and rested his hands on his knees. "So everything is okay now?" he said. "Like, with us?"

"You don't understand anything," Helen said and began to pack her bags.

But he did understand. They would never go swimming together in the blue ocean. He would never make a wish with her beside a two-thousand-year-old Roman fountain. She would never stand still beneath a streetlight while he gently searched her eye for an eyelash as the prelude to a kiss. All of the stock yet endearing intimacies of love had been revealed, once again, as unattainable. It didn't matter what he tried, what animal he lost or found, there was no dog cute enough and no cricket repellant enough to distract her from the man he was or from the man she had lost.

A cab arrived to take Helen to the port. The receptionist had booked her a ticket on the midnight catamaran to Piraeus. George carried Helen's suitcases out to the cab for her and loaded them in the trunk. When he leaned in the open window to kiss Helen goodbye, she raised Millie between them. Millie licked his mouth and barked once with wild delight. They drove away in a cloud of dust.

He slept poorly that night. Everything reminded him of Helen. The floral hush of her perfume clung to the scratchy sheets. The pillow curled in his arms recalled the silken contours of her body, now gone forever.

At dawn, he fled the hotel. Expecting an empty beach, he was surprised to see a gathering of elderly Greeks milling in the sea. The men scooped up water with their palms and poured it onto their gray chests. The women patted their hair with the solicitude of young nurses. George watched them from a ledge of volcanic rock. As the morning sky brightened, the men and women drifted out of the water. Wordlessly, they wrapped each other in towels and left. George came down from the ledge. He lay down on the gray stones. They were small and cool and hard. He curled up and tried to forget where he was.

He woke at noon, surrounded by families eating lunch out of plastic containers. The left side of his face was hot. He brushed away the pebbles clinging to his calves and walked back to the hotel. As he passed reception, the receptionist's mother called out, "Your room is need change!"

"It's okay," he said. "I don't want maid service."

The girl appeared in the doorway. "You do not understand. You must move to another room," she said.

"Why? I still have two more days in the reservation."

"Your room is for a double occupancy. You are a single occupancy now."

George packed his suitcase and was led to a miniature, whitewashed crypt at the edge of the hotel.

"There's no shower," George said.

The girl leaned into the lavatory and pointed at a bare showerhead hanging above the toilet seat. There was a small silver drain in the center of the floor.

As he slipped the new key into his pocket, he felt Millie's replacement ID tag against his fingers. He dropped it into the empty bathroom trash can.

The girl strode over and snatched the tag out of the trash. "I am glad Millie has left you," she said and walked away.

This room did not remind him of Helen. The bedroom smelled of bleach, and in his arms the flat pillow offered the anonymous discomfort of an office chair. The room was poorly ventilated, with only a single window, and in the middle of the night, unable to sleep from the heat, George got out of bed and propped open the front door with the bathroom trash can. He lingered on the hotel landing for a moment to cool off, staring up at the stars. They were sharp and plentiful, undimmed by artificial light.

If there is a mathematical model for loneliness, it is not an infinitely ascending line—it is a parabola. Though often it seems that loneliness will never end, that it will only grow greater and more hopeless, at a certain point it catches, like the end of a pinned elastic, or the gang rush of the expanding universe, and comes hurtling back. This doesn't happen only once. Loneliness recurs, followed by fellowship, friendship . . . then more loneliness . . . more love. These arcs of loss and discovery repeat themselves throughout a lifetime, a chain of parabolas, a wavelength that mirrors the frequency of the human heart.

Outside, George surveyed the sky with a weary absence of recognition. The constellations were different in this part of the world. Eventually he found Orion, and Libra, and what he thought might be Andromeda, although he wasn't sure about that one. Then he felt something brush against his bare foot. He looked down. A small black shadow had emerged from the bushes. It circled his foot and then curled up around his ankle like a misplaced comma.

He bent down to reach the cat. He moved slowly so as not to scare her. She was shivering, either from hunger or exhaustion, maybe both. He felt her tiny head brush against his palm, and then her warm dark fur was rubbing against his wrists, pressing closer, safer, tighter, home.

The Flower of One's Heart

Yoshi Takamata moved from Kyoto to Connecticut at the age of fifteen, and his three years of American high school, followed by four years at local college and two decades in New York City, had done little to soften the severe Japanese accent he greeted me with after I had climbed a flight of stairs on Chambers Street to find my new master.

It was Yoshi's accent that assured me I was in the right place. The dojo itself was dishearteningly rundown, a converted dance studio with water-damaged ceilings, a warped wooden floor, and a wall of tall, dirty windows, only half of which opened. There was no visible training gear other than a blue multipaneled gymnastics mat and a curved wooden sword propped in the corner. A flimsy cloth curtain separated the two locker rooms, each looking to fit no more than a half dozen people at a time.

"Come in to my office," Yoshi growled, bowing. I bowed in return, slipped off my shoes, and padded behind him in my dark socks.

Yoshi's office was as sparsely furnished as the rest of the dojo. On the walls hung framed photographs of Yoshi at different ages, flinging opponents through the air by their wrists and shoulders, and kicking apples off of swords while blindfolded.

Yoshi gestured for me to sit in the visitor's chair. I faced him across the slim wooden desk. He folded his hands, interlacing his fingers. Where his starchy white uniform had been rolled up at the cuffs, I could see his smooth forearms, like the skin of a mannequin.

"I'm looking for a new master," I said.

He nodded.

"It's been almost ten years since I last trained. I don't know how it happened. I stopped just after college. I had a red belt but I moved for work and then somehow the years went by."

"Are you married?" he said.

"No. Why?"

"That's usually how it happens."

"I'm engaged," I said.

"Congratulations. I was engaged once. Very nice girl. She plays violin for an orchestra."

"But you didn't marry her."

"My family was disappointed." Yoshi shrugged. "What can you do?"

He plucked two hard candies from a ceramic bowl on his desk and offered me one. A student of his, I later learned, worked for a candy distributor and kept Yoshi's office supplied with treats. Most of the students provided free services to the dojo at one time or another. A red-belt lawyer had drafted the insurance release form. A blue-belt carpenter had built the shelves in the women's locker room. Another blue belt, a computer engineer, had designed the website.

Yoshi rolled the candy around in his mouth and asked me what it was, exactly, that I wanted to learn. Why had I come back? To get in shape? For self-defense? Was I bored of the gym?

"I'd like to be able to put someone in excruciating pain," I said.

"You want to fight."

I shook my head. "That's just kicking and punching. I want to learn how to incapacitate someone. So painful they can't even think."

"That is a . . . unusual desire."

He stood and walked out of the office. A moment later, when it was clear that Yoshi wasn't returning, I followed him out. I regretted offending him. I should have said that I sought spiritual enrichment. Standing by the door, I slipped my shoes back on and tied the laces. "Sorry if I've wasted your time," I said.

Yoshi smiled. He seemed acutely relaxed, his round, wide face displaying the expressionless gaze of serenity etched into the sculptures of gods. We shook hands.

Then my thumb exploded.

It's a bad habit to shut your eyes when you're attacked. Maybe it comes from the childhood belief that if you don't see it, it will hurt less, as if viewing pain were necessary to its transmission. Or maybe it's just the opposite, and shutting your eyes is a kind of dedication, a devotion to the momentary annihilation that agony brings. Either way, I suffered in astonished blindness. When I finally reopened my eyes, I found myself kneeling on the hardwood floor, freshly released from Yoshi's vicious grip. I could feel a circle of heat throbbing around the distressed bones of my limp hand.

"Welcome," Yoshi said.

I began studying under Yoshi that autumn. Although my previous master had been a triathlete who demanded a brutal level of conditioning from his students, Yoshi possessed something beyond a physical excellence that, with enough diligence and training, I hoped I would one day achieve. There was a fluidity and ruthlessness to his movements that made him seem impossible to stop. His speed was careless, his strength inscrutable, his touch adhesive and pitiless. He was shadowy, emotionless, disinterestedly cruel. At times, when facing him, I felt like I was facing death. Only unlike the invisible figure that had recently claimed my father, for all my new master's terrifying skill, Yoshi was tangible, reachable, even interrogable.

But he did not always answer the questions asked of him. Many times he would ignore them, or else answer an entirely different question. One evening, I was struggling to understand how to move an opponent who was resisting me. I had failed to predict the difficulty of inflicting great suffering, that what life had meted out casually to my family I had to labor to reproduce and, consequently, control. Yoshi told me to create a space for the person to fall into. "But how do I *get* them into that space?" I asked.

We were standing alone on the thin blue mats. Class had just ended, and a few students were waiting outside the overcrowded locker rooms for their turn to change, checking their phones for missed calls and messages.

"Look at Oriana's feet," Yoshi said.

I craned my neck to see them. "You mean the way she positions her toes?"

"They are sexy little feet," he said.

"I guess," I said, confused.

"Haven't you ever noticed them?"

"Not really."

"You must learn to look down. Where the eye goes, the mind follows."

"Yes, Sensei."

Yoshi raised an eyebrow. "Tonight I think it is time we celebrate your promotion. Too much seriousness is not good for a man, Mr. Wallace!"

Only a year had passed since I had joined Yoshi's dojo, but my devotion, along with my previous training, had sped my advancement, and Yoshi had recently made me an assistant instructor. After changing out of our uniforms, we went to the Irish pub across the street. The bartender was one of Yoshi's students, a handsome young yellow belt with a shaved head. He brought us a round of free drinks.

"Thank you, Billy," Yoshi said and scooped a handful of peanuts from a dish. He turned to me. "What do you think of the new Italian student?"

"Gabriella or Oriana?"

"Both of them," Yoshi said.

I shrugged. "Gabriella has that dancer background, so she's disciplined, flexible, good core strength. But then she's slow, the way dancers are. Everything's a performance and—"

"Oriana has very good spirit," Yoshi interrupted.

"I guess."

"Did you see last week when she saw a nail sticking up from the floor? She went straight to the office for a hammer and flattened it. Because she is raised *European.* American but European. They have family values." He motioned for Billy to bring a round of shots. "Really, you never noticed her feet?"

"I try not to get distracted by the students."

"The pinky toe has a very small nail. It is very sexy."

Billy came over with our shots. He placed them on the bar and asked Yoshi to correct his finger lock. "I was trying it on my mom last night and it wasn't working," he said.

"Which finger did you use?" I asked.

Yoshi shook his head. "Finger selection is unimportant. Of course, it is easier to pick one of the weaker fingers, but with proper technique all will work. Give me your hand."

Billy stretched out his palm. A moment later, his face was flat against the bar and he was breathing loudly out of his mouth.

"Always, you must strike a *kyusho,* a vital point, to attack a joint," Yoshi said. "Our *ki,* our energy, flows through these *kyusho.* They connect the body's energy system. Every joint is controlled by at least four—many to choose from."

After Billy staggered away, Yoshi raised his shot glass.

"To your tremendous achievement, Mr. Wallace."

"Thank you," I said, though I felt undeserving of the praise. Whatever skills I had developed were insignificant compared to Yoshi's. I was capable, even proficient, in certain situations, but I lacked the holistic devastation Yoshi routinely demonstrated. Wrists slipped out of my grip. Partners reversed my locks. I muscled through technique that should have been effortless.

"What is very important for you next . . ." Yoshi said, and I nodded eagerly. It was the first time that I had ever been out alone with Yoshi. He had often invited me for a drink after class, but always in a group of students, and we would sit around him while he entertained us with anecdotes about his boyhood training in Japan, rigorous drills in which he was forced to run barefoot in winter around the icy fields until the skin on the soles of his feet tore free. To sit together on our own, side by side, seemed an almost daunting privilege.

"Yes, Sensei?" I prompted.

"Another shot!" He laughed and motioned for Billy to bring us a round.

"But Sensei, doesn't drinking weaken your *kyusho*?"

"Well . . . yes." He picked up the shot glass between his thumb and forefinger and sniffed the contents. "But pleasure is a discipline too."

The following Saturday morning, Yoshi called. My wife handed me the telephone with her eyes still closed. She rolled over and fell back asleep.

"Sensei?" I whispered, climbing out of bed as quietly as possible.

"Come meet me at the dojo!" Yoshi cried.

"Now?"

"It is part of your training!"

"But Sensei, it's seven a.m."

"I am a night bird. I never went to sleep. Bring your car."

He hung up. I changed into sweatpants and a tee shirt, left my wife a note on the bathroom sink, and swiped the car keys from the self-adhesive hook by the front door. It was a long walk to the outdoor parking garage on Eleventh Avenue, and I had underestimated the cold. A dog walker in a knee-length coat blew onto alternating hands, her breath white in the September morning. Outside an apartment building, I passed a series of soil beds full of purple and black-striped flowers. The blooms looked startled and hunched over, as if interrupted while stepping out of the shower.

When I arrived at the dojo, I found Yoshi asleep on the mats. He wore a baggy, charcoal suit, the sleeves wrinkled from having been rolled up. One of his socks had a hole by the big toe, which I could see because Yoshi had taken off his shoes to use as pillows.

"Sensei, I'm here," I said and bowed.

Yoshi yawned.

"I'm here," I repeated, louder this time.

"Excellent, excellent." Yoshi sat up. His eyes were red and irritated. The radiator in the corner of the dojo spit out wet, petulant heat.

"Should I change into my uniform?" I asked.

"No, no," Yoshi said, rising off the mats. "Do you know New Jersey?"

"I guess so."

"I am unfamiliar with New Jersey. It is better if you drive." He stumbled toward the door, carrying his shoes in one hand like a sleepy child dragging her doll.

I had parked the car halfway down the block from the dojo. The lock on the passenger-side door was broken, and while waiting for me to climb in and open his door from the inside, Yoshi leaned his forearm against the roof and rested his head on it. Flecks of gray had begun to sprout in his black hair. Behind him, in the second-story window of an apartment building, pigeons were cooing. I put my shoulder into the door and popped it free.

"Where are we going in New Jersey, Sensei? Is there a *kyusho* seminar?" I asked hopefully, while we idled at a stoplight.

"We go to the mall," Yoshi said.

"The mall? Why?"

"The heart wants what it wants," he said and passed out.

I took a roundabout route to the Lincoln Tunnel, wandering through the red and yellow awning-filled labyrinth of Chinatown, up through Little Italy, and all the way over to the Meatpacking District, passing the French brasserie where I had taken my parents out to dinner on their first and only visit to the city. My father instantly disliked New York; he found it noisy and congested, and insisted it smelled of sewage. My mother, out of loyalty to my father or perhaps out of agreement, remained silent. I got angry at my father for his criticism and his reluctance; I felt that his disapproval of the city that I had fallen in love with was, through a commutative property to which sons are particularly receptive, a disapproval of me. I even snapped at him for picking at his meal, calling his conservative tastes childish. Had I known then that my father was already dying, that his mild appetite and the dull intermittent ache in his stomach and lower back were the result of metastasizing pancreatic cells, I might have kept quiet. None of us knew, however, what was coming. We couldn't anticipate the next five years with their radiant pain.

Yoshi slept fitfully while I sped southward along the New Jersey Turnpike. I don't suppose it's fair to expect grace from someone asleep, but it bothered me to watch him fidget, and after a while I turned on the radio to distract myself.

"Blondie. I love her voice," Yoshi said, stirring in the passenger seat.

"Sensei, how much farther until we get there?"

"This song reminds me of high school. The good old days. Smoking pot." He chuckled and slapped my shoulder, the impact of the blade of his hand against my body sending us halfway into the passing lane. I jerked the wheel and we swerved back. "Let's see," Yoshi said and pulled a cocktail napkin out of his pocket. He unfolded it, squinted, and then flipped the napkin upside down. "Can you read this?"

I took it from him. "We passed this exit five miles ago."

"Good, then we're almost there." He flipped down the sun visor to check himself out in the compact mirror. "It is a good thing Oriana likes long hair. I need a haircut very much."

"Is that who you went out with last night?"

"Of course not." He snapped the mirror shut. "I went out with Gabriella. Aerosmith!" he said, and spun the volume dial. "Even their later material is catchy. Aerosmith has a tremendous longevity. As a band, they are very reinventive."

"I don't understand. You went out with Gabriella? I thought you were interested in Oriana."

"It is always wise to befriend a woman's friend. A woman's heart, and not just her body, has *kyusho.*" He slid his crumpled tie free of his collar and began to retie it.

A few minutes later, we pulled into the parking lot and entered the mall. It didn't take us long to find Oriana. She was easy to spot. Oriana's job was to stand just inside the entrance of the NordicTrack store and demonstrate how to use their exercise machine. She wore a black leotard, a black tank top emblazoned with the store's logo, and sneakers so big and white and clean that it looked as if she had just stepped out of a snowbank in Aspen. She moved precisely but happily on the machine, her blond ponytail bouncing above her shoulders. A queasy cross between jazz and flamenco music accompanied her efforts.

Yoshi asked me to keep an eye on Oriana while he visited the bookstore on the second floor. "Do not let her see you," he instructed.

I leaned against the mall's information board and watched Oriana from a distance. Many of my friends were getting engaged, my wife and I had just had our wedding in June, so I was becoming increasingly familiar with the difficulty of understanding another person's romantic enthrallment. And while Oriana was hardly an inscrutable object of desire—she was attractive in the way that any blonde in her early twenties with healthy skin and an athletic body can be—I'll admit I expected something more from Yoshi, a hunger for exoticism and sophistication. The most exotic thing about Oriana was her slightly upturned nose of questionable authenticity.

Yoshi returned with a slim brown bag and motioned for me to follow him into the store.

"Miss Odenna," he said, nudging past a woman pushing a twin stroller.

"Master Takamata?"

"What a coincidence," Yoshi said. "I am just doing some weekend shopping with Mr. Wallace. You remember Mr. Wallace from the dojo? He is an assistant instructor now."

I glanced in the mirror that should have been projecting Oriana's taut figure across the store but instead reflected Yoshi in his rumpled baggy suit and me beside him, swaddled in sweatpants and a workout shirt.

"Wow," Oriana said. "You guys look different out of, you know, class."

"You too," I said.

"They make me wear this. It's like a uniform."

"Black is very sophisticated," Yoshi said. "Is this a difficult job?"

"Not really. The commute's the hardest part. My roommate moved out and she was the one with a car, so now I take a bus from Port Authority and it's about an hour and a half each way. What are you guys shopping for?"

"I am buying Mr. Wallace a book," Yoshi said. "To provide him spiritual guidance. It is easy to improve the body, but the spirit is much more difficult."

"Cool," Oriana said.

Yoshi opened the brown bag and extracted a thin black paperback entitled *Hagakure: The Book of the Samurai.* "There is surely nothing other than the single purpose of the present moment," Yoshi read aloud. "A man's whole life is a succession of moment after moment. If one fully understands the present moment, there will be nothing else to do, and nothing else to pursue. Live being true to the single purpose of the moment." Yoshi closed the book. "These are very inspiring words. When do you eat lunch?"

"I usually just get a salad. I don't know. Around one?"

"You must have lunch with us."

"Oh wow. Really?"

"I insist. Live true to the single purpose of the moment."

"I don't know if I can take a half hour. They're super strict. I'm not even supposed to talk to people."

"I will take care of it," Yoshi said.

"Wow. Thanks, um, Sensei." Oriana's smile was toothy and girlish, rapturous and a bit clumsy, the kind you see young women direct at their undeserving boyfriends.

"Do you like gyros?" Yoshi asked Oriana and handed off the book to me. I took it without thinking, distracted by the sense that something was wrong—something besides my having ended up in a mall in New Jersey, or Yoshi's successful wooing of Oriana with nothing more than a Japanese paraphrase of carpe diem. Then I realized: Oriana had stopped moving. She was standing still, one foot a half stride ahead of the other, her hands folded atop the plastic and metal control panel.

I wasn't the only one to notice.

"Everything okay over here?" asked a man in khaki pants and a black polo shirt, marching over to us. He was broad shouldered and thick, with a fat, ex–college football player's build. Monogrammed on the pocket of his shirt was the store's insignia and, above it, the word *manager.*

"Sorry. We were just talking for a second," Oriana said quickly.

"Do you have questions about the machine?" His face was soft and a little sweaty. It looked like if you stuck your finger in his cheek, the indentation would stay.

"Miss Odenna is a marvelous representative," Yoshi said. "She deserves a half-hour break with us as a reward."

I had once heard that only seven percent of communication was verbal, and that the remainder consisted of body language and facial expressions. Confronted by Oriana's glowering manager, for the first time I was obliged to consider this statement as more than an inflated statistic.

"Get back to riding the machine," he said.

With an anxious glance over her shoulder at us, Oriana resumed her pacing.

"Excuse me," Yoshi said, "you may not talk to Miss Odenna in this way."

The manager ran his tongue over his front teeth. He might have been irritated or he might have been bored. He certainly wasn't intimidated. "Why don't you two go somewhere else to pick up girls? Try Abercrombie and Fitch. There's a cute Chinese girl that works one of the registers." Finished with us, he turned to Oriana. "A little slower, honey. You can't sell this thing if you look like a hamster."

"I have not completed speaking with Miss Odenna," Yoshi said.

"Yeah, you have," the manager said.

"Excuse me, there is a misunderstanding. We have not been introduced: I am Yoshi Takamata. I am Miss Odenna's master." Yoshi extended his hand to shake. His disquieting, serene half smile had returned. The manager stared down at him with apparent bewilderment. Then, reflexively, he took Yoshi's outstretched hand. He would have been safer lowering his hand into a pot of boiling water.

After security released Yoshi, the three of us drove back to the city. Yoshi sat in the back seat to comfort Oriana, reading aloud from *The Book of the Samurai* to her. Oriana listened without reply, like a child being sung a lullaby. "For a samurai," Yoshi recited, "a single word is important no matter where he may be. By just one single word martial valor can be made apparent. In peaceful times words show one's bravery. In troubled times, too, one knows that by a single word his strength or cowardice can be seen. This single word is the flower of one's heart. It is not something said simply with one's mouth."

The changes at the dojo began soon afterward. A potted ficus plant appeared on the windowsill of Yoshi's office. Pine-tree-scented air fresheners hung in the locker room. The floors were swept, the mouse holes plastered over, and the mats mopped. Along with the addition of a miniature refrigerator and a cube-shaped portable speaker, these renovations were discreet and welcome, and at first I took them as indicators of a blossoming in Yoshi's life, as he courted Oriana in every venue that he could.

A few weeks after they had become a couple, Yoshi confessed the news to me in his office, though he needn't have bothered. He was in his early forties, and the pace of dating a girl in her early twenties was taking an obvious toll on him. His eyes were puffy with sleeplessness. His skin looked waxy. An aged slackness had overtaken his handsome, once-boyish face.

Gradually, he stopped teaching many of the classes. Oriana was now working as a cocktail waitress, a job Yoshi had secured for her through a former student who managed a Midtown nightclub, but he liked to be there at the start of her shifts, and since her hours were unpredictable and her schedule likely to change without warning, he often abandoned his teaching duties at the last minute. Naturally, this wasn't how Yoshi described it when he called in a panic half an hour before class, begging me to take over for him. Instead he invented emergencies, repetitive lies about late-running meetings and sudden dinners with clients—besides owning the dojo, Yoshi claimed to help at his father's insurance business—lies that would be forgotten hours later when my phone lit up with a midnight call from Yoshi, who was now at home, waiting for Oriana to get off work. I could hear the television babbling and the metallic click of a bottle opener. "She is so shy. She is an angel," Yoshi would tell me.

From the contact I'd had with Oriana, I didn't think she was an angel. She was shy, that was true, but she was also vain, and when people paid attention to her, the shyness vanished, and in its place came a brassiness that could easily be misinterpreted as something more inviting. While Yoshi was aware of the agitating effect Oriana could have on men, it didn't mean that he endured it with any grace. When they went out at night, he glared at men who eyed Oriana and threatened the intrepid ones who dared speak to her. Luckily, most of the bartenders knew Yoshi and prevented any real confrontations—except for one instance when Yoshi squeezed an overly solicitous man's jaw and brought him to the ground in flustered, agonized tears.

Oriana had asked him to keep their relationship secret from the other students. Consequently, Yoshi was careful not to favor Oriana in class and avoided eye contact with her if she asked a question. Yet his fascination was impossible to wholly conceal. He grinned whenever he spoke her name. He answered her too quickly, repeating himself and gesturing wildly. There were moments when I felt that everyone could sense his enchantment, that it was noisy, incandescent, flagrant—as love, perhaps, should be. One night I caught him staring through the rear window of his office, a diamond-shaped sliver of glass that looked out onto a corner of the dojo. When I reminded him that we had been waiting ten minutes for him to begin class, he whispered, "Mr. Wallace, you must come see this."

I closed the office door and came up beside him. He gestured to where

Oriana stood with her back to us. Her long blond hair was piled on top of her head and speared through with a chopstick. Inside her bulky white cotton uniform, she was winsomely petite, her neck as thin as a dandelion stalk. She reached high with her right arm and let her left arm slacken at her side. Slowly, tantalizingly, she stretched the tiny intercostal muscles running between each rib and the lean latissimus muscles of her lower back. She had been in the office plenty of times and knew precisely where the window was positioned.

Yoshi shifted in place, continuing to observe her. I could see the reflection of his eyes in the glass, and for a moment, I had the disconcerting sensation that I was once again in my parents' boxy old Volvo, looking up at the slashed reflection of my father's face. As the youngest of three, I sat in the small middle seat while my brothers sandwiched me, my arms pinned, with nowhere to go and nothing to do but stare ahead, either at the unspooling road or up into the rearview mirror. The angle of the mirror created a spooky superimposition, projecting my father's mouth onto his forehead, so that he looked like a Greek titan, ready to consume us.

It was strange to think of him like that now—my most recent and final memories of him were of a shrinking old man in a hospital bed, weak and pale, as bitter as an almond. That there had been a time when he was all powerful was almost unimaginable to me.

After class that night, when Yoshi announced that we were having a holiday party, I should have realized how far gone he was. Food, drink, even excessive conversation was forbidden in the sacred space of the dojo, where one forges one's soul through strict discipline. Yoshi kicked open the miniature refrigerator and pulled out two six packs, then told the candy distributor to run to the corner deli for beer. The windows that could open were opened. The radio was switched on to a classic rock station. Oriana came out of the dressing room, carrying a bag of votive candles under her arm and, without any warning, flipped off the overhead lights. Darkness stretched across the room. Then she lit a candle and placed it on the wooden floor, and lit another and another, each white circle spreading its new, urgent luminescence.

It was the time of year between Thanksgiving and Christmas, when a night in the city often becomes a matter of celebration, despite the unpleasant personal and professional facts of one's life. In those busy weeks, dozens of parties are attended, most of them happily—evidence of what might just be the enduring resoluteness of life, which doesn't care much for facts. And the forty students who milled around the dojo that night did seem genuinely cheerful as they drank beer and talked about their lovers, spouses and children—those essentials we ignore every night while we strive to inflict agonizing pain with ever greater ease—but I was gloomy and worried. I felt edgy, tethered to something I could neither recognize nor, accordingly, protect myself from.

After a while, I snuck into Yoshi's office. It was quieter in there, the radio muffled by the heavy wooden door, and much darker. The only light came through the small diamond-shaped window, and this light was a diminishment, the faint glimmer of distant candles. Holding my hands out in front of me, I navigated around the sharp edges of the desk and sat down behind it. It was uncomfortable on the floor, but it would have been disrespectful to sit in Yoshi's seat. I crossed my legs and shut my eyes, assuring myself that I was meditating, though really I was drunk and sleepy.

The creak of the door jarred me awake. I wasn't sure how much time had passed. I blinked in anticipation of brightness, but the light stayed off. Then the door clicked shut and two black shapes tiptoed across the office. The smaller shape approached the file cabinet and removed a bottle from the top drawer. It was the scotch that, I thought, Yoshi had told no one else about except for me. The bigger shape sat on the edge of the desk. He had his back to me, but I recognized Billy's shaved head.

"Did you bring cups?" whispered the smaller shape as she handed over the bottle. It was Oriana's voice.

"You don't drink Glenlivet from a *cup,*" Billy replied. Oriana giggled and rubbed Billy's shoulder. She ran a hand along his developed triceps and cupped his elbow, pulling him close to her.

I stood and turned on the green banker's desk lamp.

"Mr. Wallace!" Oriana said, jerking away from Billy. "Jesus, you scared me!"

"We were just getting something for Master Takamata," Billy said.

"But we couldn't find—" Oriana said.

"We need real glasses," Billy explained. "Then we were going to bring it out to him."

"I'll bring it," I told Billy. "Why don't you go? Oriana, stay for a minute."

Billy hurried out of the office. Oriana sat down in Yoshi's chair and crossed her legs. She pursed her lips into a small pout. There was something charming even in her sullenness, and I suspected she knew it. "What?" she said. It was an old story, maybe the oldest, and I wanted nothing to do with it.

"Don't hurt him," I said.

Yoshi pushed open the door with a grin. He had decided to grow his hair long, but instead of a masculine wave, it puffed out like a hedgehog's back. When he saw the bottle in my hand, he swatted my shoulder with affection. A nerve near my scapula went numb.

"Mr. Wallace, you have been hiding very unseasonally. But you are forgiven because you found my special treat."

Yoshi took the bottle from me. He filled three cups and gestured for us to raise them in a toast.

"To the flower of my heart," he said.

On Christmas Eve, my wife told me that she was pregnant, and a week after the new year, I stopped training with Yoshi. I explained that with a baby coming, I couldn't risk an injury that might put me out of work. He accepted my excuse with regret but didn't try to change my mind. Perhaps he worried that there was something else to my sudden resignation, some behavior for which he was responsible and that he didn't want to confront.

I was surprised by how little I missed the dojo. My wife encouraged me to continue my training, concerned that I was abandoning my only outside interest. Like my father, I had no hobbies, and when the illness overtook him, he'd had nowhere to go for diversion.

"I'm not like my father," I told her.

"I didn't say you were. Just that . . . people need something else."

"I don't need it anymore," I told her.

"But you like it."

I wondered if I did. When I was nine years old, desperate to impress my older brothers, and exchanging the first and most valuable currency of boys, which is bravery, I had jumped off our roof. When our father heard me crying, he came outside to the backyard and, shaking his head, told me to get into the car so he could take me to the hospital. "I can't walk," I'd cried, crumpled on the grass. My brothers came over to help me up, but our father waved them away. "He does it himself or he doesn't go." It took ten minutes for me to drag myself across the yard and to the car, and another five to settle into the back seat, wincing as I struggled to position my leg in a way that didn't make me want to scream. When I was done, my father climbed behind the steering wheel and lit a cigarette. He looked over his shoulder at me, exhaling smoke as he spoke. "If you're going to be stupid, you'd better learn to be tough."

But training with Yoshi hadn't taught me anything about being tough. And perfecting the painful manipulation of a stranger's *kyusho* now seemed equally senseless. Whatever minor skill I had gained only rendered me more aware of how vulnerable we are. It was an impossible task. There was no training, no expertise, no level of mastery that could ever truly protect us.

*

I saw Yoshi one more time, at the end of February. He had been locked out of his apartment and called to ask if I would come downtown and give him my keys to the dojo, which I had forgotten to return.

"It's almost four in the morning. Why don't you just take a cab up here and sleep on our couch?" I offered.

"I must get into the dojo."

"I'll pay for the cab."

"My keys," he repeated. "Please."

I put on a sweater and a pair of jeans and thick black boots. Softly I kissed my wife's warm cheek. Her forehead was damp with sweat and her lips chapped. She often woke in the middle of the night and had trouble falling back asleep, but that night her breathing was heavy and deep. She was growing, changing, becoming. It was a strange new process, tasked with its own variety of pain, and I kissed her again, full of gratitude. Then I found the keys and hailed a cab to help my old master.

Yoshi was waiting for me in the Irish pub. It closed at four, but the bartender, a heavyset man in his fifties, had let him stay inside until I arrived. Yoshi sat slumped in a booth in the corner. His eyes were gray and unfocused. He hadn't shaved in a few days, maybe a week, and a wispy mustache was sprouting above his lip, giving him the appearance of a catfish.

"Master Takamata," I said.

"Excellent, excellent." He waved to the bartender. "A great student!"

The bartender handed me Yoshi's tab. I paid it and we left.

Outside, Yoshi paused at the curb of the sidewalk. The cold night air seemed to have roused him, and he began to bob his head slightly, as if he were a boxer weaving in a fight. "The night is still young, Mr. Wallace. I know a Japanese bar . . . very high profile. I introduce you to a Japanese girl." He took an accidental step off the sidewalk, flinging his arms wide to reassert his balance. "Japanese girls—very loose. They pretend the opposite, but they are island girls. A history of many sailors."

"I brought your keys," I said and led him across the street.

He labored up the two flights of stairs to the dojo, and then I unlocked the door for him. The air smelled dusty. Plaster littered the edges of the floor where the mouse holes had been chewed back open. I switched on the light but Yoshi switched it off.

As I kneeled in the doorway to untie the laces of my boots, Yoshi pushed past me and lay down on the mats. He stared at the ceiling, stained with years of water damage.

"Oriana is gone," he said.

"I'm sorry."

"She leaves me for her yoga teacher." He kicked off one shoe and tried to pry free the other but couldn't do it. I walked over and unlaced it for him. Then I placed both his shoes alongside the edge of the mat.

"Thank you," he said.

"Are you going to sleep here?"

"I don't need to sleep. I am a night bird."

He blinked.

"Do you think she loved me?"

"Why don't you try and get some rest?" I said.

"Did she?" Yoshi sat up, leaning on his elbow to face me. "Tell me the truth."

I hesitated. I thought about the icy fields of Yoshi's youth, the skin tearing from his feet as he chased after bravery and strength.

"No," I said.

He smiled. It was the smile that I had so often confused with serenity, but which was only familiarity, a muted recognition of the transference of pain. Yoshi closed his eyes. I placed his jacket over his shoulders, left the keys beside the door, and went home to my beautiful wife.

Girlfriend

Neither handsome nor outgoing, of unknown employment and shabbily dressed, Nicholas Jenson was an unlikely candidate for infatuation. It was weeks into the school year before Hannah even noticed him, though this had less to do with any specific absence of appeal than a disregard for men in general. Since her divorce four years ago, she had gone on a number of dates, a few arranged by friends, the rest brokered online, but regardless of initiative or responsibility, the results had been similarly disheartening. It wasn't just that most of the available men her age professed themselves uninterested in commitment. She, too, when newly divorced, had had little interest in resuming the chain of suppressing and withholding that had characterized her eleven-year marriage. It was that when these men did, at last, decide to commit again, they chose partners who were ten, twelve, even fifteen years younger. Dismissing everything that they had learned through the agonizing collapse of a marriage about the necessity of parity and mutuality, they scooped up a twenty-nine-year-old and blithely started over. Had it not been for her son, Mitchell, Hannah would have written off the entire male half of the human race. Thanks to Mitchell, she merely seethed at it.

She first met Nicholas during parent volunteer pick-up duty at Corsair Private Elementary. Pick-up duty did not actually consist of willing volunteers: the school ran and enforced a random-selection process—a lottery in which you won an inconvenience, like jury duty, or a cancer scare. On the day that it was Nicholas's turn, he stood by the chain-link fence, waving children through the gate, a red-and-white-striped electric bullhorn dangling by a strap from his wrist. As a new parent, he didn't know many of the families, and his failure to quickly match the children to their parents was holding up the line of approaching cars. In the midst of this slowdown, a third-grade boy snatched a girl's knapsack and, hooting with triumph, scrambled up a tree. Hannah watched Nicholas hesitate, besieged on one side by impatient drivers, on the other by an eight-year-old girl already well acquainted with the influence of tears.

"It's okay, we'll get it back," he reassured the crying girl, but the instant he took a step away from the gate into the schoolyard, he was blasted with a honk. "Hang on," he called out. As he hurried to the base of the tree, additional honks followed him like little goslings.

"Excuse me. Um . . . excuse me," he said, but whether the boy couldn't hear Nicholas's voice over the rising clamor from the indignant drivers, or simply didn't care, he clung to the branch.

Hannah slipped her phone into her purse and walked over to the contested tree. She grabbed the bullhorn, still attached to Nicholas's wrist, and yanked his arm upward so that she could comfortably reach the mouthpiece. "Get down, Jackson. Right now. Or I'm calling your mother." As the boy scrambled down the trunk, proclaiming his innocence, Hannah led Nicholas back to the gate by the wrist. She swiftly dispatched the waiting students while he stood on the library steps, fiddling with the thirty-watt bullhorn.

"Let's go, Corsair Seagulls!" Nicholas announced with an augmented boom, startling a fourth-grader en route to the after-school soccer program.

"Give me that," Hannah said and reached for the bullhorn. "And your vest."

He wriggled free of the reflective orange vest. Hannah wrapped it around the bullhorn and tucked them both into the unlocked volunteer bin.

"Thanks," he said. "I'm Nicholas, by the way."

"Hannah."

"That was good teamwork."

"You didn't actually do anything."

He laughed amiably, straightening his back. He was taller than she had first thought, and his bottom teeth were crooked, like a foreigner's. He had thin but persistent blond hair and an easy smile, and he was not bad looking, in the simplistic way that any man could be acceptable if you were angling for competence. For a moment, Hannah recalibrated her opinion of him, dismissing awkwardness and diffidence as the by-products of intelligence. Then she caught him nodding to a young mother dressed in yoga pants and a tank top, and a flash of anger singed her.

"I'm late to pick up the twins from their after-school class," he said, "but maybe—"

"No," she interrupted.

"No what?"

"No to anything. To everything. Not interested," she said and walked away.

Hannah glimpsed Nicholas a few days later, after dropping off Mitchell at school in the morning. Nicholas was shepherding his son and daughter to kindergarten, and he briefly let go of the boy's hand to wave to her from across the blacktop. It was a big, broad canvas-covering stroke of congeniality. Hannah ignored him. Her friend Melissa waved back.

"You know him?" Hannah said.

"He's one of the dads from Chloe's class. Nick Jenson."

"What do you know about him?"

Melissa shrugged. "Divorced. Straight."

"His sneakers tell me that," Hannah said. "I mean his background. Job, education, interests. Who is he?"

Melissa widened her eyes and jerked her head at Mitchell.

"Hey, off to class," Hannah said, smacking her son on the rear.

"*Mom.*"

"And don't forget your father's picking you up today. I want you home by eight-thirty, homework done."

As Mitchell slouched away, Hannah turned to Melissa. "Well?"

"I really don't know very much," Melissa whispered. She led them toward the Parent Association Meeting Room, a converted teachers' lounge now used for committee gatherings. Beside the door hung a bulletin board to which colorful sign-up sheets had been pinned like extracurricular butterflies.

Melissa switched on the light and entered the room. "I think he's some kind of musician?"

"Then how does he afford two kids at Corsair?"

"His ex-wife's a corporate lawyer," Melissa said, slipping out of her beige trench coat and laying it on the counter, folded in half. She placed her purse beside it.

"Attractive?"

"So-so. She has bad skin. She gets peels too often. Ends up looking papery."

"Does she come to school a lot?"

"I only saw her the first day," Melissa said and sniffed the coffee pot, wrinkling her surgically reduced nose. "It's either him or a Filipino nanny. He's a very involved dad. Seems like a good guy."

Hannah grunted. She didn't believe in good guys. Men were just monsters in varying states of revelation and collapse.

"Filters . . ." Melissa muttered and began rummaging through the low cabinet.

Through the window, Hannah saw Nicholas coming back across the school courtyard alone. The Parent Meeting Room was adjacent to the campus exit, a common place for parents to stop and talk. Hannah made brief eye contact with him, then turned away, tilting her chin downward slightly. Her college boyfriend had told her that her left side was the more attractive, nearly the only thing that she still recalled from their two-year relationship. She held the pose, waiting for Nicholas to enter the room.

"Got it," Melissa said and waved a coffee filter in the air like a white flag. "So how do you know him?"

Hannah gave in to curiosity and looked outside.

Nicholas was gone.

A rush of embarrassment overtook her and was instantly replaced with irritation.

"Ugh," she said and rolled her eyes. "He's obsessed with me."

Despite being the cochair of the school fund-raising committee, Hannah skipped Corsair's annual Oktoberfest fund-raiser event that year. She had been invited to a "girls' getaway" in New York City with five friends she rarely saw any more. They had all met in Los Angeles when in their early thirties, most newly married and some of them pregnant or soon to be pregnant with their first children. Since then, everyone but Hannah had moved from Southern California, and everyone but Amanda and Celine—who was hosting the weekend at her home in New Jersey, on the outskirts of the city—had gotten divorced. Hannah anticipated a wild, vaguely vengeful weekend of heavy drinking and dancing in Manhattan, and at the expense of considerable interpersonal capital, she secured Melissa as a fill-in for the fund-raiser and her mother as a fill-in with Mitchell.

The morning of Hannah's departure for the proposed debauchery, two of the women dropped out due to emergencies. Hannah was not particularly well versed in statistics, but the odds of two out of six women felled by an emergency on the same weekend seemed highly unlikely. Worried about the virulence of defection, Hannah sent a rallying group text as she boarded her LAX-Newark flight: *Forget those bitches. Onward, ladies!*

She slept on the plane and touched up her makeup in the airport bathroom before getting a cab. When the taxi pulled up to Celine's home, Hannah glanced around the suburban Bergen County neighborhood with apprehension. This looked nothing like the outskirts of Manhattan, more like its ankle socks. She rang the doorbell and was disconcerted when Celine's husband opened the door. Behind him, Celine's eight- and ten-year-old sons were chasing each other up the carpeted stairs.

"I thought this was a girls' weekend," Hannah said as she entered the kitchen, where Amanda, Celine, and Kelly each hugged her with one arm, careful not to spill their red wine.

"It is," Celine said, brushing aside a loop of her curly hair. "But since it's just the four of us now, there was room for David and the kids to stay. They won't get in the way."

"As long as they're not *my* kids and husband," Amanda said.

Everyone but Hannah laughed devotedly at this minor joke, eager to dispel the sudden tension. Hannah had always liked Celine least of the five. Hannah considered Celine self-satisfied to the point of complacency and resourcefully passive-aggressive. "Half-French and half haircut" was how she had once described Celine to her ex-husband.

Whether she had developed some form of heightened pattern recognition that came with turning forty, or if she had simply befriended three women who had since become woefully predictable, in that moment Hannah knew exactly how the weekend would turn out. She could have scripted it, so accurate were her disappointment and resentment: the noisy Italian dinner swimming with pinot noir; the strident babble about children and husbands, ex-husbands and boyfriends (everything they had endeavored to escape that weekend); the enthusiastic suggestion to go out dancing and, as soon as they saw just how young the crowd was, the equally enthusiastic decision by the married women to head home to Celine's so as "not to ruin tomorrow." For Hannah, who back in Los Angeles was routinely besieged with an anxiety about aging so great that, were it an airplane, it would have sucked every bird in the Southern California sky into its engines, the girls' night out in New York City had been intended as a glorious countermove, a celebratory parry to this tedious, unnerving thrust to remain young. Instead, she found herself at two in the morning dragging Kelly by the hand along Seventh Avenue, both of them gloomily drunk and disastrously underdressed for the autumnal cold. As Hannah hunted in vain for a taxi that would ferry them to New Jersey, Kelly huddled close behind, bemoaning her latest breakup. "Why is everyone off duty?" Hannah demanded, waving her arms at distant yellow cars.

"He didn't want a partner. He wanted a distraction," Kelly said.

"This is unbelievable," Hannah said, as another car flew past with its overhead light switched off. Both of their cell phones had run down an hour ago, leaving them at the mercy of uncommitted drivers.

"He's still going on the New Orleans trip," Kelly said. "Even without me."

The traffic lights flashed to red. Hannah strained to see down the avenue, searching the idling cars for possibility.

"He cc'ed me on the hotel email. That he didn't need a suite anymore but still wanted a room. Isn't that crazy?" Kelly said.

"You deserve better than him," Hannah said. She stamped her feet against the concrete sidewalk to warm her legs. Shivering, she cupped her hands to her face and breathed onto them. "We're catches. *Catches,*" she said, as a new unsympathetic fleet of cars for hire sped past.

Hannah returned to Los Angeles late Sunday evening, flush with a feeling of relief that bordered on happiness. She thanked her mother for watching Mitchell and quietly began to unpack so as not to wake her son, asleep in his room. She was carrying her cosmetics bag down the hallway when she noticed her mother standing by the bookshelf in the living room.

"You're still here," Hannah said.

"Oh." Her mother smiled and leafed through a biography of Sylvia Plath. Unlike Hannah, her mother was not a reader, and the large hardcover book looked as implausible in her hands as a bugle.

"Did you want something?" Hannah said.

"Oh it's . . . maybe we should discuss it another time." She folded shut the book and slid it onto the shelf.

Hannah dropped the cosmetics bag on a chair and crossed the room. She removed the book from the novels among which her mother had slotted it and returned it to its correct shelf.

"Did something happen with Mitchell? I know he can seem aloof sometimes, but he's just spacey."

"No, no, Mitchell was wonderful." She inhaled in that deep, Yogic, nostril-flaring way that always subtly shamed Hannah, since the closest thing she had to a spiritual practice was screaming "Fucking Christ!" when she stubbed her toe.

"If you don't want to talk about it, I'm not going to force you."

"I met someone," her mother said, exhaling at last. "A man."

Hannah shrugged, not particularly surprised by this revelation. Men had always been attracted to her mother. As a young woman, Hannah's mother had occasionally been approached by modeling agents—though Hannah's father, a jealous and fearful man, would never allow his wife to pose for photos—and even now, a widow in her early sixties, her mother remained athletic, tall, and slim, with silver-white hair halfway down her back and an austere bone structure that prompted frequent yet inaccurate speculation of Native American ancestry.

"What does this have to do with me? Wait—is it getting serious? Are you guys talking marriage?"

"Oh, no, no!" her mother said, trilling. "We just met yesterday, Hannah. At the pumpkin patch event you asked me to bring Mitchell to while you—"

"Oktoberfest."

"Oktoberfest, yes. But it was a very interesting conversation, he's a nice man, and he invited me out for coffee, and I didn't want to respond until I'd discussed it with you. After all, it's Mitchell's school, and I didn't—"

"Mom, it's fine," Hannah said, waving her hand as if dispersing an unpleasant odor. "I don't care what you do. Go ahead, get coffee with random grandparents. It's your life."

"Oh no, he's not a grandparent, he's a parent," she said. "He says he met you recently. Nicholas Jenson?"

*

Joyce was surprised by her daughter's restraint. Almost a full week passed before Hannah asked her mother if she had ever met with Nicholas, this from a girl who had been so determined to figure out what she was getting for Christmas that one year, after spying her mother leave the house with a small, unmarked box, Hannah had inadvertently dug up the body of her dead hamster in the backyard.

Now that curiosity was trained on her mother, and Hannah peppered her with questions.

Where did they go? What time of day was it? What did he wear? What did he drink? Did he sit facing the door? Did the people there know him? Did he excuse himself for the bathroom? Multiple times? Did he cover his mouth while speaking? Did he talk about his ex-wife? Did he take out his cell phone and place it on the table or leave it in his pocket?

"Oh, I can't remember," Joyce insisted, though in truth, it had been a memorable encounter, not because she had assessed a series of behavioral maneuvers that, together, signified a great probability of romantic intention, but for the simple reason that it had been pleasant. Nicholas had a patient demeanor, he smiled often, he paid attention when she spoke, he did not continually redirect the conversation toward himself, and perhaps most notable of all, unlike the handful of men she had met with socially since her husband's death, Nicholas did not seem to be auditioning for a caretaker or looking for an audience. He just liked her.

"Well, I've got to hand it to him," Hannah said. "He's creative."

"Oh, have you heard his music?" asked Joyce, prying the lid off the blender and dropping in a handful of watercress, a Persian cucumber, and a quartered green apple. "I've been curious to hear it."

"No," Hannah said. "I mean creative about this."

"This?" Joyce peeled a banana and dropped it inside the blender, placing the peel beside the squeezed lime and the apple core in the compost container under the sink.

"Getting on my good side. Cozying up to the mom and then, bam, you're in. It's a little old-fashioned. Not to mention kind of creepy."

"Honey," Joyce said gently, "I think you misunderstood. Nicholas didn't meet with me to . . . sway you."

"Well, he's not going to come right out and say what he really wants. Men are a little more devious than that, Mom." Hannah rolled her eyes, flashing the same expression of pleased superiority as when she had helped her mother create a Facebook profile (whose friend request Hannah had swiftly ignored).

"If he bothers you again, just let me know," Hannah said.

Joyce nodded unhappily. Her excitement had been contaminated by her daughter's distrust, and doubt slowly crept into her heart. She did not believe that Nicholas had intentions for her daughter—whenever Joyce had brought up Hannah, Nicholas had merely blinked, as if waiting out a television commercial—but it occurred to Joyce that neither did it mean that Nicholas had intentions for her either. Had she misinterpreted his kindness and attention, his curiosity and friendliness, as something romantic?

When a week had passed and still Nicholas had failed to contact her, despondency overtook her. She had imagined everything. Though she'd engaged in but the mildest flirtation, she punished herself with made-up visions designed for maximum humiliation: sprawled across the coffee-shop table like a desperate supplicant while this man, twenty years her junior, courteously struggled to hide his horror and disgust. She had become precisely what she'd feared all these years: a joke. In her midfifties, even before her husband had died, Joyce had understood that she was no longer allowed the same desires that had once begrudgingly been permitted a woman. She was considered too old for lust and for longing. Gradually, inexorably, the world had come to view her sexual interest as untoward, distasteful, or, worst of all, ridiculous—so unlikely to be reciprocated as to be amusing, a pratfall of desire.

Then, the following Wednesday, Nicholas called.

Although Joyce had told herself that she would have preferred he never contact her again, the alacrity with which she answered her phone belied this assertion. Nicholas began with a fumbling apology for the belated call, something about work and coordinating childcare, and then asked if she was free on Friday night. A musician he liked was performing at a jazz club in Pasadena.

"I don't care much for jazz," Joyce said.

"It's not traditional jazz. It's got elements of almost . . . minimalist classical? Hard to put into words. But trust me, he's really good."

"I don't doubt it," Joyce said. She was surprised by the coolness in her own voice; she hadn't consciously summoned it, and she was unsure whether it revealed actual, suppressed anger or whether it was an instinctual imposture meant to chasten and entice him. It had been so long since she'd been courted—if, God forbid, that's what this even was—and she'd forgotten how warlike these things were. The feints and the flattery, the tactics and the tactlessness, the sincerity bleeding into affection, the affection bleeding into fear. Nicholas tried once more to persuade her to accompany him, but Joyce made it clear that she was uninterested, a front of indifference that haunted her the moment the call ended and she realized what she had just done.

It took all of her restraint to keep from calling Nicholas back and shouting that she would come with him to Pasadena. Drawing on the lifelong reserve of a beautiful woman, for whom rejection is an especially bitter flavor, she successfully resisted calling him for three days. On Saturday morning, once there was no longer any risk of undermining herself, she dialed his number.

"It's Joyce," she said. "What did I miss?"

He had a soft laugh, and over the phone it had a way of sounding like something whispered just out of earshot.

"You didn't miss anything," he said. "I didn't go."

"Why not?" she asked with satisfaction.

"I didn't want to go alone. It would have been depressing."

"Oh."

She hadn't expected honesty, and it briefly disarmed her.

"Well, I'm on my way to the beach," she said, recovering her levity. "If you're interested in coming along, we could meet there."

"In November?"

"It's sixty-five degrees outside."

"Clearly you're new to the West Coast," Nicholas said. She did not remind him that she had moved to Los Angeles over six years ago—after the death of her husband, to help raise her grandson—since except for widowhood, she hadn't been called new in reference to just about anything for quite some time.

"I'll bring the body boards. Do you have a wet suit?" she said.

"Sure. One wet suit coming up."

They agreed to meet at noon by the lifeguard station on the border of Santa Monica and Venice. Joyce arrived early and sat in the shade. It was November, and the beach had been mostly abandoned. The volleyball courts lay unattended, the lifeguard stations boarded up for the season. When she spotted Nicholas crossing the bicycle path on foot, she stood up from the sand and waved unnecessarily.

"Where's your wet suit?" she asked as he approached. He was dressed in his usual sloppy outfit: worn jeans, a yellow tee shirt so old it threatened transparency, and an unzipped navy-blue hoodie.

"My what?" he said, tossing his knapsack back onto his shoulder like a girl flipping her hair.

She motioned to the two body boards she had stacked alongside the lifeguard station, atop of which lay a wetsuit.

"I thought you were kidding," he said.

"Why would I be kidding?"

He tugged at the drawstring to his hoodie.

"Why would that be a joke?" she said.

"Well, it . . . wouldn't," he stammered. "You're welcome to own a wetsuit. I just thought . . . I figured . . ."

Joyce watched him continue to fidget with the drawstring. She had always been active, a dedicated runner, a strong swimmer, and an aggressive tennis player, and over the past few years the frequent visits to the beach with her grandson had led her to take up bodyboarding. Of course none of that was imaginable to him, she thought with chagrin, a man whose reference point for a sixty-two-year-old woman was a Warner Brothers cartoon widow in a black housedress and tight gray bun, waving a cane. She felt her confidence and excitement implode once again, the tenuous structure of hope collapsing in upon itself.

"It's fine," she said. "You don't have to keep explaining yourself."

"I've just never been into surfing, or any water sports for that matter. I don't like to be cold and wet. But I think it's great you like waterboarding."

"Bodyboarding," she corrected. "Waterboarding is a form of torture."

"Right." He laughed his soft little whisper. "Freudian slip."

Joyce blushed. When anticipating meeting a younger man, she had tried to purge certain words from her lexicon so as to avoid any discomfiting moments; foremost among these words were Freud and Oedipus.

Nicholas knelt in front of his knapsack and removed an oversized beach towel. He laid it on the sand, anchoring two corners with his shoes and a third with the bag itself. Squinting up into the sunlight behind her, he motioned for Joyce to join him. She removed her sandals and walked toward the towel, the cool sand displacing beneath her bare feet.

They sat and faced the ocean together, watching the white-hemmed waves tumble with rough constancy onto the beach. It was a senseless and comforting sight. They spoke easily and intermittently, neither trying to enchant nor failing to endear, and at some point, after the wind had blown her hair across her face yet again and she had reached up to tuck the wild silver strands behind her ear, she laid her head on his shoulder.

The next time they met, they went out to dinner. Then it was his turn to have the twins, and she did not hear from him for a few days. When he called her up again, it was to invite her to a photography exhibition at the Hammer Museum. Another dinner followed, then another daytime outing, this time at the Getty. Joyce was pleased with the invitations but wondered what, exactly, Nicholas wanted. Except for that single moment on the beach in November, the physical intimacy between them had been tentative to the point of near absence. Nicholas did not try to kiss her, hug her, or hold her hand, blurring the already shadowy line between friendship and attraction. So a week before Christmas, she invited Nicholas over to her home for dinner. She picked up a vegetarian entrée and two sides from Whole Foods and reheated them in the oven, not bothering to cook from scratch, as her intention was to sleep with him, not to impress him with a quiche. Besides, she reasoned, if she succeeded, he wouldn't care what they ate, and if she failed, then she would have wasted her time cooking an elaborate meal.

He arrived with a bottle of red wine, a romantically indefinite gift—no flowers?—and she was so nervous that she drank half of the bottle before they had even begun their meal. For his part, Nicholas was more talkative than usual. Recently he had taken a job at a software company, composing soundtracks and incidental music for video games, and the corporate experience seemed to alternately agitate and intrigue him.

"I don't know what I expected exactly," he said. "But it's not—I don't hate it. I thought I would."

"You're not very hateful," she said.

"They really like what they do. The people working there. That might be the difference. What I wasn't expecting."

"It's good to like things," she said and then cringed at her blandness. All night she had been worrying about coming off as chaste or asexual, and here she was dispensing mild homilies. She poured herself more wine, thinking of her daughter's unfailing provocation. How she had raised a girl like Hannah, who would say or do just about anything that entered her mind, had often flummoxed Joyce—now, however, she envied her daughter's fearlessness.

Thankfully, it was not an unattainable state, as Joyce confirmed an hour later when she tossed the empty second bottle into the recycling bin and tottered back to the table. Nicholas had pushed his chair back a few inches and, without thinking, Joyce sat on his lap.

"Oh," he said.

"I'm on your lap," she said.

"You are. Hello."

"I sit sidesaddle—like a lady."

He laughed and finally, mercifully kissed her. She placed her hands on his shoulders to steady herself. She could feel a flush of heat spreading from her face to her neck and across her chest, and then it bloomed throughout her body without order or passage, on the soles of her feet and the backs of her knees and the palms of her ringless hands.

She led him out of the dining room into her dark, low-ceilinged bedroom. They slipped under the covers and undressed without speaking. She had done everything possible to get him to this place, yet now that he was here, she was seized by a staggering fear that almost caused her to call it off. What if he didn't want her? What if he found her creased and sun-damaged skin unseemly, her wrinkled neck repellent, her sagging breasts shameful? What would he think when he saw her flaccid stomach, the gray smudge of her Cesarean scar nearly as old as him?

It was a world of youth, and while years ago she had indignantly reconciled herself to invisibility, the prospect of visibility and all its attendant judgment and rejection suddenly upset her even more. Then she felt him beside her, excited, straining, she heard his shallow breath in her ear, and the persistence of male desire reassured her. Her husband's tendency to stray had once tormented her; she had despised his biological rationalizations masquerading as apologies, thinking his self-portrait of lust cowardly and juvenile; and thus it was an unexpected gratification to benefit from this same ineradicable lust all these years later.

Nicholas, to his credit, was nothing like her husband. He was as gentle and thoughtful in bed as he was out of it, though unfortunately he was also exceedingly affectionate afterward. As much as Joyce still enjoyed making love, her interest in postcoital cuddles had diminished, and after a polite request from Joyce, Nicholas dutifully pulled back.

As the weeks passed, they continued to see each other whenever Nicholas's busy work and parenting responsibilities and Joyce's grandparent duties allowed them the time. There was a second and more severe impediment to their relationship, however, that had nothing to do with schedules: Hannah. Joyce did not want her daughter to know about Nicholas, and she avoided going anywhere together where they might run into Hannah, Hannah's friends, or parents from Corsair. It was an impossible dodge to indefinitely sustain, but Joyce had kept secrets from her daughter for a lifetime, and Joyce believed that she could do so again. Then one day in late February, she received a phone call from Nicholas asking her what kind of car her daughter drove.

"Hannah's car?" Joyce said. "It's a . . . Civic. Honda Civic."

"Is it blue?"

"It's cobalt."

"What's cobalt?" Nicholas said. "A kind of green? I'm bad with colors."

"Dark blue. Why do you ask?"

"Because I think she might be following me."

Nicholas first spotted Hannah behind him in the Starbucks drive-through line. He had come from dropping off the twins at school and wouldn't see them again for three days, and distracted by that confusing collaboration of sadness and reprieve particular to divorced parents sharing custody of their children, he initially failed to notice Hannah crouching slightly behind the wheel of her car. He glimpsed her in his rearview mirror just as he was accelerating back onto Lincoln Avenue, hot coffee in hand, and came across her an hour later filling up her tank at the gas station and, again that evening, pushing an empty cart around the supermarket. For a moment, Nicholas wondered if this was the universe telling him that it was time to dispense with secrecy. Joyce's insistence on her daughter's ignorance had always bothered him; his three near encounters with Hannah seemed serendipitous, signs that they needed to become friends, that all of this subterfuge was silly. It was the kind of dreamy, upbeat, magical thinking that had initially charmed, then gradually incensed his ex-wife, who'd argued that his childish, imprudent outlook had ensured her having to work nonstop as she shouldered the family's financial burden.

"So work less," Nicholas had replied. "We don't need money to be happy."

"You're kidding, right? You're not really saying that."

"We can manage."

"How? We have a mortgage. We have two car payments. Insurance. Utilities. The cable bill alone is two grand a year. Then there's—"

"We'll stop watching TV."

"Nick, we have kids! That means preschool. Then twelve years of private school. Then college. Not to mention all of the extracurricular activities, gymnastics and karate and ballet and soccer . . . There's clothes, there's toys and bikes and birthday parties. Do you have any idea how much all that costs?"

"A lot. I know, I know," Nicholas had said gently. He was accustomed to giving reassurance. The youngest of five children, it had always fallen on him to smooth things over in his family. As a child, he'd often relied on the pacifying charm of innocence and sweetness, and he had carried it on into adulthood. But just as the coquettishness and petulance of the starlet are endearing at eighteen and unbearable at forty-five, so are the goofy optimism and sunny persistence of the indigent musician.

"We can figure this out," Nicholas had assured his ex-wife, even after she'd begun suggesting divorce. "I can try to get a regular job. I don't know who would hire me, but if you put yourself out there, the universe will listen."

"The universe? Don't talk to me about the universe, Nick. The universe fucks you. That's what it does."

Now, a year after the divorce had been finalized and six months after finding the steady employment that might have saved—though more likely, merely prolonged—his marriage, Nicholas still believed that things had a way of working themselves out. He was not immune to melancholy, but he had a resistance to it that could almost be called a talent, and upon glimpsing the profile of his girlfriend's daughter at the distant end of the soup aisle, he hewed to this cheerfulness and approached her.

"Hannah!" he said, waving, but she had already turned the corner. He hurried down the aisle and rounded the corner. The only person there was a white man with dreadlocks somberly comparing nut butters. He skipped to the next aisle, then the next, then still the next, but there was no sign of Hannah anywhere. Nor was she in the produce section, the bakery, or either of the frozen foods aisles. When, at last, he tried the checkout counters, she was missing from there too. Had he imagined her?

But he was more concerned about Joyce. Since she'd proposed they take a vacation together in Hawaii—Nicholas's ex was flying the twins to Idaho for spring break to visit their maternal grandparents, leaving him free for the week—Joyce had become almost unreachable. She'd never been very communicative, relishing her privacy and independence, but this was something else.

On the night before he was due to get the children back for three days, he impulsively set out for Joyce's house. She'd failed to return his calls all day, and he wanted to be sure that nothing had happened to her. At least, this was the excuse he gave himself for the unsolicited visit when he pulled up to her small, darkened house in Playa Del Mar and knocked on the door. The truth was that he missed her, and he expected her to open the door, to shake her head with bemusement, and to pull him inside.

Except there was no answer.

He knocked again, listening for the approach of her footsteps.

Silence.

She was probably out, he reasoned as he retreated onto the lawn, out running errands or dropping off her grandson, or else she had driven down to the beach for an evening walk.

The headlights of a car turning onto the street momentarily lit up the windowless garage door and Nicholas wondered if there was a way to determine if her car was inside. He went over to the garage door and pressed his ear to it, rapping it with the back of his knuckles, and straining to hear some reverberation or quickening of sound that might indicate an emptiness within. Of course, there was none, and feeling stupid, he pulled his head away. This wasn't like him—the anxiety, the impatience—he ought to go home, he told himself.

But instead of returning to his car, he rooted around the herb garden that Joyce had planted below the kitchen window and located the spare house key. He tucked the key into his palm and waited by the door while a pair of high school kids in reflective orange vests jogged along the sidewalk out front. Once they were out of sight, he inserted the key into the lock and pushed his way inside.

"Joyce?" he called out. The living room was murky and indistinct, a mass of soft shadows. "Hello?" he said, advancing past the black body of a couch. In the kitchen, he found an unfinished green shake in the blender, and the cutting board dotted with parsley. "Are you here?" he asked, but the only answer was the refrigerator's motorized hum.

When his mother had died, three years earlier, it had been in a hospital, surrounded by machines and people and the cold bright efficiency of fluorescence, and yet the darkness and loneliness of that time seemed to Nicholas, even now, like a primer on the inescapability of solitude. The idea of coming across Joyce unconscious on the floor somewhere in her house alternately horrified and saddened him. The discomfort of the thought was exceeded only by Nicholas's confusion as to its origins. Where had this moroseness come from? Why such grimness? With her yoga practice, her bodyboarding, her vigorous, leafy diet, Joyce was arguably in better shape than he was. But the eighteen years separating them suddenly seemed ruinously mortal, and wandering around inside of her dark, gloomy house, vainly calling out her name, Nicholas found all of his childhood fears resurrected, and none more prominent than death, that arbitrary, inexplicable theft.

He was in Joyce's bedroom, squinting down into the two-foot canal between the bed and the wall, when he heard the click of a light switch from the living room. Brightness flooded the hallway outside. "Joyce!" he said, running out to meet her.

Only it was Hannah who stood by the front door.

Nicholas's relief to learn that no harm had come to Joyce, that she had simply taken her grandson to the movies, was quickly displaced by embarrassment. He glanced around the living room, innocuous and pedestrian in its illumination, and shook his head.

"I'm sorry, I shouldn't have come inside," he said. "I don't know what happened."

"You're lucky I didn't call the police," Hannah said.

"Thank you. That was very . . ." he trailed off, unable to complete the thought. He felt disoriented and foolish, and the heavy dulling fatigue that follows shame was pressing down on him. He went over to the windowsill and placed the spare key beside the scored incense burner. The cedary scent of sandalwood rose from the caterpillar ashes of an incense stick.

"Why are you doing this?" Hannah said, shutting the door with a backward press of her heel.

"I don't know," Nicholas said with a sigh. "When I hadn't heard back in a couple days, I guess I—that wasn't me," Nicholas said, noticing the mess in the kitchen. "It was like that when I came in, the cutting board."

"I mean this thing with my mother," Hannah said.

"Oh. Well . . . we . . . I mean . . ." He struggled to articulate why they had gone to such lengths to shield Hannah from their relationship without sounding dismissive or infantilizing. "The thing is . . ."

"She's not rich. I don't know what you think my dad left her, but it's not that much."

"Excuse me?"

Hannah rounded the couch and approached Nicholas. She stood in front of him, her right elbow resting on the back of her left fist, appraising him as if he were a newly acquired sculpture of unknown value.

"Can't be more than what your ex-wife gives you, anyway."

"I think there's been a misunderstanding," Nicholas said. A cold draft had escaped from beneath the windowsill and was curling around his wrists and up his sleeves. "Is this because of Hawaii? The trip wasn't my idea. And I plan to buy my own ticket."

Her expression brightened at this. Hannah only broadly resembled her mother, alike in height and a general shape of the face—absent the striking cheekbones—but her eyes were eerily similar, and for an instant, Nicholas had the disconcerting sensation of looking into Joyce's stark blue eyes.

"No, not money," Hannah said, "and not to get to me—unless . . . ?" she reached out and placed her hand against his chest. He jerked back, landing on the windowsill and knocking the incense holder to the ground.

"What are you doing?" Nicholas said. "Joyce—"

"Right, your sixty-year-old girlfriend. The old woman who, unlike your ex-wife, won't ever leave you. She'll just be grateful you come around now and then, using her when you feel like it." Hannah scuffed the ashes into the carpet with the toe of her boot. "That tale of true romance."

"I understand you're upset," Nicholas said evenly, drawing on a marriage spent enduring his wife's frustration. "And I'm sure it's hard for a child to watch a parent move on—"

"I'm not a child! I'm your age. Do you even get the—I mean, fuck, do you have any idea how disgusting what you're doing is?"

Nicholas took a deep breath before speaking, pausing to assemble his thoughts. He knew that he had only one chance to describe his gratitude at having met Joyce. And from the moment that he began, he could feel Hannah's skepticism, could see it in the acetylene glare of those familiar, hateful eyes. She did not want a tale of affection and admiration, care and kindness, amusement and respect; she wanted the annihilation of young love, the violent upstart that takes us by the throat at sixteen and shakes us, over and over, while we misinterpret the bruising as happiness. But if what Hannah required as proof of love was irrationality, what he felt for Joyce was also obviously, stupidly imprudent. It was as reckless and senseless as any love that preceded it. Wasn't this precisely the glorious error that she demanded?

When Nicholas had finished explaining, Hannah leaned forward. He crossed his hands in front of himself like a defender preparing for a penalty kick. But Hannah seemed to have no interest in touching him again. Her canines flashed when she opened her mouth and spoke.

"I. Don't. Believe. You."

After Nicholas left, Hannah waited on the porch for her mother and son to return. It was warm, even for spring in LA, but she kept her scarf wrapped around her neck. Soon a station wagon pulled up, long and trundling. A deliveryman got out and carried a stack of pizza boxes to the brightly lit house across the street. Belatedly, Hannah noticed the pink balloons lashed to the mailbox.

Though it only vaguely resembled the family car from her youth—the delivery vehicle had a narrower body, tinted windows, and no wood paneling—the discrepancies did nothing to ease the vertiginous sensation that overcame her, of riding inside the car as a young girl, all the way in the back. Alone, loose and unprotected, she would roll around and around, moaning, exaggerating the turns, goading her parents to shush her.

The deliveryman exited the house and climbed back into the station wagon. He glanced over at Hannah, or at least she thought he might have, it was hard to see through the car's dark windows, and then revved the engine. As he drove off, she heard the door to the bright house swing open again. A girl, four years old, maybe five, raced outside in a new dress and no shoes. Tiny guests streamed out after her, laughing and carrying hot, thin slices on paper plates. All along the front lawn the boys and girls chased each other, the triangles slipping unnoticed from their hands. Those who could not bear the pleasure screamed out joyful threats. It is a world of children, noisy, desirous, and brief.

Murmur

When I met Anabel, she was standing on the subway platform and talking to herself. She was tiny, less than a hundred pounds, with dark circles beneath her eyes and unwashed brown hair. We were nearly alone in the station. I leaned against a metal strut to listen, but her words were indistinct, a blur of gentle, self-directed noise, and soon enough a train charged in from the darkness to silence her. It thundered along the track, and as we approached the stippled yellow edge in anticipation, it kept hissing and racing until, at last, it disappeared with a shudder. We were left side by side, introduced by disappointment.

"You were eavesdropping," she said to me.

I blinked too many times, flustered. I glanced down at her white canvas sneakers and back up into her tired smile, those two rows of small lopsided teeth.

"Anabel," she said.

When we boarded the next train, there were empty seats, but we stood side by side, holding onto the same fingerprinted pole. I spread my feet and felt the train twist beneath me like the spine of a cat. We were new at being New Yorkers so we talked about home, the places we had fled.

"I didn't know people actually lived in Arkansas," I said. "I thought it was one of those states they made up so there would be fifty. Like Oklahoma."

"You're just upset because we call you Yankees."

I told her I was going downtown to buy an album by the Terrifics that was being released exclusively in vinyl format. I didn't own a record player but I wanted the album anyway.

"I have a record player. Ah'm not sure if it works," she said, her accent briefly revealing itself.

"Does it have a needle?"

"I think so. My mother gave it to me."

"Ask her if it has a needle."

"She's dead."

I changed hands on the pole, startled, though I shouldn't have been. Flirtation usually involves precocious familiarity, asking and telling things ordinarily unshared with a stranger. They aren't grand secrets, they're things any friend would know, but it's through the swift progression of revelation that intimacy arises.

"I'm picking up a friend at Penn Station," she told me as we transferred to the S train. "He's in the air force."

"You don't seem very excited about it," I said, carrying her bag for her.

"He just called this morning to say he was coming up from DC for the weekend. I wasn't expecting it." She scratched her neck, leaving a pink mark like the smear of a pencil eraser. "We went to college together. Medical school."

"You're a doctor? You look eighteen."

"I'm an intern at Sloan Kettering."

"I'm healthy," I said.

"Terribly," she said and reached up to fix the collar of my shirt. We were melting, with a kind of instantaneousness that had little to do with each other and more to do with ourselves, a mutual affinity for being saved.

I tried to convince her to leave her air force friend at the station and come downtown with me but she wouldn't agree to it, though it seemed she wanted to. When we got to the Penn Station stop, I got off the train early and walked her to the turnstile. She paused to write her telephone number on my hand in red ink. Then she raised her jacket up over her head so I couldn't see her face.

"What are you doing?" I said.

"I don't know," she said, her voice issuing out of the improvised tent. "Come here."

I leaned in, nervous, worried that the sweat on my hands would smudge the numbers. She turned her head and pressed her lips to my ear, as if she were going to whisper a secret. We were breathing in that dark, silent space, surrounded by the fever of strangers, and then she slipped the jacket back down off of her head and walked away to meet her unwanted friend.

They took your shoes at the restaurant. As Anabel pried her sneakers off, she held my forearm for balance, each bony finger serious as a handcuff. In the dining room the wooden floors had been scooped out to let you dangle your feet, in case kneeling was too difficult.

"Order for both of us?" she said and folded her menu. "But I'm not too hungry."

"It's Japanese food," I said. "It's little."

She was wearing pale frosted lipstick. It looked as if she had kissed a mirror and the reflection had peeled away onto her lips. Her legs were short and her bare feet pedaled in the hollow beneath the table.

"So how was your friend?" I asked.

"I should have gone with you," she said. "He left early, on Saturday. Do you drink?" she asked and split her chopsticks.

"Sure. Should we order sake?"

"I'm on medication," she said, shaking her head. "You're the healthy one."

She did look a little unhealthy, I noticed later, as she ignored the broiled eel and yellowfin tuna to squeeze the plump green heart of an edamame into her mouth. Her bare arms had the muscle tone of a marathon runner, a survivor's decay, and her neck was so skinny it looked precarious. The natural slimness of her girlish body was exaggerated; her eyes looked larger, the sockets almost aggravated by leanness. There was beauty there, in the prominence of her cheekbones, the softness of her brown eyes, the graceful curve of her clavicle, but it was shadowed by a vague impression of self-cannibalism.

After dinner we walked along Fifth Avenue, high in the seventies and eighties. I had fallen out of love only recently, for the first time, and was still suffering from the punishing conscience of youth that believes, exclusively, in the singular romantic phenomenon. Because of this, it felt like a kind of betrayal when Anabel wound her fingers through mine and I experienced, rather than a simple and permissible erotic charge, tenderness. It was nearly midnight and Fifth Avenue had emptied out, leaving the city to us. On the corner of Eighty-First street, I kissed her. She pressed herself against me, so fine and slight I felt I could have folded her up and slipped her between the pages of a book.

"I love the Met!" she said and pulled me over to the stone steps. We sat beside each other, our shoulders touching, as the sky opened up. Raindrops misted past the streetlights.

"I was raped," she said into my neck. "Two years ago. You ought to know."

"I'm sorry," I said.

"It's a bad story," she said and told it to me.

We stayed on the steps until the rain had stopped. It passes fast in the summer in New York.

The streetlights made the puddles look like powdered glass as we walked to my apartment. Anabel came inside without asking. I wandered around the living room, lighting candles with wicks that were too long, so that the flames trembled and sent uncertain shadows onto the bookshelves. When I kissed her neck, I located that tiny vein flickering beneath the skin, hurrying life, and I pressed my mouth to it.

We pulled our soaked shirts over our heads. I stuck a finger through the belt loop of her jeans and pulled her to me. She was braless, small breasted, but she didn't cross her arms like other girls. I carried her into the bedroom, enjoying the lightness of her. I threw her on the bed and she bounced once, laughing. Then she screamed.

"What is it?" I said. "What wrong?"

She pointed at the window where a knife lay along the sill.

"It gets stuck," I said. "The window gets stuck."

She whispered something I couldn't hear.

I picked up the knife and she scurried to the end of the bed. She watched me with the sheets wrapped around her body. I wrenched open the window and flung the knife onto the rooftop of the movie theater next door.

I lay down beside her and she wriggled into my arms. Her hair tickled my shoulders as she tucked her head into my neck. I could feel the warmth of her cheek against my bare chest, and her breath moving across my ribs. We slept for a while.

"You have an arrhythmic heartbeat," she mumbled when we rolled onto our sides.

I raised my head off of the pillow. "Is it serious?"

"It's probably nothing," she said, closing her eyes again. "But you should have it checked out."

After that night, we always met in her apartment. Anabel lived in an elegant high-rise tucked along the East River, where the doormen treated her like a favored child, offering her candy and beaming, even when she came home dressed in blue surgical scrubs. They soon learned to recognize me. I typically visited after her midnight shift had ended, and the late-night doorman would shake my hand with an affection that I found disconcerting to encounter in the city, which seemed an escape from the considerations of geniality.

She didn't cook, and her freezer was filled with unpleasant soups her grandmother sent, so I would bring dinner. Failing that, we would sit on the couch and eat cheese and pretzels while she flicked through the channels, or skimmed magazines, her foot rocking tirelessly on the table. Nothing seemed to hold her attention, and while there were always new books appearing on the shelves, I don't remember her ever finishing one. Her single consistent distraction was a crippled kitten she had adopted; its spinal injury had left it with a hopeless nervous system. It moved like a rabbit crossed with a sidewinder snake. Whenever it tried to pounce on my bare foot, it jumped the wrong way, or collapsed onto its back, before hissing and hurling itself backward into a wall.

So she cradled weakness, that was obvious to both of us, and in whatever manifestation it arrived, including me: young and bruised, quietly hiding, fit only to remove her from the outrageous loneliness of the city. And there was, beyond our shared reluctance to pry, or a survivor's appreciation for the barest kindness, a mutual attraction that bordered upon absorption. I spent almost every night in her four-poster bed, wandering along the narrow bones of her body, the adolescent chest, the wiry legs, the unsoftened hips; we fondled and caressed each other restlessly. Yet when it came to penetration itself—impossible. Though Anabel insisted she wanted to, no matter how hard I tried, there was simply no entering her.

"You're sure you want to do this," I said, during another unsuccessful attempt.

"Yes."

"Because I'm trying and it doesn't—"

"I'm sure."

After a discouraging few minutes, she shrugged and rolled me off of her, then climbed on top. I could feel the slight weight of her pressed against my stomach, like a bag that's been leaking from a tiny hole for days until it's almost empty. Some awkward moments passed as she positioned and readjusted her knees on the bed. I reached up for her and there was sweat on the inside of her elbows, though her skin was cold. She sighed and sat back on my thighs. "I . . . I don't know why it isn't working," she said. "I want to."

"You do," I said.

"Maybe we just have incompatible genitalia," she said and playfully swatted my hip, to distract me from a widening uneasiness.

*

For a while the nights continued with their domestic comforts, the midnight cereal and careless television, and I quit my attempts. Instead I enjoyed the ardor of her guilty attention, the earnest, apologetic affection. I absently suspected—with the vagueness that overwhelmed me that first city winter—that her physical refusal mirrored an emotional reluctance, but her initial candor made this a little unbelievable. The ordinary contradictions of a personality somehow seemed unlike Anabel. She was too extreme, I thought, too strident—as she accompanied her senile neighbor to the movie theater bathroom, or cried when passing a gibbering homeless man—too easily disturbed to bother hiding herself. Her focus was bigger, and just as impossible: the immense and endless pain of the world.

I was the one who worried about smallness, about sexual satisfaction and occupation. The desire for possession surged with the arrival of spring; after a heartbroken fall and a catatonic winter, I was hungry for strength. Strength requires a sacrifice.

"Have you even looked into why you can't?" I asked Anabel one night.

It was April and warm, and coming through the screen windows was the wet, sooty smell of the city returning to us. She was playing with the cat. Even with its funny spine, it had grown long and skinny.

"I mean professionally," I added, after she still hadn't replied. "Not like some online search. Have you discussed it with someone at the hospital?"

"It's not something I'd feel comfortable bringing up."

"If you're worried about anonymity, blame the disorder on a friend."

"It isn't a disorder," she said and righted the cat, who then, ungratefully, clawed her.

"Well, what is it then? It's not . . . normal."

She put the cat down. We'd been together long enough so that we didn't have to be nice to each other anymore and could opt for honesty instead. This was what I told myself to justify cruelty.

"If you were your patient, what would you recommend?" I said.

"You want to try again," she said, sucking on the skin between her thumb and forefinger, where the cat had sunk its claws. "You're annoyed."

"We're talking about you."

She sat down beside me on the couch, the confused animal rolling on its back and clawing the air, its mouth open.

"Are we?" she said.

There was a brief sensation of enormity as I slid my arm around Anabel's tiny shoulders and pulled her close to me, the hard knot of her runner's knee pressing against my thigh. Then the telephone rang. Anabel glanced at it.

I stood up quickly, irritated by her skittishness—her rocking foot was unsteadying the coffee table; she was whispering to herself again—and found my clothes. While I was dressing I could hear her on the telephone with her grandmother, who was shouting because someone had broken into her house and stolen sixty pounds of sirloin she kept in a basement freezer.

"They come in," I heard her grandmother say. "I was asleep."

"It's okay it's okay," Anabel cooed, while with her free hand she calmly pulled the cat's claw out of her foot. "We'll call the police. It's okay."

"Somebody taked my meat!" her grandmother moaned.

I laughed, and Anabel glared up at me. She was crying, I saw, two wet little streaks across her cheeks. I blinked furiously and walked over to the stereo. The record player did have a needle, and one night after I had hooked it up, we had listened to the Terrifics' album, though halfway through the first song Anabel had wandered off to the bedroom to rearrange her sundresses, and I'd soon turned the player off. I tucked the album under my arm and stood by the front door. I was dressed in a tie after midnight, my posture was stiff, and the formality wasn't—as I'd thought at the time—so much a seriousness of intent as a complicated and anxious relationship to cowardice.

Her grandmother was loud and inconsolable, and Anabel shot me apologetic looks. As I waited, the cat stalked me, weaving clumsily across the floor. It leapt for my toe and I snatched it off the ground. I held it in the air with one hand. Its head rolled back and from side to side, the sharp white teeth exposed, and with my thumb I stroked the soft fur of its belly. The cat's head continued to thrash as if it was in agony, while it made a low, purring sound.

I left without saying goodbye.

She called me from the hospital, between shifts. I didn't return her calls or her texts. What had begun as momentary sullenness soon transformed, with little effort, into a parting. We had always been imprecise about our relationship, and I relied on this indistinctness to protect me from any accusations of unkindness. But there were none; after two weeks of silence had passed, she left a final message: she was sorry I was gone, she was lonely again, and I should remember to have my heart checked out. She suspected it was nothing, but it was best to get a second opinion and be certain.

I spent my weekend nights in bars, catching up on my drinking. I was startled by how big other women were. Their skin seemed thicker, their fingers as large as Anabel's wrist. They didn't stand on their tiptoes to talk to me. A woman took me home on her birthday, and we had sex in the living room while her roommate pretended to be asleep. I woke up before dawn on the couch. The air smelled of cigarettes and steamed broccoli. Her curly hair, longer and darker than Anabel's, itched my bare chest. I missed the shape of Anabel's nervous mouth and the lock of her fingers. I dressed silently, putting my shoes on in the elevator, and within an hour was standing outside Anabel's apartment.

It had been over two months but the doorman still recognized me. He shook my hand.

"Long time," he smiled. "You must be busy busy."

"Is she home?" I said.

He shook his head. "No luck, boss."

"Can you tell her I came by? I'll call her but can you tell her too?"

"She moved," he said. "Last week."

"Moved where?"

He shrugged. "Home."

"Arkansas," I said.

He smiled and spun the revolving door for me. "She's a good girl."

I tried Anabel's number but it had been disconnected. I called the hospital but the receptionist wouldn't release any information. I didn't bother looking for her online; she had purged her profiles in March after reading an article about social networks aiding in abductions.

At home, I sat on the couch and thought about how much I missed her. An hour later I had a competing revelation: had she stayed, we would have simply exchanged the tedium of abstinence for the tedium of sex. There are moments when youth is leaving you, and everything becomes a motion toward shame.

The following Christmas, Anabel sent me an email that said she had taken a semester's break after her grandmother had died. Now she was living in Boston and studying at Mass General Hospital. She signed her name and the cat's name. I wrote her back and we arranged to meet in February, when she would be coming to the city for a weekend conference.

I arrived at the café just as a corner table was being deserted. Hurrying over, I placed my bag on the chair to claim it. The service was quick and surly and the coffee mediocre, but the light was unrivaled, flooding through the picture windows and onto the many small, contested tabletops. Anabel answered her cell phone from the cab.

"I'm just crossing the bridge," she said.

"I'm by the window," I said. "Impossible to miss."

"See you in fifteen minutes."

I waited an hour and a half but she never came. I left a series of bewildered text messages and a single annoyed voicemail and then paid the bill.

A week later, an email arrived. "I don't remember if I mentioned it," she wrote, "but I've been trying electroshock therapy to cure depression and it inhibits short-term memory. It's a sorry excuse for missing our date, and I hope you can forgive me. I'll be in the city for another conference this September if you can make it." This time, Anabel did not sign the cat's name.

But when fall came, I had left New York. I had grown weary of the quiet derangement that life in the city provoked in me, with its heaviness and its hurry, its agitated, lonely provocations. Too often I had caught myself cursing as I passed an old woman struggling up the subway stairs. I was the man in the elevator who stabbed the "close door" button, glaring at newcomers. I wanted everything immediately, and without blemish, and the distance between this desire and its failed delivery was cracking me open wider and wider, splitting me like firewood.

One summer day, just before leaving, I closed my office door and lay on the floor. As I stared up at the ceiling, a sound came out of my body, a quiet, steady hum, like the rhythmic hiss of a needle after a song has ended, and the record keeps spinning.

After a while, someone knocked on the door. She knocked again, then said my name. The light beneath the door changed when she walked away.

That night, I carried my furniture out onto the street. I was taking only what would fit in my car: two suitcases of clothes, a milk crate heavy with vinyl records, and a shopping bag of books I had never gotten around to reading and probably never would. On my final trip down the stairs, I had to stop halfway to catch my breath, exhausted from the effort of repeatedly descending and ascending six flights. My legs ached. My shirt clung to my neck and back with sweat. I swore I could hear my heart, it was racing so fast. Take it easy, I told myself and placed a hand along the center of my chest, thinking—hoping—there's time.

How to Get into Our House and Where We Keep the Money

ETHAN HAD ALWAYS been a bad swimmer. As a toddler, he revolted when his mother carried him into the ocean, screaming and thrashing in her arms, then clambering onto her shoulders as if she were a sinking ship. At the YMCA where his parents signed him up for swimming lessons, he refused to get into the pool for five months, decimating the unofficial "sea slug" record (three weeks) previously held by a boy who ended up becoming a junior national swim champion and was paraded as a model of success—and, implicitly, the folly of childhood rebellion. Ethan, however, was unmoved by this story of triumph, and finally the instructors resorted to outright bribery. In month six, he retrieved candy from the bottom of the shallow end with his toes and ate it in a crouch, the sweetness of the butterscotch tainted with the blanching slickness of chlorine and acquiescence.

In every other part of his life, he was an obedient child, and the ferocity of his defiance first mystified, then angered, and finally exhausted his parents. On the day of Ethan's final swim lesson (they had paid for one year, and would never pay again), his father pointed to a redheaded toddler climbing the ladder to the high dive. Her blue swim diaper peeked out from behind her bathing suit bottom as she scaled each step. When she reached the top, she ran toward the edge of the diving board and fearlessly hurled herself out into the air. "You should be ashamed of yourself," his father said, as the girl plunged into the water with a small, echoing splash.

He got his wish. It was a moment of humiliation so potent that it nearly assumed a physical shape, and from then on, except for a brief stint of rebelliousness involving an earring in his senior year of high school, Ethan redoubled his efforts at filial compliance. He studied well, tested well, worked well, married well, and even parented well, despite being raised in a household in which a father's parental duties consisted primarily of belittling, and the end result was one of respectability, decorum, and stability—"the good life," as Ethan referred to it on occasions of immodest self-reflection.

It was this hard-earned, pleasant existence that Ethan cited when explaining to his wife, Lydia, the many reasons why they shouldn't have a second child. Together, they had arranged their financial, professional, and parental ambitions and obligations to an exquisitely calibrated state—adding another child would tip the mechanism into disorder. Financially, they would suffer: either Lydia would have to take time off from work to raise the baby, depriving the family of her significant salary, or they would hire a full-time nanny they could barely afford. Lydia had only just resumed employment after their daughter Jesse had started preschool last fall, and did Lydia really want to indefinitely delay her career again—after months of hunting to find this job? As for the issue of parenting, already Jesse cried when they left each morning for work, begging for more time with them; were they ready to halve her allotted time to accommodate a baby and its endless demands? Would they willingly recreate the families that they had sworn to avoid, clashes of hungrily contending siblings chasing after overworked, distracted parents who tossed out attention like farmhands scattering dried corn to the animals?

As discourses go, Ethan thought his was measured and reasonable, even compassionate. When Lydia failed to respond, he crossed the bedroom to where she stood beside the dresser, working to release the trapped wick of a candle with a ballpoint pen. She was wearing a white nightgown that in length and cut resembled an evening dress and left most of her back exposed. He placed the palm of his hand on her warm bare skin. Without acknowledging the gesture, she continued to jab at the candlewick. Shavings of white wax were piling up like ice scraped from a car windshield.

"I know it's disappointing. I'm just trying to be sensible," Ethan said.

"Bullshit. You just don't want another kid."

"I love Jesse."

"I never said you didn't." She flung the pen aside and stalked past him toward the bathroom. Lydia had been a dedicated ballet dancer well into her teens, and twenty years later she still walked like one, her hip rotators turned out and a slight waddle to her gait, as if the cost of fleeting onstage beauty and grace were a lifetime of duckish inelegance. He followed her to the bathroom. She shut the door before he could enter.

"We're not in a position to be impulsive," he said through the door.

This was followed by the wheeze of the shower coughing and spattering awake.

"I'm just being sensible," Ethan repeated, though by now he was sure that Lydia was no longer listening. Not that he blamed her. It *was* bullshit. Yes, everything he'd said about the economic strain, their career aspirations, and the attentional deprivation were true, but the greater truth was exactly what his wife had intuited, which was that he didn't want a second child.

Specifically, he did not want a son.

If he could have been assured of another daughter, he might have considered it. Ethan loved everything about his daughter: her solemn, spookily adult facial expressions; the swell of her belly pushing out her tutu; the way she hung from his neck while hugging him, suspended like a trapeze artist; even his daughter's petulant complaints, when pronounced with her sweet, high-pitched voice, had been known to charm him. But whereas his little girl was a compilation of adorable features and behavior, boys seemed to be composed of nothing but aggression, insubordination, and screams. Of the boys that Ethan had come across at playgrounds and birthday parties, the majority were spastic, charmless idiots engaged in what seemed like a constant and thoughtless struggle for dominance. Ethan didn't understand why people compared boys to puppies, which were sweet and endearing, when boys were actually much more like mean-spirited, intoxicated donkeys. Nor was Ethan ignorant of the troubling insight that a son's fundamental purpose in life was to replace his father. Wasn't it enough that obsolescence was inevitable? Did they also have to invite it into their home and tousle its golden hair?

He was watching television when Lydia returned from her shower. She was no longer wearing her white evening-gown-looking nightgown but a periwinkle short-sleeved pajama set with wide lace and lettuce trim. She pulled back the blanket and silently climbed into bed. Ethan turned off the TV and slotted the remote control into the space between the wooden bedframe and the mattress. He fumbled with the bedside lamp, pinning the small metal legs in his hand and squeezing the switch with his index finger as if pulling the trigger of a gun. Then he rolled onto his side to face Lydia.

"You awake?" he said.

"No."

She was not awake the next night, or the night after that, and on Saturday morning Ethan drove to the supermarket to buy her an enormous bouquet of flowers. This gesture was usually reserved for significant marital apologies, and he felt a little embarrassed entering the kitchen with two dozen yellow-and-red-flanged French tulips swathed in paper, as if he had come overarmed to a fight, but though Jesse circled his legs with delight, Lydia merely flicked out a perfunctory smile and reached for the cutting board. Laying the tulips on their sides, she sawed at the long stems with a bread knife, taking what Ethan thought was a disheartening pleasure in their severance. Placing the reduced flowers in a vase, she added a burst of cloudy tap water.

"Jesse," Ethan whispered. When his daughter came close, he stuffed a penny into her palm and instructed her to drop it into the vase. He was hoping to endear himself to Lydia with a moment of father-enabled adorability, but Lydia had already left to answer her cell phone.

Not that the maneuver would have helped, as Jesse refused to do it.

"It's my penny," she lisped.

"I'll give you another one. Just put this one in the vase."

"Why?"

"It's for the flowers."

"Why?"

"They eat it. The metal."

Jesse eyed the tulips with horror.

"They drink it," Ethan amended, but this too failed at reassuring Jesse, who was pressing herself against her father's chest, mouth tight with suspicion. "Okay, forget it," Ethan said, and lifted her off the stainless steel counter. The moment that her feet made contact with the floor, she skittered out of the room.

He looked for Lydia in the bedroom but there was no sign of her, and after two laps of the house, he noticed her car missing from the driveway. Resigning himself to another day of emotional retrenchment, he sat on the couch beside Jesse, who was watching a Saturday-morning cartoon about magical, bitchy ponies attending a wedding. It was hard to say whether this was an improvement on the *Peter Pan* DVD that had been in heavy rotation for months—occasionally Ethan, forced to watch *Peter Pan* again, would feel an existential panic stealing over him, as if Disney's animators had inadvertently channeled Nietzsche's horror and paralysis at the prospect of eternal recurrence.

They were a few minutes into a story about a pony that had mischievously devoured the flower arrangements, when the doorbell rang. Ethan craned his neck and saw Maggie, Jesse's swim teacher, framed by the central glass panel of the wooden door. She was a short but stocky girl, with the broad shoulders, spanning back, and powerful legs of a devoted athlete. She paused from waving to pull a strand of curly, black hair away from her face. Ethan climbed off the couch and answered the door with an apology. His wife had forgotten to tell him about the lesson, he explained. Lydia had arranged for twice-weekly swim instruction at the start of summer, determined to combat Jesse's inherited fear and loathing of the water, but the schedule was in constant revision.

"It's all right," Maggie said. "Oh wait, can Jesse not do it right now?" She reached up and fingered the strap of her bathing suit, dark blue beneath her white tee shirt.

"It's fine. I just have to get her changed."

"I can wait at home and you can shout when she's ready if you want."

Maggie's family had recently moved into the house next door. Their yard was poorly maintained, with the casual neglect increasingly characteristic of the houses in the neighborhood, and its steady shift from owners to renters. It was easy to forget that people lived within the unruly confines of shrubbery and overproducing lemon trees, and on occasion, while taking out the trash late at night, Ethan would glimpse their porch light and feel a flush of unease, wondering if they had been watching through their windows, and what indignity might have been witnessed.

"That's all right, it'll only take a minute," he told Maggie. "Come on in."

"Great," she said, and smiled.

After Lydia's resentment, Maggie's steady cheerfulness was a relief. Since beginning to instruct Jesse, a reluctant and difficult student, Maggie had demonstrated an otherworldly immunity to frustration, anger, and impatience. It didn't matter what Jesse did or didn't do, Maggie remained encouraging. She was like a perpetual-motion machine of kindheartedness, gently violating the first and second laws of emotional thermodynamics.

Maggie slipped out of her flip-flops and padded barefoot into the house. She waved at Jesse on the couch. "Hey there."

Jesse snarled, "I'm watching ponies."

"I loved this cartoon when I was a kid," Maggie told her.

All of five years ago? Ethan thought. But he resisted the urge to comment on the prematurity of her nostalgia. Besides, he didn't know exactly how old Maggie was. He had reached that age when visually distinguishing between high school and college students was like one of those find-the-hidden-object video games that he routinely caught his assistant playing at work.

After helping Jesse into her bathing suit, he reclined on a chaise longue set near the deep end of the pool. He opened the hardcover biography that had sat, unread, next to his bed for the past year, and within minutes the bright heat of Los Angeles in August pulled his eyes shut. It wasn't a deep sleep at first—he could still hear the sounds of his daughter splashing and hooting in worried defiance—but gradually the tenor of the slumber changed.

His face slackened and his left shoulder rounded as he slumped to the right. He was falling, engaged in a dream that carried with it the qualities of premonition and loss, and when he felt a cool presence pass in front of him, he opened his eyes to see Maggie standing above him, replacing the sun.

"Is it over?" he said.

"A little while ago," she said. "I was going to go home but I didn't want to leave you out here asleep."

He licked his dry lips. His body felt dull and hot. He wondered if the top of his head had gotten sunburnt, but didn't want to draw attention to his bald spot with Maggie standing right there.

"Maybe you should go inside? Your face is really red," she said. "Better yet, cool off in the pool first?"

He squinted up at Maggie and the golden arc of her athletic shoulders.

"I don't swim," he said.

"Seriously?"

"Seriously."

"But you have a pool."

"Wasn't my idea. I don't even know how to swim."

"That's crazy. You should know how to swim. Everyone should."

"And yet."

"At least to float."

He stood up from the chair too quickly and dizziness overtook him. Stumbling backward, he flung out a hand for balance. Maggie grabbed onto it, pulling him in close and steadying him upright with her body. "Are you okay?" she said.

Dark spots flickered across his eyes. For a moment, inhaling the heady chlorinated scent of her, he was sure that he was hallucinating. He gazed in blank confusion at the sliding glass doors that led to the house. Tall and scallop-shouldered, with a mass of stringy black hair, a boy was slouching across the living room. He moved in silhouette, his features dimmed to obscurity, his intentions, desires, aggressions—all of it unknown.

*

It had been six years since Ethan had last seen his nephew, Timothy, and even after Lydia made the introductions on their poolside deck, he found it hard to reconcile this lanky, tattooed, lip- and eyebrow-pierced nineteen-year- old with the short, chubby boy who had spent an entire Thanksgiving holiday playing his Nintendo DS. Ethan had heard the stories of Tim's metamorphosis, of course, bemoaned to Lydia by her sister, Tim's mother—the struggles adapting to high school, the bullying, the ADHD diagnosis, the scholastic intervention (where Ethan first heard the deceptively unironic phrase "gifted underachiever"), the talk therapy, the group therapy, the art therapy . . . but all of these earnest efforts at redirection and assistance had failed to redirect Timothy. Born to young parents—Lydia's sister and her soon-to-be husband were freshmen in college when she got pregnant; both dropped out and never rematriculated—Timothy had caused them considerable difficulty with his arrival, but nothing compared to the upset that he brought his parents in his adolescence. The delinquency, the defiance, the truancy, the vandalism, the school expulsions, the embittered self-seclusion, the run-ins with the police: it was a performance as costly as it was incomprehensible for Timothy's demoralized parents, high school sweethearts whose marriage rattled and shook and finally collapsed in the wake of their child's unremitting insolence.

In those six years Ethan, too, had changed. He was no longer a thirty-two-year-old newlywed with an unstoppable work ethic and the belief that life was a sharply ascending slope, like those hockey stick graphs his new boss, Garrett Morse, liked to populate his presentations with—market size ramping up exponentially, year-over-year revenue growth unchecked, and consumers seemingly unable to say no. Lately, Ethan had been realizing the smallness and insecurity of his position. While both friends and rivals continued to come into enormous professional success, exploding like careerist supernovas, Ethan was a brown dwarf, a failed star condemned to float in space, cooling off for a few million years.

With a growing alertness to his diminished status, and the sight of his young nephew beside his shimmering swimming pool, attended to by his wife, marveled at by his daughter, and studied by her nubile swim instructor, Ethan felt a territorial response well up so viscerally he nearly bared his teeth at the boy.

Wiping the sweat from his forehead with the back of his hand, Ethan trudged into the kitchen for a beer. He pulled a Red Stripe from the fridge, along with a package of salami, and drank at the counter, occasionally pausing to stuff a folded slice of lunch meat into his mouth, tamping the wad against his cheek like a plug of salty, fatty chewing tobacco. After finishing the beer, he hid the empty bottle under a flattened royal-blue box of tampons in the recycling bin and got another. He was halfway through his second beer when Lydia entered.

"Why are you eating in here?" she said. "We're all out at the pool."

"Salami," he said, chewing.

"So?"

"I didn't want to upset Tim's vegetarian sensibilities."

"He doesn't care what you eat," she said, refilling the pitcher with filtered water from the tap. "And he goes by Scudder now."

Ethan snorted. "That's a ridiculous name."

"It's what he wants to be called."

"Sounds like a G.I. Joe character."

"Can you take this out to the pool?" Lydia said, gesturing to the pitcher.

"Not one of the tough ones either, like Roadblock. Scudder's the guy who drives the supply truck."

"It's getting heavy, Ethan."

"Or the munitions clerk. That's a guy, you know. They actually sell that guy."

"Forget it," Lydia said, switching off the faucet. She placed the pitcher on the stovetop, and the weight of the water and glass made a cracking sound against the ceramic surface. "You're acting like he crashed our party," Lydia said, snatching a lemon from a bowl and slicing it in half, then dropping both halves into the pitcher. "I invited him for lunch."

Ethan nodded. He didn't believe in coincidence, and his nephew's sudden arrival now made much more sense. It was neither happenstance nor serendipity, but that old handmaiden of causality—retribution. And why not? Instinctively, he'd been waiting for Lydia's punishment since their argument days ago.

Lydia dried her hands with a bar towel. She hoisted the pitcher and smiled. "Can we please just try to have a good time?"

"You bet," Ethan said. "Here we go."

Lydia set off down the hallway with her small duckish steps. Ethan remained behind, drinking his beer and staring out at the pool. Everyone had relocated to sit along the edge and they were dangling their bare feet in the water—even Scudder, who had rolled up the cuffs of his black jeans to expose pale, hairy shins. With a shrug, the boy flicked a green diving ring into the water. It skipped twice, then began to sink. Submerged, the ring looked misshapen and bent. There is a point of contact where light, slowing in response to the greater density of water, initiates an optical distortion. It's nothing more than a trick of refraction, Ethan reminded himself, as one by one the girls hopped off the edge and dove for the ring. He wasn't seeing what he was seeing.

Ethan thought no more about his nephew until the following week, when he received an urgent text from his wife—*emergency call me pls*—while in a meeting with his new boss. Garrett Morse, the recently appointed marketing director, was the twenty-seven-year-old son of Kenneth Morse, the CEO of Madison-Morse-Malick, a consortium of small but durable consumer-goods brands. Garrett possessed the studied exuberance of the freshly minted Ivy League MBA, exhibiting a charged but mechanical affability, as if graduate school had programmed him for congeniality along with business strategy and data analysis. Like a truly gifted egotist, Garrett seemed oblivious to the resentment that he inspired in Ethan, a man who had spent the past fourteen years crawling his way up the ranks from marketing assistant to officer for promotional jobs to product manager to marketing manager, then waiting patiently for the ultimate position, marketing director, to finally open up—only to have it stolen from him by a candidate whose claim rested on nepotism and privilege.

Ethan wondered if Garrett ever put aside his omnipresent smile, shelving it during moments of solemnity, significance, or misfortune. But as his young boss sunnily explained that Ethan had been given "a one-of-a-kind opportunity to raise the brand awareness around "FatCat"—MMM's languishing line of cat treats, renown for killing careers—Ethan understood that his speculation was in vain. The exuberance was real: the performance was the man.

Issuing a series of awkward, resentful apologies for the interruption, Ethan rushed out of Garrett's office and called Lydia. "What happened?" he said. "Is Jesse okay?"

"Jesse's fine," Lydia said. "She's okay."

"You said it was an emergency. Are you okay?"

"I'm fine. We're both fine," Lydia said. "It's about Scudder."

Ethan stopped pacing. Already he didn't like this. He had that itchy, panicky feeling you get when you suspect you've stepped into the slowest line at the supermarket.

"What about him?"

"His friend Andre got arrested for burglary."

"Was Scudder driving the car or something?"

"No, no, he wasn't involved."

"So . . . what does this have to do with us?"

"Well, with Andre in jail, Scudder doesn't have anywhere to stay now. And since we're his only family in the area—"

"We haven't seen the kid in six years! And now he's going to live with us?" A coworker glanced up from his desk. Ethan made an apologetic face and stepped into the empty conference room, drawing shut the heavy glass doors.

"It would just be for a few days," Lydia said.

"It's a bad time right now, Lyd. The timing is just—Garrett put me on the worst assignment," he whispered. "Deliberately. He's setting me up to fail, it's obvious. He's the kind of guy who masturbates to Sun Tzu's *Art of War*. The last thing I need is additional—"

"Who's Garrett?" she said. "What are you talking about?"

Ethan exhaled. In his panic and frustration, he'd forgotten that he hadn't yet told Lydia about losing the position to Garrett. For weeks now he'd tried, but at the moment of revelation, the intensity of his humiliation would silence him.

"No one. Forget it," Ethan said. "Why can't Scudder go live with your sister?"

"He doesn't get along with her husband. James pretty much banished him. And his father—well, you know what he's like these days. The boy just needs some time to figure out his next steps."

"Doesn't he have other friends besides his little burglar buddy?"

"Friends aren't family. He's my nephew, and I'm not going to let him live on the street! You don't get to say no to everything, Ethan."

"What does that mean?"

"I think you know exactly what it means."

Ethan ran his tongue over his right incisor. They were here again, circled back to this place of discord. What did wives expect from their husbands? Ethan wondered. You were punished for refusing to communicate, for stonewalling and stoically maintaining the peace at the expense of your own happiness—and then, when you submitted to their pleas for expression and opinion, when you convinced yourself, at last, that they meant it when they petitioned for your honest feelings, if what you wanted contradicted their desire, well, you were punished for that, too.

"We're both very busy right now," Lydia said, "so I'll have him take a taxi to the house and use the spare key under the deck. Then he can pay the driver with cash from the drawer in our bedroom."

"Great," Ethan said. "His friend gets arrested for burglary—let's tell him how to get into our house and where we keep the money."

Ethan returned home that evening, anticipating scenarios of robbery, destruction, and ruin, but when he entered the living room, he found Jesse and Scudder placidly watching TV and eating microwaved popcorn. They were halfway through *Peter Pan,* at the moment when Peter throws his voice to rescue Tiger Lily. Ethan bent over the edge of the couch to kiss Jesse's cheek, but she pulled away from him, retreating toward her cousin, who lay sprawled along the L-shaped corner of the couch.

"Hey," Scudder said, making a small upward motion with his chin that Ethan presumed meant hello.

"Where's Lydia?" Ethan said.

"Kitchen." He grinned. "Yo, have you seen this movie? Peter Pan is crazy racist."

"It's a kids' movie."

"Yeah, racist kids."

Lydia emerged from the kitchen wearing an apron and carrying a glass of red wine. Lydia rarely cooked—one of them either picked up something on the way home from work or ordered in—and as they all sat down to eat a homemade turkey-noodle casserole, Ethan wondered why his wife had prepared this wildly traditional meal. Was the performance of old-fashioned domesticity intended to charm their houseguest, riddled with piercings, insolence and, most recently, criminal displacement? Or was it for Ethan's sake, a manner of apology?

"So Tim—Scudder," Ethan corrected, observing Lydia's frown, "what brings you to LA exactly? You're a long way from Philadelphia."

"On tour," Scudder said. He slouched in his chair, a fork dangling from his left hand like a cigarette.

"You're a musician?"

Scudder shook his head. "Following a band on tour. We started in Chicago, like, three months ago."

"What band?" Ethan said.

"You won't know them," Scudder said.

"Try me."

"Hollow Asian Fashion."

"Sure, I've heard of them," Ethan lied.

"You have?" Lydia said.

"Yeah, I heard them on the radio," Ethan said.

"They don't play HAF on the radio," Scudder said, scooping a forkful of casserole into his mouth.

"What's a radio?" Jesse said.

"Well, this station did," Ethan said.

"A radio is a machine for playing music," Lydia said. "People used to use them a long time ago but now they're mostly in cars."

"Can I have one?" Jesse said.

"You don't need a radio, sweetie," Lydia said.

"What song did they play?" Scudder asked Ethan.

"I didn't catch the title." Ethan slid the spatula under the casserole and dragged a layer onto his plate. "This is delicious, Lyd."

"What was it about?" Scudder said. "If you tell me, I can figure out the song. I know every HAF song."

"It was about . . . an indie record store," Ethan guessed.

"What's an Indian record store?" Jesse said.

"A record store is a place where people used to buy music," Lydia said.

"Can I have some?" Jesse said.

"You already have music, sweetie," Lydia said.

"You're definitely thinking of another band," Scudder said.

"The DJ said Halloween Asian Fashion," Ethan insisted.

"It's Hollow," Scudder said.

"That's what I said."

"Ethan, let it go," Lydia whispered. She turned to face Scudder. "Was it a good tour?" she asked and gave him a look packed with such maternal warmth and comfort that Ethan could practically feel the production of oxytocin surge in her brain.

"Yeah, it was cool—until Dylan met some chick in Seattle. He went off with her and then that was the end of it. He like *moved in.*" He yawned. "I went to the LA show with Andre but it wasn't, like . . . HAF is Dylan's and my thing."

"Andre the burglar?" Ethan said.

"He's a street artist," Scudder said. "The cops just busted him because his crew's been tagging heavy lately. It's a bullshit B and E."

"What's a bullshit B and E?" Jesse said.

"Bacon and eggs," Ethan said. "And you can't have any."

While Lydia continued to ply Scudder with polite questions, Ethan picked at his casserole. Despite the vague awareness that he'd been creeping toward cultural irrelevance for years, this latest demonstration of his ignorance and exclusion was impossible to ignore. He glanced over at Scudder, irked by the boy's oblivious cultural entitlement. With his nineteen-year-old, quasi-hipster, quasi-street-kid identity, he lived in that charged, desirable space of subcultural preeminence, a hidden, coveted, rapidly shifting locus to which mainstream culture looked for the emergence of the next great thing . . . a thing that would, of course, be contemptuously abandoned by Scudder and his friends the instant that the mainstream got hold of it.

It was maddening that the boy and his peers defined the cultural avant-garde—it was only due to a confluence of the accidental (their age), the economic (young people make art because they're often supported by parents and, as importantly, don't have to support their own families), and the arrogant (young people haven't failed enough to realize how ordinary they actually are). Yet most maddening of all was that even while aware of all the vicissitudes behind it, Ethan wasn't immune to the effect. As he was rinsing the dishes that evening, his phone connected to the kitchen speaker and quietly playing "Down to the Wire," Ethan held his breath when Scudder passed by, steeling himself for the inevitable dismissal. Instead, Scudder nodded approvingly and said, "Neil Young . . . cool." Ethan blushed, and hauling the trash bag out of the house afterward, he felt alternately proud of Scudder's endorsement and ashamed to care so much what a nineteen-year-old delinquent thought of his musical choices.

He slung the garbage bag into the black plastic container beside the house and slammed shut the lid. As he turned away from the sweetly rotting smell, he caught a competing scent, skunky and vegetal. From behind the bushes that separated their yard from their neighbors', a tiny red light flared. It bobbed at head level, wavering slightly in the darkness.

Slowly, Ethan advanced toward the small red light. "Is someone there?" he said.

The light blinked out. He heard a rustle of leaves and then saw their neighbor, Jesse's swimming teacher, standing with her arms crossed against her chest.

"Maggie?"

"Boo," she said.

He sniffed the air, smelling it again, that pungent skunky odor.

"Everything okay?" he said.

"Yeah," she said, and laughed. "I was just out for a . . . walk."

He glanced at her bare feet, then up at her plaid flannel pajama pants and ivory camisole. He'd seen her in a bathing suit a dozen times, but dressed for bed, she seemed somehow more exposed than ever before. He wondered if he ought to look away but couldn't quite make himself.

"How's that trash going?" she said. "Gotta love trash night, right? Trashy trash night."

"Most of it's recycling," Ethan said.

"I stand corrected." She gave him a thumbs-up, the candy-red shell of a lighter peeking out from within her fist. "Well, good night," she said, and turned away.

"Wait! I have a question for you."

She turned back to face him, a look of curiosity on her uncharacteristically animated face.

He smiled to hide his apprehension. There was no question, of course, he just hadn't wanted her to leave. He scrambled to come up with something, but everything he thought of sounded either too pedestrian or too intimate. As the seconds ticked by and he said nothing, impatience began to replace her curiosity. At last, she sighed and took a step back toward the bushes. In a panic, Ethan blurted out, "What kind of cat treat do you like?"

Maggie paused in midstep. She tilted her head to the side. "Did you just offer me a cat treat?"

"I meant *if* you were a cat, what would you want from a treat."

"I don't know. I've never . . . do you mean, like, turkey? Is that an answer?"

"Not a very good one."

"Hey!" She placed her hand on her hip in mock indignation. "You're the one asking weird cat-food questions."

"Yeah, forget it," Ethan said. "I don't know what got into me."

"Me."

"Excuse me?"

"Me," Maggie said. "My cat wants whatever I have. If it's on my plate, he gets obsessed with it. He ate a raspberry once. Well, licked it. But that's eating for cats."

A wind moved through the bushes, rustling the waxy, dark leaves that concealed the space between them.

"Why don't you ever wear your hair like that during the day?" he said.

"Oh God," she said, patting the bun of kinky black hair piled atop her head. "I just do this at night because it goes flat the next day if I don't. And

I don't like washing my hair every day since it's kind of dry. I tried braids but they leave these . . . waves." She laughed. "I can't believe I'm talking to you about my hair routine."

"If it'd make you feel any better, I can forget that this conversation ever happened."

Maggie eyed him thoughtfully, biting at the corner of her lower lip.

"No," she said. "I don't think so."

Ethan woke the next morning earlier than usual. He shaved briskly and carelessly while humming a TV jingle for tacos, and even the two bloody slits on his neck couldn't staunch his giddy confidence. After placing the razor back on its curvaceous magnetic pedestal, he lowered himself to the bathroom floor and forced out ten uneven push-ups—his right arm was notably stronger than his left—then he leaned against the bathroom counter, wheezing with triumph. Once he could breathe again, he washed away the pink smear of blood along his throat and applied an aftershave that promised to make him smell like a cleaned-up version of a Caribbean pirate.

While Lydia made coffee, Ethan rooted through the refrigerator for something healthy to eat. "I can't find the eggs," he said. "Did you put them somewhere?"

"I used them all in the casserole."

He pulled out the Tupperware and ate a forkful of cold tuna-noodle mix. "You sure there's eggs in here?"

"Yes, I'm sure. Oh, I forgot to tell you: you're carpooling with Ryan today." The lines in Lydia's forehead thickened as she effortfully plunged the French press. "Scudder needs a car to get his things from Andre's, and I have to pick up Jesse from camp after work, so I can't lend him mine."

"Why can't he just go at night?"

"No one'll be there at night. Andre's mother can only meet him at three."

"Why didn't he bring his stuff with him yesterday?" Ethan pierced a black mushroom cap and flung it into the cat's dish.

"I don't know. Not everyone's a planner. Besides, how many times has Ryan offered to carpool? I think he wants to be friends."

"I don't have time for friends." He watched the cat approach the mushroom. She sniffed it, paused, sniffed again, and padded away. "Why won't she eat it?"

"Cats don't eat mushrooms."

"I thought maybe if it was from my plate," Ethan said.

Ryan was a talkative companion and on both legs of the trip Ethan did his best to nod his way through the conversation. After a long day of struggling through FatCat meetings, however, Ethan's morning cheerfulness had hardened and grown stale, and it was only when he saw Maggie standing at their front door that Ethan came back to life. He bolted upright in the passenger seat.

"You OK?" Ryan said.

"I'm great," he said, lunging out of the sedan. "Thanks for the ride!" He strolled up to Maggie, suddenly buoyant. "Need help getting in?"

"Oh, hey. I rang the bell but, yeah, no one answered."

"Maybe camp went late," Ethan said, shouldering open the door. "Come on in."

Maggie followed him into the kitchen. While he texted Lydia, she sat at the table and placed her hands on the smooth blond wood, palms down, like a piano player. She was wearing gray athletic shorts and a pink shirt with faded lettering on the front. Ethan could see the dark stripes of her bathing suit top beneath the thin fabric of her tee shirt. She tilted her head to read the titles of the cookbooks stacked along the top of the kitchen cabinets.

"You guys must cook a lot," she said.

"No. Every few months one of us decides we should start to save money, so we go buy a cookbook. But we never end up using it."

"My mom is like that with yoga books."

"The purchase satisfies the intention," Ethan said. Maggie flexed and released the ball of her left foot, activating the strong muscles of her leg. Ethan went to the cabinet for a glass. "Wearing your hair up today. Guess I changed your mind."

"Oh." She laughed and patted her bun. "Yeah, no. I was just running late. And since I'd be getting in the pool I figured . . ."

"Looks good. Not just a nighttime thigh anymore." He blinked. "Thing," he corrected.

Maggie pushed away from the table. "Maybe we should just reschedule the lesson? If they're going to be a while? It's not a big deal."

"I'm sure they'll be here any minute. Camp probably detained them."

As Ethan soon learned in a text, however, it wasn't camp but Scudder that had detained them. While returning from Andre's house, Scudder had rear-ended another car and then fled the scene, abandoning the car on the side of the road.

"Unbelievable!" Ethan shouted, flinging aside his phone. Maggie stared at him with obvious curiosity. He didn't know what to say, overcome by warring impulses to rage and to charm.

"What happened?" Maggie said finally.

"Scudder crashed my car."

"Oh my God," Maggie said. "For real?"

Without knowing it, Maggie had voiced the question that Ethan and Lydia would debate endlessly over the next few days. According to Ethan, the whiplash that Scudder sustained from the accident was a counterfeit claim to elicit sympathy and forgiveness. According to Lydia, the headaches and jaw clicks, the muscle spasms and the difficulty turning his head to the left were as real as the crumpled fender.

"Fake, fake, *fake,*" Ethan insisted. "And even if it were real—and it's not—but *even if,* that still doesn't justify sitting around the house sleeping all day."

"One of the common symptoms of whiplash is fatigue," Lydia said.

"By an amazing coincidence, fatigue is also a common symptom of laziness."

"He's in pain, Ethan. And pain is pain."

Ethan couldn't disagree more. Pain had a variety to it that was staggering, and the childish whimpers of his nephew were insignificant in comparison to the greater agonies and distresses of adults—they certainly didn't merit his wife and daughter rushing around the house, fetching Scudder ice packs and blankets. On Sunday morning, Ethan prepared Jesse a bowl of Honey Nut Cheerios with slivers of sliced banana, and when he ventured upstairs to wake her, he found Scudder asleep in her bed. His nephew lay sprawled atop the covers, his long dark hair fanned out across a heart-shaped pillow, while curled up in the pink beanbag chair at the foot of the bed was Jesse. She saw her father and smiled, waving the fingers of one hand.

"He said my bed is more comfortable," she whispered.

"Get him out," Ethan announced to Lydia, who, changing in the corner of their bedroom, motioned for Ethan to close the door. "What? Don't give me that face. He kicked Jesse out of her bed."

"No he didn't. She loves having him there. She's always begging for him to hang out with her." Lydia wriggled into a vintage red-and-white dress that, in the fifties, had been salacious, but now looked docile.

"This is exactly what his father used to complain about. No sense of responsibility. No work ethic. I worked my way through college. I didn't just have things handed to me."

"Then take him to the office with you," Lydia said. "He could be an intern."

"So he can screw up there too? The kid's an idiot. He crashed my car *and ran for it.* Like no one's going to know who did it?"

"He's not an idiot, Ethan. He's actually very sharp. He's just unmotivated. I think a lot of Scudder's troubles come from being an only child. You learn to expect special treatment all the time. It's something I'm seeing already with Jesse, the way you spoil her."

"What? Jesse's nothing like Scudder."

"Not yet." Lydia smirked. "Just take him with you. He'll be so impressed once he sees you in charge and in your element. Maybe it'll motivate him to make something of himself. More than anything he needs a stable male role model, someone he can look up to."

"Fine, I'll bring him," Ethan said. He knew where this conversation was going. He'd been married long enough to understand when his wife was going to get her way. And it was so clearly a mistake, so obviously a bad decision, that for a moment he imagined it would all work out, since in a universe of unknown complications and implications, how often can a thing become exactly what we expect?

On Monday, Ethan and Scudder left for the office together. It was early morning as they climbed into Ethan's loaner car. The sky was radiating a flat white light that no painter has ever bothered to capture, except possibly Monet at his bleakest and most cataract ridden. Scudder immediately began scrolling through his phone, and didn't look up until they were a mile from the house, idling at a red light.

"Holy shit," he said, "I can't believe nobody's tagged that yet."

"What are you talking about?" Ethan said.

They were at the intersection of Market Street and Dearborn Avenue, where the residential area gave way to commercial endeavors. It was here where the neighborhood kids came to loiter, buying donuts and energy drinks from the small market while wishing for cars, or rides, or simply to be seen. Scudder pointed up to a papered-over billboard perched on the roof of an abandoned six-story commercial building. "You can see it from, like, every direction. You couldn't miss it."

"Maybe no one thinks it needs to be vandalized."

"Yo, it's not *vandalism.* It's freedom of expression. First Amendment shit."

"The First Amendment doesn't entitle you to spray-paint your name on someone else's property."

"That's the corporations talking. They want to own everything we see. So like it's all Doritos and Coca-Cola and Adidas. But people have messages—they should be able to share them too."

"Right. Important public contributions like 'My gang is going to murder you,'" Ethan said.

Scudder shook his head. "Most of it's just guys, you know, showing off. Or saying where they're from. Or writing to their girlfriends, 'I love you, bitch, take me back.' Romantic shit like that."

Scudder craned his neck to examine the billboard as they drove past.

"It's harder to reach than it looks," Ethan said. "Somebody tried it."

Once they arrived, Ethan stashed his nephew in his office and hurried to the small conference room. He was alarmed to see that Garrett had brought along his father, and Ethan shook the CEO's hand with the excessive, defiant cheerfulness of someone who has just been betrayed. The meeting had been represented to Ethan as an informal strategy preview, and Ethan remained committed to this premise, chatting and joking as he breezily clicked through the first few slides. His simple presentation had been built around Creamsicle, the newly imagined mascot for the brand, a chubby, mischievous orange-and-white cartoon cat. Ethan was only three slides in when the CEO waved for him to stop.

"Yes?" Ethan said.

"It's Garfield," the CEO said.

"You mean Creamsicle."

"I mean it's a fat orange cat," the CEO said. "You can call it whatever you want, I know who it is."

"I can see why you might initially get them confused," Ethan said. "But actually, they're very different. Creamsicle is *spotted* orange and white, not striped. And his ears are triangular, not rounded like Garfield's. Also, his teeth are—hang on . . ." He clicked ahead on his laptop.

The CEO picked up his cell phone. He scrolled through an email, making a puffing noise with his mouth.

"Here we are," Ethan said. "Whereas Garfield has square human teeth, Creamsicle has a more authentic feline smile. That's intentional."

"That's fucking Garfield," the CEO said, putting down his phone. He turned to Garrett. "What else do you have?"

"This is Ethan's show," Garrett said with an innocent shrug. "Since I'm still new to running the team, I gave him first run creatively."

"Ethan?" the CEO said. "This all you have?"

Ethan gazed down at his laptop, where a queue of unwatched slides featured Creamsicle delightedly cavorting in an ice cream parlor, at a piano bar, and in front of the Eiffel Tower. "We're in active brainstorming mode right now . . . the team's exploring concepts around . . . how to connect with the emotional needs of existing consumers." It was panicky market-speak babble, as meaningless as it was obvious, but before he could save himself with a slug of data—Friskies, Purina, Pounce, and Greenies relied on photographic imagery with their packaging, whereas the only other cartoon-based approach was from Whiskas, and Whiskas lacked a single dedicated character like Creamsicle—he heard Scudder call out his name.

That Ethan had been easily and expertly set up by Garrett, Ethan didn't dispute. But was it really necessary, at that susceptible moment, for his delinquent nephew to wander into the conference room?

"Excuse me," Ethan said and rushed to intercept Scudder, who, dressed in a black tee shirt printed with the name of what was either a band or an STD—possibly both—was slouching toward them. "What are you doing here?" he hissed.

"I need to borrow your computer. Someone stole my iPhone last week and now all I have's this, like, drug-dealer burner that can't even go online."

"I'm busy. Go back to my office."

"It's boring in your office." Scudder glanced up at the projection screen. "Garfield. Right on."

"I'm in a meeting right now," Ethan said. "We'll discuss this later."

"Actually, the meeting's over," Garrett said.

"It's not Scudder's fault what happened," Lydia told Ethan that night, as he railed to her about his nephew's intrusion.

"The CEO was there!" Ethan said. "Do you have any idea how unprofessional it was to have my screwup nephew stumble in?"

"All he did was ask to borrow your computer. If the CEO has children, I'm sure he understood."

"Oh, he's got kids. The new marketing director: twenty-eight years old with a shiny Ivy League degree and a gutting knife in his pocket."

"Wait. The director position got filled? When?"

"June."

"June!"

"It doesn't matter now. I had one shot to turn the meeting around and Scudder destroyed it. He's a walking disaster. I told you bringing him in was a bad idea. He's an agent of destruction."

"He's just a kid."

"By his own admission, he's a vandal! He's *proud* of it. 'Yo, I tagged some shit with my crew.' That's what you've invited into our home, Lydia. A vandal!"

Lydia went over and locked the door. "Calm down," she whispered. "What's gotten into you lately? He's got his issues, sure. But let's try to be a little understanding of the challenges he faces."

Challenges? As far as Ethan could see, Scudder's life was nothing but rewards. Day after day, people lined up to help him: Lydia with her maternal fussing and cooing; Jesse with the adulatory surrender of her room and toys; even at the office, Scudder was the recipient of largesse. The office supervisor bought him snacks from the vending machine, the IT department loaned him a company laptop, and one morning the head of the HR department surprised him with one of her ex-husband's suits. Ethan watched in quiet, stupefied envy as a constellation of minor benefactors seemed to appear wherever Scudder went. No, Lydia was wrong, very wrong. The world didn't challenge his nephew—it favored him.

Why? Ethan wanted to know what his nephew did to earn such generosity. How did he elicit such interest? With his obscure references and juvenile jokes, his sullen slouch and casual boredom, Scudder offered nothing of value that Ethan could recognize. If you were to believe Scudder's tediously apathetic rhetoric, he was impressed by nothing. Desirous of nothing. Concerned with nothing. Unlike Ethan, who spent so much of his time worrying over what to say, or to whom to say it, not once had Scudder expressed any embarrassment, anxiety, or regret about what he was saying or doing.

Which was, of course, exactly what made him so appealing. This was the belated realization that occurred to Ethan as he stood between the border of his house and Maggie's on Thursday night. He had taken out the trash every night that week, lingering by the bushes where he'd encountered Maggie, in the unfulfilled hopes of another run-in, and now, when he heard her voice at last, it came not from the edge of her yard but, curiously, from his own swimming pool.

"Come on in, it's warm!" Maggie cried.

Ethan felt his stomach spasm. With that terrible presentiment of the body, he understood what was happening. He lowered the lid onto the blue recycling bin and trudged back into the house with dread. From the dark kitchen, he watched them through the window, their figures lit by moonlight: Maggie treading water in the deep end and Scudder sitting along the edge, bare chested in a pair of black basketball shorts, dangling his feet in the water.

"How can you call this shit warm?" Scudder said.

Though they were speaking quietly, their voices skipped along the surface of the water like stones.

"Don't make me pull you in," Maggie said and swam up to him. Her head bobbed above the surface.

"Hey!" Scudder said, splashing at her with his foot.

Maggie grinned and slipped out of range. She circled around from his left. "There's no escape . . ."

"Yo, you're relentless. You're like that crocodile that ate Captain Hook's hand," Scudder said.

"Crocodile," Maggie said. "That's flattering."

"Better than some stupid-ass pirate. What does he even need a hook for? When do people use a hook?"

"Are you seriously not coming in?" Maggie said.

"If I was Captain Hook, I'd put a bottle opener where my hand used to be. Or a coffee mug. Something useful. A spoon."

Maggie laughed. It was a terse, excited little fox-bark, and with a pang of sadness, Ethan understood that he had never heard her true laugh before.

"What are you doing?"

Ethan spun around. His wife was in the entryway of the kitchen, her arms crossed.

"Me? Nothing. I'm—nothing."

"Just standing in the kitchen with the lights off," she said.

"I was coming up to bed. I don't need light for bed. That would be weird. That's what the weird thing would be." He hurried over toward Lydia, putting his arm around her waist in an attempt to steer her out of the kitchen before she looked through the window, but then a splash erupted from the pool.

She shrugged free, stepping past him. "Is somebody out there?" she said.

"I don't know. It's pretty late. I'm *tired,*" Ethan said. "Let's go to bed."

"Oh, it's just Scudder," Lydia said. "He played Marco Polo with Jesse today during her lesson. She loved it. Wouldn't get out of the water." Lydia smiled. "Maybe she doesn't take after you after all."

Another splash erupted from the pool, followed by Maggie's delighted fox-bark.

"They're cute together," Lydia said, gazing out the window. She placed her hand in Ethan's. "He's so tall now. Do you remember what he used to be like? With his floppy haircut? He was such a little boy."

What about me? Ethan thought. So was I.

Near his sternum, just above where his ribs connected, there was a curious circular indent in Ethan's chest. In his youth, this spot—where the skin pushed inward an inch as if someone had fired a bullet into his chest only to have it, miraculously, repelled—had served as the focus of all of Ethan's vanity and insecurity. Every time he stepped out of the shower, he eyed it with shame and indignation.

If only he had known, at fifteen, at eighteen, at twenty-one—hell, even at thirty—that this strange little divot in his chest would one day become endearingly trivial when compared with the other physical indignities awaiting him: the fatty, lugubrious roll around his waist; the dark ever-present bags beneath his eyes; the retreat of hair at his temples and, conversely, its malicious arrival in unwelcome places, white strands sprouting in his chest hair, coarse black strands popping up on his shoulders and inside his nose and even, on occasion, along the outside of his ear, as if his body were a strip of soil seeded with wild grasses. If only he had known what was to come, he would have . . .

What? What would you have done, Ethan asked himself, while staring unhappily at his naked reflection. Appreciated it? Admired it? We're built for ingratitude, not love. Everything, even ourselves, especially ourselves, goes unrequited.

He left the bathroom and sat on the bed, perching his laptop on his naked thighs. He was a loud and clumsy typist, and at that moment he enjoyed the angry clatter of his fingers driving the keys. He was just beginning to lay out his new concept for FatCat when the doorbell rang.

The owner is the "parent" and the cat is the "child," Ethan typed. *The owner does everything for the cat and the cat doesn't care.* The doorbell rang a second time. Ethan kept typing. When he entered "Morse" in the address line, two possibilities popped up: "Morse, Garrett" and "Morse, Kenneth." The doorbell rang a third time. Ethan hovered the arrow over Garrett's name but then, impulsively, slid his finger down and clicked on Kenneth. He hit send, pulled on shorts and a tee shirt, and went to answer the door as the bell rang a fourth time.

Ethan felt a flutter of hapless excitement when he saw Maggie behind the panel of glass. She was in terry cloth shorts and a bikini top, a fuzzy towel hanging around her neck. Her head was cocked slightly to the side, and she smiled with a careless luminosity, and though Ethan knew that the radiance he was receiving was merely a reflection of the true thing, like the tangential arc of moonlight striking the earth, he couldn't resist its allure.

"You just missed her," he said, opening the door. "Lydia took Jesse to the county fair for the day."

"But you're here?"

"I decided to stay behind."

"Wasn't today supposed to be a family thing?"

"It was an impulse. I'm very impulsive. I almost bought a motorcycle in college."

She rose up on her toes and peered over his shoulder into the empty living room.

"Hey, so I just had an idea," he said. "You teach adults how to swim, too, right? Why don't you teach me? Since you're already here, I'll just swap places with Jesse today."

"Actually Sundays aren't the regular—I mean, Jesse didn't have an official scheduled—"

"I'll pay you double," Ethan said. "Because I'm older—not old. Just, you know, an adult. We're both adults. So it's an adult rate. Come on!" He grinned hopefully. He could see the discomfort in her eyes, the sidelong glances of a pedestrian looking for rescue when cornered by an importuning stranger, and while he couldn't blame her for shying away from his babble, what choice did he have? Surrender? God, how he longed for the overconfidence of youth, that sweet and delicious arrogance. But it was long since extinguished in him, gone extinct, along with the Levuana moth and the Liverpool pigeon and the western black rhinoceros, all the many lost creatures the world would never see again.

He led Maggie toward the swimming pool, reassuring her that despite his lifelong fear and suspicion of the water, he would reward her efforts with swift progress. When they reached the deck, he handed her a water-damaged women's magazine to keep her occupied and hurried to the bedroom to change into his bathing suit. He struggled into the blue and orange Hawaiian-print board shorts Lydia had gotten him for some Father's Day, cinching tight the braided draw cord with a gasp. He didn't want to show up bare chested—every inch of his torso embarrassed him now, not just the divot—and yet he understood that swimming with a baggy cotton tee shirt was what fat boys did, so he rifled through his tee shirt drawer to find his most athletic-looking shirt and rebrand it as a rash guard. But he couldn't find anything made out of nylon or rayon or even polyester, and out of impatience and desperation, Ethan pulled on a snug red tee shirt with a fading logo for Heinz barbecue sauce and sprinted back downstairs.

"Have you ever heard the expression: 'When the student is ready, the master appears?'" Ethan asked as he stepped onto the pool deck. He strolled over to the chair where Maggie had placed her sandals and towel and glanced down into the water, expecting to find her gliding gracefully beneath the surface.

But the pool was empty.

"Maggie?"

Leading away from the shallow end was a trail of dark wet footprints. They were small and misshapen, resembling a series of shrinking yet vital internal organs. Ethan followed them into the house. The floor of the hallway did a poor job of capturing the dampness from Maggie's feet, but then Ethan didn't truly need the guidance. He knew where she was going.

Scudder looked up from the foldout bed as the door to the study swung open. He yawned and scratched his belly. Beside him, her feet resting on a black duffel bag disgorging spray paint cans, Maggie stared out the window with nervous attentiveness.

"Maggie, why did you leave?" Ethan said.

"Yo, she's not feeling well," Scudder said, following this pronouncement with an upward tick of his chin.

"Sorry," Maggie mumbled.

Ethan nodded and shut the door. A weary resignation overtook him, his embarrassment at being beaten by a nineteen-year-old tempered only by the belief that this, at least, was the end of his humiliation.

But it would not be the end. Humiliation has a way of reaching out for more, the way salt calls out for water, only to dissolve in its own compulsion. Early the next morning, while toasting a bagel, Ethan accidentally dislodged Lydia's cell phone from the charging cable that snaked along the kitchen counter; when he plugged the phone back in, a picture of Scudder glowed awake. Ethan stared at the screen, perplexed as to why his wife would replace a photograph of their daughter with a grainy, poorly lit image of their troubled nephew. Ethan keyed in his wife's password—2468—and swiped to the menu screen, searching among the unknown apps for an explanation, until he came to the Messages folder and saw the name "Andre." He clicked on it.

Andre: hey man Sunday u in? trial in 1 wk gotta enjoy myself
Scudder: if I can get a ride
Andre: yo use the bus mister privleg
Scudder: i know a girl who said she might drive me
Andre: the swimmer?
Scudder: yeah

Andre: thought you said she was fat
Scudder: no such thing as a free ride
Andre: lol

It wasn't Lydia's phone—or, at least, it wasn't her phone any longer. Yesterday, Ethan remembered, she had upgraded to a new model, and most likely she had passed the old device on to Scudder. Ethan ran his thumb over the web of tiny white cracks in the lower left corner, impact damage from last Easter, when Jesse had tripped over her laces and dropped the phone face-down onto concrete.

What he ought to do, Ethan knew, was to put the phone aside. Instead, he scrolled to the Messages folder marked "Maggie."

Maggie: u asleep?
Scudder: hey
Maggie: cant sleep still thinking of u
Scudder: me 2
Scudder: can still smell u on my hands
Maggie: dirty!
Scudder: i meant klorine
Maggie: oops
Scudder: haha ur bad

Ethan frowned and kept scrolling. He didn't know why he was still reading, or what he hoped to gain by scanning the ceaseless, misspelled, enigmatically abbreviated exchanges of his nephew (what did JFC even mean?).

Then he found it, and he realized what he had been looking for all along: himself.

Maggie: where ARE you? swimmer answered now im stuck at ur pool

Scudder: sorry wuz sleeping
Maggie: he wants to learn how to swim
Scudder: why? fat floats
Maggie: lol im serious what do i dont
Maggie: do
Maggie: for real hes getting changd now
Scudder: speedo time ;)
Maggie: gross not funny
Scudder: bet he tries to hug you
Scudder: "thx so much!"
Scudder: HUG
Maggie: omfg id rather die
Maggie: how are u 2 even related
Maggie: pls help
Scudder: come up
Maggie: hell get mad
Scudder: ill protect you from pervs
Maggie: k ur sweet brt

Ethan had always thought of rage as a hot emotion, full of blood and energy and wildness, but what he felt that morning in the kitchen at 6:45 a.m. was an overwhelming coldness. It was as if a glacier had formed just beneath his skin, constricting every capillary in his body. He navigated to the Andre folder and took a screenshot of their conversation, careful to ensure that their final exchange was visible. Whistling softly between his teeth, he swiped to Maggie's name and sent her the image. Then he placed the phone back where he had found it, pocketed his car keys, and left for work.

Ethan had worked in an office long enough to know that the sentence, "I'm glad you could join me," when spoken by a superior at the start of an unplanned, closed-door, one-on-one meeting, meant that you were in trouble. Just as in the realm of the heart, where excessive kindness preceding a romantic discussion signifies an impending breakup, in business, excessive politeness and civility signify an impending reprimand.

Garrett didn't deviate from this rare corporate truth. In a mannerly, scripted fashion, he articulated a list of Ethan's many disappointments, oversights, and missteps—including, most recently, emailing the CEO rather than Garrett. "That's just sloppy, Ethan. Always proofread your address field." Ethan nodded. He didn't bother to explain that he had intentionally sent the email to Garrett's father in the misguided hope that he would back Ethan's new marketing strategy around cats and ungratefulness, since parents are intimately acquainted with the concept of ingratitude. He didn't bother because it wasn't a discussion but a scolding. When Garrett transitioned into suggesting "best practices" and stating step-by-step resolutions for future situations, it was so blithely condescending, so wantonly patronizing, that Ethan had to bite the inside of his lip to silence himself. As Garrett rattled on, Ethan increased the pressure until the salty, metallic taste of blood slipped across his tongue.

After the meeting, Ethan returned to his office and sat at his desk with the door closed. His mouth ached, the swollen flesh below his lip throbbing. He felt wounded, slighted, degraded. What had he ever done to deserve such contemptuous treatment? He sat for awhile, simmering in his unhappiness, refusing to do any work, until his office phone rang. Ethan glanced at the caller ID and recognized Kenneth Morse's assistant.

He had never been called by Kenneth before. Was the CEO apologizing for the pedantry and fussiness of his son? Or Maybe Garrett had been so touchy not because Ethan had sent the email to Kenneth, but because Kenneth had liked his idea.

Ethan picked up the receiver and cleared his throat. "Hello," he said with forced calm.

"Is that you, Ethan?" drawled Gail. Despite the casting tendencies of

TV sitcoms, the executive assistants in the office were not cute twenty-somethings but women in their late fifties and sixties like Gail, intelligent, intuitive women who had made careers out of being matronly, omniscient, and discreet.

"Of course it's me," Ethan said.

"Well, I'll tell you, actually I was looking for your nephew. Is he there? Or is he wandering about the floors again?"

"What do you want Scudder for?"

"Mr. Morse asked me to find a time with him and Garrett to discuss some viral video ideas. Did you see the one your nephew sent with the bulldog riding the skateboard?" She chuckled. "How does he stay on?"

Ethan stared at his desk in enraged disbelief. Everything on it, from the chrome-plated swing-arm lamp to the mesh container of dry-erase markers to the stack of yellow sticky notepads was as replaceable as he was.

"Where would you even buy a helmet for a dog?" Gail said.

"I'm going to have to call you back," Ethan said and reached for the markers.

It hadn't been called the executive washroom in over a decade, and though a plaque marked "Guest" had been applied to the door for egalitarian appearances, everyone knew that the bathroom on the fifteenth floor belonged to the CEO. Glancing down the hallway first to ensure that no one was watching, Ethan gently pushed open the door.

Inside, it was dark and cool and smelled, oddly, of the lavender oil that Lydia used to apply to Jesse's crib pillow to help her sleep. Groping blindly along the wall, Ethan located the switch and turned on the lights. He had expected a certain degree of lavishness, amenities like Egyptian cotton towels and a glass bowl of individually wrapped mints, but what greeted Ethan was not so much luxury as domesticity. A lace doily lay draped across the left side of the counter, atop which rested freshly cut flowers in a glass vase, while to the right, surrounding the sink, a menagerie of turtle-shaped hand soaps looked on in innocent configuration. Behind the turtle soaps, a ceramic toothbrush holder, painted in a delicate lilac and purple palette, contained a single toothbrush. Ethan ran his thumb over the soft bristles, observing in the mirror's reflection, just below the monogrammed hand towels, a metallic toilet-paper-holder statue in the shape of a spaceship, with the toilet paper roll serving as the nose of the shuttle.

It was here, Ethan decided, to begin Scudder's reign of vandalism.

Fuck you he scrawled in red marker across the spaceship's fuselage. *Eat me* and *Eat shit* followed, rather predictably, as he reproduced the simple profanities he'd observed in bathrooms over the years. He had no prior experience with defacement, and as he moved among the surfaces of the washroom with his markers, dispensing insults and sketching genitalia, a feeling of potency gradually rose up in him, similar to what he imagined a cave painter in Lascaux felt when first smudging and staining the bare rough walls of his world. With every embittered phrase, he was taking control of the room, discrediting its presumed authority. *Fat ass* he wrote on the toilet seat, then drew an upward arrow on the cistern and, switching markers, scrawled on the rear wall in blocky blue letters *Corporate scum*. He attacked the mirror above the sink next, swatting the turtle soaps out of his way as he populated the surface with slurs and abuses, each one increasingly furious and decreasingly comprehensible, exchanging urgency for legibility, outrage for clarity, until finally he gave up on coherence all together and flung aside the marker, climbing up on the sink and, with his bare hands, began spreading the ink around in muddy whorls.

It was hard to say who was more surprised when Gail entered the washroom, carrying a new lavender candle and a striped box of matches. Squatting on the counter, his hands covered in purplish-brown ink and the mirror nothing but a murky smear, Ethan had the disorienting and shameful sensation of a child caught playing with his feces. He jumped off of the counter, knocking over the vase of flowers. Miraculously, he caught it before it shattered and he smiled reflexively, as if expecting admiration. Then he saw the rest of the room, and realized that there would be no admiration coming his way. "Scudder . . ." he stuttered, but in the disgraceful and furious lexicon that he had contributed that day, *Scudder* was the one curse missing, the only word that held the chance, however slight, of saving him. And in his mania he had forgotten it.

Gail had four children and eleven grandchildren, and out of this vast maternity of dependency, wildness, and error came a weary manifestation of mercy. At least that was what Ethan imagined saved him when, instead of reporting him to Kenneth, she furnished him with cleaning products and the pronouncement that he had thirty minutes to erase all evidence of his disgraceful actions or she would escort him out of the building herself.

"Thank you. Thank you. Thank you," Ethan said.

"Get to cleaning," Gail said. "And be grateful you didn't use permanent markers."

When he returned home that evening, he went immediately to find Lydia. He was embarrassed by all that had occurred, his derangement, his humiliation, but dwarfing this shame was enormous relief for all that he had not lost, and he urgently wanted to hold in his arms the bounty of his family. He came across Lydia in the hallway, piling fresh, hot laundry onto the wooden folding shelf. It is often in times of trauma that a man's hidden sentimentality is revealed, and he demonstrates a fierce, affectionate devotion for the life that he once railed against. As he watched his wife fold a towel, her dancer's head held high, her spine straight, her elegant, tired profile possessing the same distracted, intelligent expression as that of the girl he had fallen in love with twelve years ago, Ethan was overcome with a dizzying gratitude. He ran over and threw his arms around her.

"What's wrong?" she asked, reaching up and pulling free her white ear buds.

"Nothing," Ethan murmured. He buried his face in the curve between her head and shoulder with a stooping motion reminiscent of a man lowering his head into the stocks.

"Are you sure? Did something—"

"I missed you. That's all. I just . . ." Glimpsing Jesse coming down the stairs, he waved for her to come and join them. He disengaged from Lydia and bent down, waiting for his daughter to leap into his arms.

"Where's Scudder?" Jesse said, running past Ethan. She scanned the empty living room, disappointment pinching her tiny features.

"He didn't come with me to the office today," Ethan said. "He's probably still up in his room."

"He's gone," Jesse said. "I checked his room."

"Then he's somewhere else. Maybe the bathroom."

"I checked there too. He's gone, Daddy."

Ethan nodded and ignored her. His daughter had been known to trip over toys for which she was searching, and it wasn't until a few minutes later, when Scudder failed to appear for dinner, that Ethan considered Jesse might be right. He ascended to the second floor and knocked on the door of the study. When there was no answer, Ethan twisted the knob and entered. The room was in its usual disarray: the foldout bed entangled in sheets, the window propped slightly open with a yellow, rolled-up bag of potato chips, and the modular wall calendar fragmenting into pretty, discontinuous tiles on the floor. Yet in the midst of this, Ethan detected a new sloppiness, the disorder amplified by agitation or clumsiness or some other cousin of haste.

Maggie, in her sadness and anger, corroborated that Scudder had left.

"I'm glad he's gone," she said, standing inside her front door with her arms folded, hands tucked into her armpits. "I never want anything to do with him."

"Did he say where he was going?"

"He just kept saying he was sorry. But I hung up." She huffed. "Then I blocked his number. My mom had this antirape app installed on my phone for when I leave for college. It lets me block thirty people."

"Before you blocked him, did he say why—"

"He just said I needed to listen to him and 'It's just guys talking' and he was sorry and didn't mean it and he really liked me and whatever. I told him all he does is lie. Like I would *ever* listen to him again." Her eyes were swollen and red from crying. In her expression, Ethan saw a saddening blindness to all the pain still coming for her in the name of love. "I hope he dies," she said and shut the door.

He was halfway down Maggie's steps when it hit him. He ran back to the study in a panic, Maggie's heartbroken wish echoing in his mind. He almost didn't bother to check under the bed for the backpack in which he had once glimpsed a cluster of spray paint cans. Of course it was missing.

It was just after eight when Ethan arrived at the corner of Market Street and Dearborn Avenue, and though the commercial area had emptied out for the evening, the streetlights would remain lit until midnight. He couldn't wait hours for concealment. By then, Scudder would have accessed the roof and attempted to scale the antique billboard upon which, Ethan suspected, his nephew intended to spray paint an apology to Maggie. Where better to display his sincere contrition than the most visible public space within miles? Maggie would have to see it and, admiring Scudder's boldness and devotion, forgive him. Only what Ethan hadn't told his nephew when riding in the car with him that morning was that a pair of teenagers had once tried to climb up to the old billboard and the platform had given out, breaking the back of one boy and killing the other.

There had been no explicit reason to inform Scudder of the structure's unsteadiness, but as Ethan hurried toward the building, he understood that his silence on the matter had been intentional, a petty dark fantasy. That he had wished death upon his nephew, however abstractly, now horrified him, and he anxiously circled the building in search of access.

It was a clutter of abandoned commercial spaces, and none of the obvious doors were open. Ethan struggled to open a side door that seemed promising, but ultimately he couldn't budge it. A second side door, announcing a derelict photography studio, remained similarly sealed. Despairing, he grabbed a golf-ball-sized rock and approached a low window in the rear of the building, out of sight from the road and the occasional car shuttling past. He was about to shatter the window when he spotted a third door, partly sheltered by shrubs with pinkish-purple flowers, propped open an inch. He dropped the rock and, wrestling with the stiff door, wriggled his way inside.

Almost immediately, Ethan was plunged into darkness. All around him he smelled urine and beer and, beneath that, something fouler, maybe a dead mouse—or, from the potency, an entire family of mice. Holding onto the cool metal rail in the stairwell to guide him, he hurried up the steps, tripping slightly in the dark. He paused at each landing, listening for the sounds of approach, beset with a fear that he would come across deranged and violent men without homes. As a child, he had feared goblins, trolls, demons, and all sorts of supernatural creatures, but now that he was grown, the only thing he feared was ordinary human desperation.

No one swam out of the darkness to claim him, however, and after a few minutes he emerged onto the roof, unharmed. He took a sharp, grateful breath of fresh air and then rushed over to the billboard, reminded of why he had come. "Scudder!" he called up. There was no answer. "Scudder!"

He circled to the front of the billboard, a blank, untouched pastiche against the blue-black California night. He had made it in time. He circled around to the back again and shouted for his nephew to come down. It was at least fifteen feet to the base of the billboard and, due to the construction of the metallic lip and the shabby fraternity of original and repair beams, impossible to see where his nephew was standing.

"Scudder!" he hollered again, cupping his hands around his mouth.

After a few more cries had gone by with no reply, he understood that his nephew had no intention of revealing himself. For all his idleness and sloth, Scudder was a stubborn kid, and Ethan knew he would hide out all night if it came to that.

The prospect of climbing up after his nephew was terrifying, and for a moment Ethan hesitated, but then he thought about his daughter, trapped one day in some similar defiance. He pictured her as a little egg perched on a shelf, with all the world rattling and shaking below. What would happen to her? How could he desert his nephew and then expect someone to save his daughter from tumbling, unguarded, into the precarious clamor?

Ethan placed his foot on the bottom rung of the skinny metal ladder and, exhaling twice in quick succession, began to climb. It was an awkward and difficult ascent, the width of the ladder so narrow that his knees brushed against each other with each step. As he reached the second rung from the top, just before clearing visibility with the platform, the metal joints anchoring the ladder to the beam groaned. He paused, reminded that he was suspended near the edge of a six-story building. He could feel the entirety of his weight burdening the rusted ladder, decades of indulgence, inactivity, and denial conspiring to adult heaviness. Sweat beaded along his forehead and prickled on his palms as a queasy vertigo overtook him.

"Scudder," Ethan shouted. "The platform isn't safe. It can—"

The joint groaned again.

He froze.

"You need to come down right now," Ethan said, softer this time. "Please."

He raised his left forearm and wiped the sweat from his eyes.

Click.

The joint snapped free. Abruptly, the ladder swung down and to the right. Ethan was jolted backward, clutching the rung with one hand. He grabbed on with his left hand as the ladder jerked to a stop and, panting, wrapped both arms around it, as if clinching his opponent in a boxing match.

Dangling at a thirty-degree angle, staring down at the concrete sidewalk six stories below him in shock, he felt his phone vibrate. The buzz wrested him from his daze. He pushed away from the ladder to which his face had been pressing, so close that he could taste flakes of rust on his lips, and with great care, he lowered his left foot. Ignoring the menacing moans of the ladder, he forced his left hand to mimic the motion. He continued, step by step, until he touched the rooftop and, with a burst of gratitude, lurched away from the edge of the building. Wiping his sweaty palms on the fronts of his pants, he peered up past the damaged ladder to the platform. Then he took out his phone and called Lydia back.

"Where did you go?" she said.

"I'm on the roof of the building on Market and Dearborn."

"What are you doing there? I thought you were circling the neighborhood—wait . . . did you say the *roof*?"

"I'm trying to get to Scudder. He's hiding on the back of a billboard."

"Why would he be on a billboard?"

"He's going to tag it with graffiti to prove to Maggie that he's sorry. It's the perfect location, he told me once. She'd have to see it."

"Ethan, Scudder just texted me."

"Then tell him to come down! The platform won't hold! The ladder's half broken already. Tell him I'll secure it from the bottom and then he can—"

"He's on his way to San Francisco."

"What?"

"There's a show tomorrow night with that band he was following around. Apparently his friend in Seattle changed his mind and is meeting him there."

"I don't . . . understand. He's . . . how?"

"Hitchhiking probably. I can't bear to think about that part." A truck passed below on the street, its engine gasping. "Isn't Market and Dearborn that condemned building?"

"Let's just forget about it," Ethan said. "Doesn't matter now."

"So you went to a condemned building and climbed up onto the roof—"

"I know, I know, can we drop it? It was stupid."

Ethan stepped around to the front of the unmarked billboard.

"It *is* a pretty good view."

"Please be careful, Ethan."

"I'm always careful."

"Are you?"

He cleared his throat. "Yes. But I'll be more careful."

"Good," she said. "Now come home."

He hung up and slipped the phone back in his pocket, his cheek warm from the call. He could almost, but not quite, see his house from the roof. He rose up on his toes, squinting, and for a moment he thought he spotted the shimmering reflection of his swimming pool. It was an illusion, of course, but a kind one, and Ethan descended the dark stairs of the building imagining a pool full of children, his daughters and sons splashing toward each other, wild and careless, stupid and brave, every fearful, frozen fragment of their inheritance dissolving in the water.

But first, him.

Runners of San Vicente

WHILE OUR WIVES were upstairs, Sean asked me if I ever considered running away.

"I was a pretty happy kid," I said.

"I mean as an adult," Sean said. "Maybe disappear is the better word. Vanish."

"Is that even possible? With security cameras and GPS and the NSA tracking phone calls . . . I'm not a conspiracy theorist but we all seem very watched these days."

Sean turned up the heat on the stove top. A thin crust had congealed on top of the black bean soup. He used a wooden spoon to break it apart.

"People do it all the time," he said. "I read an article, said a million adults disappear every year, just in the U.S."

"I don't know if I believe that figure. A million sounds—"

"Even if it's a tenth of that," Sean said, "even if it's a *hundredth.* That's ten thousand a year. That's significant. That's a *thing.*"

"A lot of those people probably died."

"That's why you'd have to let your kids know somehow that you weren't dead. You wouldn't want them wondering. Or thinking it's their fault." He reached for the cilantro and tore the green leaves, sprinkling them onto the soup.

"They're still going to think it's their fault."

"You think so?"

"What if—" I paused as I heard the women coming down the stairs. I lowered my voice to a whisper and kept an eye on the entryway to the kitchen. "What if you got caught?"

Sean shrugged as he switched off the burner. "What could they do to you that they haven't already done?"

*

For the new year, Sean and I took up running. We lived only a few blocks from each other in Santa Monica, Emilie and I in a cramped yellow rental that we could barely afford, and Sean and Ingrid in an elegant midcentury home ringed with avocado trees, and on Tuesdays, Thursdays, and Saturdays Sean and I would meet on Twenty-Sixth Street and jog the narrow strip of grass and concrete that runs the length of San Vicente Boulevard. We ran slowly, stopping for a moment where the median ended and the Pacific Ocean appeared below the bluffs, huge and bullying, before we turned around and retraced our path. Sean had been a cross-country runner in high school and could have gone much farther and faster, but he held back without complaint, and even when I encouraged him to sprint by himself at the end, he usually deferred. Now in our early forties, we were at an age when whatever competitiveness and envy we might have once harbored toward each other had quietly dissipated, and in its place was a discreet but durable friendship, a mutual appreciation akin to what marriage is portrayed as, on its better days.

We ran in the mornings during winter break, when our kids didn't have school, and once classes resumed, we switched to evenings and weekends. Sean's wife worked in the financial industry, so she was beholden to New York hours and in the office by 6 a.m., leaving it up to Sean, who did occasional freelance Web design from home, to get the children ready each morning and pick them up at the end of the school day. Their daughter, Jenna, was now eleven—like our Catherine—and Sean had gotten in trouble the last time we had gone for a run because he had left Jenna alone in charge of her seven-year-old brother.

"When my sister was Jenna's age, she was babysitting other people's kids," Sean said.

I nodded and grunted, finding it a challenge to talk while running.

"I left them alone for *half* an hour, all the doors locked, watching TV—"

"Sorry, I have to stop," I said, holding up my hand with a grimace. "Just for a—I'll pick back up in—"

"Don't worry about it," Sean said and slowed to a walk beside me. "Cramp?"

"Skinny people get cramps. This is just fat person pain."

"Come on, you're doing fine," Sean said and swatted me on the shoulder.

We walked toward the traffic light on Seventh Street. I kept the blade of my hand pressed into my left side and forcibly exhaled. It was one of those tricks I'd seen other runners employ. It didn't seem to work.

"One more minute and I'm good," I said, while we waited for the crosswalk signal. I felt embarrassed, ashamed of my slowness and heaviness. The other day, when I had asked Emilie if she'd noticed any change in my appearance since taking up running, she'd replied, "I think it's great you're so committed to it," and hurried out of the bathroom.

"Why call a minivan 'The Odyssey'?" Sean said.

"What?"

Sean motioned to a maroon van idling at the red light. "Why not just name it 'I Give Up' ? Call it what it is. 'Wearing Sweatpants to the Supermarket.' 'Living Vicariously through My Kids Until They Break My Heart.'"

"That one might be hard to fit on the back."

Sean laughed. He had deep dimples and a strong masculine jaw, and when he laughed he made the actual sound "ha ha ha." It sounded insincere until you got to know him. His peculiar laugh was one of the reasons it had taken a while until I had warmed to him. It was also the thing everyone would describe to the police when, in the first week of spring, Sean went missing.

At first, everyone assumed it was about a woman. Sean drank, but moderately, and since drugs weren't an issue either, that left women as the third reason why a man might disappear for a few days. Sean was certainly good-looking, with a slightly weathered, grown-up California beach kid look, and considering the number of divorced and separated women in our neighborhood—let alone married women looking for an erotic diversion—he wouldn't have had too much trouble finding company. But he never expressed any interest in it. During one of our last runs together, when he had told me about a mother at Jenna's school coming on to him, it had been with bewilderment rather than desire.

"We were in the parking lot after morning drop-off and she told me she was moving to Silver Lake," Sean said. "Divorce. Then she took me aside and said she'd had an adult dream about me."

"An *adult dream*? I have *never* heard that expression before. It's like something out of *The Crucible.* Goody Mullins had an adult dream!"

"Ha ha ha."

"So what did you say?" I asked.

"Nothing. I didn't know what to say. I was shocked. Then she said, 'Don't you want to know what happened in the dream?'"

"This is crazy. If it weren't coming from you, I'd call bullshit."

"So I said—because I didn't want to be rude—"

"You're very polite. Too polite to get a real running partner."

"So I said, 'Sure. What happened in the dream?' And she puts her hand on my arm and leans in and says, in this husky voice, 'You were an animal.'"

"I'm stopping—and for once not because I'm tired. But because this deserves my complete attention."

Sean laughed his curious "ha ha ha" again as I rested against the rough bark of a tree to catch my breath. "It's a nice way to be remembered," he said.

At the time, I'd thought he had meant because the woman was moving away, but in light of what later happened, I'm no longer certain. Was he warning me, even then, of his intention to leave? Despite a conversational ease and candor, in many ways Sean was inscrutably private. I knew very little, really, about his interior life. I had inferred things from almost a decade of anecdotes and commentary, and Sean was always willing to vent his most recent marital or parental frustrations, but ours was a friendship based more on distraction than disclosure. It was Sean's way, I imagined, to be like this with everyone—agreeable, charming, but ultimately elusive—and so I wasn't surprised, two days after his disappearance, to find Sean's wife on my doorstep demanding that I tell her about any secret relationships he had been having.

"Secret relationships?" We were standing in the entryway to my house, the front door wide open and a warm spring wind sending the sheet music skittering off the piano and onto the bench.

"This doesn't have to be a long conversation," Ingrid said. "Just give me a name."

"I don't have a name."

"This is serious," Ingrid said. "You get that, right? My *husband* is missing. My children's *father.*"

"I don't know anything."

"I won't ever say where I heard it from. But I need to find him."

"Ingrid—"

"You're friends! You run together every day! You tell each other things!"

"Come in, please," I said, urging her inside and glancing anxiously around at the other houses. Ours was a quiet but nosy neighborhood, and Sean's disappearance had been the most exciting incident in its history. He had vanished on a Wednesday morning, after returning home from dropping off the kids at school. He had taken his wallet and laptop but left his car keys behind. Everybody assumed he had been picked up by someone—no one, not even the desperately unhappy, walks anywhere in Los Angeles.

I shut the door and caught up with Ingrid in the living room. "I wish I knew something that could help," I said, stooping to pick up Bach's "Musette in D," which I'd been using to teach an intermediate student. "But Sean wasn't very . . . revealing."

"No kidding."

"And he hasn't called or texted . . . ?"

"He left his phone."

"What about phone records? Anything there that might lead you—"

"Nothing. I checked his email too. But he probably had some secret account . . ." She exhaled and slumped on the piano bench. Ordinarily, Ingrid was a forceful presence—opinionated, aggressive, self-involved—and over the years, Sean had complained more than once about her ability to steamroll him. I'll confess that a part of me had quietly applauded when I first heard that he had disappeared; I had admired his nerve. Now, however, seeing his once-formidable wife hunched before the piano, dwarfed by her sadness and uncertainty, I felt a rush of regret. It had been foolish to cheer for this.

"What about the kids?" I said.

"What about them?"

"Did he say anything to them that might give any indication of where . . ."

She shook her head wearily.

"Are you sure he didn't leave a note for them? Maybe hidden somewhere in their room? Or in a school backpack?"

"I searched the whole house. There's no . . ." She stopped. Her expression darkened. "He told you, didn't he?"

"Told me what?"

Ingrid stood up from the piano bench and advanced toward me. "How long have you known he was planning on leaving?"

"I don't know anything," I stammered, backing away from her. She seemed to be growing taller, columnar, imposing, like a time-lapse video of a night-blooming cactus. "If I knew where he was, I'd tell you."

Ingrid walked to the front door, her back rigid. I followed behind, anxiously clenching and unclenching my hands. Outside, Emilie was pulling into the driveway after having taken our daughter to her Friday after-school physical therapy session. Emilie waved at us as she helped Catherine out of the car.

"Ingrid," Emilie said, "Have there been any—"

"No," Ingrid said, descending the concrete steps.

"I'm so sorry. Do you need any help with the kids while you're out looking? We can watch them."

Ingrid shook her head. "I'm going back home now. I just stopped by so your husband could lie to me. I've missed it with Sean gone."

I put off Emilie's questions by pointing out Ingrid's fragile and desperate state of mind and went for a run. It was noon on a Saturday and the grassy median was packed with weekend athletes, sporadic with their exercise regimens and yet almost all in visibly better shape than me. It was a dispiriting display and soon I switched to walking. I wandered down to where San Vicente intersects with Ocean Avenue and paused at the small palm-tree-dotted park where Sean and I would usually take a break midrun. I was reluctant to go home and face my wife. We had a good marriage overall, but there were fracture lines here and there, and Sean's disappearance had only deepened them. My quiet refusal to vilify my friend's leaving had been interpreted by Emilie as tacit approval, and the implications of this frightened and angered her.

She shouldn't have worried. Rather than encouraging a fantasy of abandoning my family, I was terrified that my wife might find inspiration in Sean's vanishing. Without Emilie, I didn't know what I would have done. The pressures and anxieties of my life often threatened to overwhelm me—our ever-rising debt as we consistently lived beyond our means, my stalled career as a musician, the perpetual disquiet of raising children in a world designed to devour or break them—and the thought of having to face these adversities alone was unbearable.

I sat on one of the benches in the park for nearly an hour, while all around me affluent women in skin-clinging yoga wear exercised among the grass and trees. I had been raised in New England, with its dark, weathery tantrums, and though I'd lived in Los Angeles now for almost fifteen years, I still didn't trust it. I found its perpetual beauty tedious and obnoxious. We all know the universe doesn't care about any of us, that our life is as insignificant as a cocktail napkin, disposable, one of billions of trivial reproductions that, if piled together, would still amount to nothing; and we bear this truth well, so long as we don't have to see bright-blue skies on the day our husband leaves us, or soaring palm trees on the day our mother expels her last contaminated breath, or a luminous ribbon of cool, white sand on the day our child's leg shatters, unfixable, beneath the thunder of a car axle, breaking like that first promise we ought never to have trusted, that all of this will hold together, peaceful and unchanging, to the end.

I walked back to our house and circled the mailbox a few times, delaying the conversation I knew was awaiting me. Catherine was sitting on the lawn, her legs in a skinny V, her crutches stacked beside her. She hadn't seen me yet. She was carefully building another playground out of cardboard for her pet mice. The playgrounds were temporary, since the mice could chew through them in minutes, and the amount of effort that my daughter put into constructing these brief palaces with a glue gun and scissors and stacks of cardboard was alternately admirable and unfathomable to me. I pulled my phone from my pocket to see how many times Emilie had tried to reach me while I'd been gone. When I scrolled through Recent Calls, however, the only missed call was from a local, unknown number.

Sean, I thought. He's trying to reach me.

I dialed my voice mail immediately and pressed the phone to my ear. Emilie came out of the house and moved down toward me with her arms crossed, awaiting an apology. I waved to her with my free hand and mouthed, "Sean."

"*Sean*? He's on the phone?"

I held my finger to my lips and listened for his voice. I had never before realized how physical an activity listening is, how your entire body conspires to hear, from the tendons in the back of your neck to the tiny muscles bridging your jaw. The phone was hot and glassy against my ear as the message unspooled. Sean had a habit of clearing his throat before he spoke, and if he timed it poorly, a phone would catch the echo of it.

But there was no throaty catch. There was just a steady staticky crackle, then silence.

After a week had passed with no contact or explanation, people began whispering the more unpleasant theories: suicide, murder, hit-and-run, drowning. These fates all seemed gaudy and sensational, and I refused to entertain them. Since the silent local phone call from Sean, I'd been searching the surrounding neighborhoods, certain that he was hiding out nearby. He wouldn't just disappear for good, I reasoned. He had left on an impulse, driven to it by some irresistible frustration, and was now waiting in shame and confusion, unsure of how to return.

"How do we know he isn't just living in another country?" asked Sean's friend Kirk, as we pulled out of the parking lot of a bakery where they used to order homemade donuts. I'd been commandeering Sean's friends to help me check out all of Sean's favorite local places, in the hopes of spotting him. It was a desperate strategy, but I didn't know what else to do. No one did.

"Ingrid had all the flight manifestos from LAX and Burbank checked," I said. "She got a guy who specializes in it."

"Sean could have rented a car."

"His name would have showed up if he rented a car. You need a credit card."

I shook the fresh bag of donuts to distribute the sugar. I'd grabbed them while inside the bakery. They were the size of plums, and still hot from the deep fryer.

"Maybe he hitchhiked," Kirk said. "Or took a train."

"He wouldn't just leave his kids forever. Think of everything he does for them. Eighty percent of the parenting is done by Sean."

"Did for them. And maybe that's why he left."

"He's here," I said, biting into a burning hot donut, huffing to let the heat escape my mouth. "He's just too embarrassed to come back on his own." I offered Kirk a donut but he scrunched up his nose. Our only connection was through Sean, who occasionally gathered up his disparate friends to watch football, and our terse, unproductive exploration was confirming how little we had in common.

"You guys used to get lunch at that Thai place on Wilshire, right?" I said. "Let's try that."

"Maybe later. I have to get back to work." He turned right and headed north along Ocean Avenue. "Where do you want me to drop you off?"

"Doesn't matter." Despite my best efforts, I had been unemployed for almost a year and a half after being fired from a job I had disliked but couldn't afford to give up. It was a perverse disgrace, a humiliation I'd thought exclusive to me—until Sean had gone missing. Only then had I realized that my enduring unemployment and Sean's tedious domesticity were comparable. It had become clear that we had both entered a period in our lives when getting what we wanted was no longer an option. Neither of us had known that life would become so thoroughly and habitually about failure, that disappointment would cling to us as enthusiasm once had, but whether it was my joblessness and indebtedness or Sean's inescapable domesticity, our futures had proved wildly divergent from our expectations.

Kirk turned onto Broadway, and after a few minutes, turned again, until we were driving along Sean and Ingrid's street. Slowly we approached their yard, the giant avocado trees leaning solicitously toward the house like reporters. A man on a bicycle, his face obscured by a navy hoodie, was rounding the corner. Impulsively, I instructed Kirk to follow him.

"Who?"

"That guy."

"What guy?"

"He just went around the corner. He's on a bike." I took off my seat belt and leaned forward to keep him in sight.

Kirk tapped the brakes.

"What are you doing—don't slow down. You're supposed to follow him."

Kirk shook his head. "Historically, following kids in hoodies hasn't worked out too well for anyone involved."

"What if it's not a kid? What if it's Sean?"

Kirk pulled over and stopped the car.

"You're losing him! He's getting away."

"It's not Sean."

"It *could* be. It could be him coming to check on his family."

Kirk rubbed his eyes. "If he cared about his family, he wouldn't have left in the first place."

"Just follow him! Some of us actually want to find Sean! Some of us actually want to help him!"

"All right, that's enough," Kirk said. He unlocked the doors and made a dismissive motion with his head.

"This is on you," I said, climbing out of the car. "Losing Sean is on *you.*"

Kirk's taillights flashed as his car receded into the suburban distance, rising and falling along the speed bumps, and then I was alone, staring up at Sean and Ingrid's home. It was a lavish, handsome house, the kind that Emilie would have loved and that I had never been able to provide her with. How unhappy Sean must have been, I thought, to abandon the extravagant comfort of this home. How lonely, if he was willing to discard everyone he knew—except for me, of course. I was the only one he had entrusted his secret to, the only one for whom the scope of his dissatisfaction was comprehensible.

He was relying on me, I understood, to stand in for him. If anyone could speak for Sean in his absence, it was me.

Sean's daughter, Jenna, answered my knock. She didn't look much like her father, except for the compactness of her mouth and the rounded shape of her forehead. She stared up at me defiantly—angered, I supposed, by the many futile visits from concerned, or maybe just curious, neighbors during these past ten days.

"My mom's upstairs," she said.

"I just came by to tell you that your dad loves you."

She shrugged and walked away.

"He wanted to leave you a note but he couldn't," I called out after her. "But he told me. He said—"

Her younger brother appeared around the corner. His glasses were enormous. The magnification of his eyes and the jerky movements of his slender frame reminded me of a mantis. "Mom!" he cried, in his reedy worried voice.

"No, you don't have to . . ."

But it was too late. He was already scrambling up the stairs, hunched over on all fours.

I hesitated for a moment, listening as the boy's hands and bare feet scurried along the distant hallway. Then I heard Ingrid's hard, sharp voice in reply. I shut the door and ran home.

Sean had been the driving force behind our daily runs, and with him gone, I'd lost interest in the activity. But that night I felt restless, and after putting on my neglected gym clothes and lacing up my sneakers, I set off at a slow jog for San Vicente Boulevard. It was past dinnertime, and the night's final wave of runners was appearing, serious men and women flitting along the grassy median, the reflective strips on their shoes lighting up like the eyes of rabbits.

I'd gone less than a quarter mile when my breathing grew labored and I thought about turning back. It was always this way, but I no longer had Sean to urge me on. As I toyed with the idea of capitulation—what was this minor shame, compared to all the other shame that came before it?—I spotted him. He was winding his bike slowly, lazily, onto Seventeenth Street. His shoulders were hunched and his head was low, concealed inside the navy hoodie.

I darted across the two lanes of eastbound San Vicente. A Lexus swerved to avoid me and climbed onto the median, nearly toppling over. The driver honked his horn, a long, enraged beat, and the man on the bike glanced over his shoulder. It was too dark to see his face from this distance, and charged with resolve, I scrambled up the side of the nearest yard and beheaded the sculptured ferns on a diagonal path to intercept him.

I made it onto Seventeenth Street about thirty feet behind him. He hadn't noticed me, I didn't think, as he was casually coasting down the middle of the road, looping from side to side like a snake. Still, I was on foot, and it took an immense effort to match his pace. I trailed behind him, the tiny muscles along my shins prickling every time my feet hit the concrete. My breath grew shorter and tighter. I was hoping for him to slow down, to pull onto the grass, but he kept rolling along. Soon my legs threatened to fail me. Strength was bleeding out of me, as if someone had made two small but precise cuts in the backs of my hamstrings. I could see Sean and Ingrid's house in the distance, beautiful in its restrained enormity, and the thought of losing my friend again inspired a terrible panic.

"Sean!" I shouted. "Wait!"

The man on the bike didn't look back, but he sat up straighter in his seat.

"It's me!" I panted, my lungs aching. "Stop!"

Suddenly his feet zipped around, he pedaled faster, and the space between us opened up into an impossible distance.

But I refused to give up. Gasping, I forced myself onward, legs burning, arms pumping, lungs roaring. The dark scenery blurred beside me. I stared at the tiny red reflector on the rear of the receding bicycle and, for the first and only time in my life, I sprinted. It was glorious. I was flying.

Then I felt a pressure in the center of my chest. It was how we describe love when we talk to our children about it. A fullness, a greatness, a noble expansion as our hearts grow to match our passion.

Only I was dying.

Emilie brought Catherine to the hospital against my wishes. I didn't want my daughter to see me like that, pale and weak, with wires crisscrossing my body like the little plastic tubes in which her mice navigated their palaces. But Emilie insisted that with everything that had happened lately, Catherine needed to know that her father was all right.

My daughter stood by the doorway, fearful and sad eyed, propped against her crutches. Roused from bed, she was wearing flip-flops and a sweatshirt over her thin cotton pajamas. It was early in the morning, and the pink California light coming in through the window, though I couldn't feel it, was trying to warm my daughter's feet.

"Hey," I said, forcing myself to smile. "It's okay."

She tilted forward and handed me a card. It was a folded sheet of computer paper on which she had drawn a hot-air balloon.

"That's nice," I said.

"Mommy says they cut you open and put a balloon inside of you. So I—"

Her face crumpled. She was eleven, on the precipice of teenhood and the vanishing that adolescence entails, and the thought that I would lose her soon caused the pain in my chest to reemerge. I remembered her at four years old, her eyes big and dark, excitedly applying rainbow stickers to my clothes with her tiny fingers. She had tried to cover me in them, resolute in her bliss as they flaked off, immediately falling away.

"Come here," I said, raising my arm, and she nestled against me, crying. I rested my bristly cheek against the top of her head. "It's okay. I'm not going anywhere."

For the first time, Sean's disappearance seemed truly inscrutable to me. I knew that Ingrid could be overbearing, that his career had collapsed, that his children exhausted him—Jenna was defiant and bad tempered, and her brother, possibly on the autistic spectrum, required constant attention—but I couldn't imagine unspooling my wife and child into the air like kites and snipping the strings so that they tossed above, wild and unprotected.

Emilie came over and put her hand on mine, careful not to disturb the oxygen-saturation wire that bound my finger. I apologized, again, for putting her through this, and she shushed me with a kiss.

After a while, she left to take our daughter to school, promising to return at lunch. I watched the morning news on television and then napped. I didn't want to stay in the hospital, but medically I was required to remain for at least one more night. Our health insurance only covered eighty percent of the bill, and this accident, I knew, would force us to move out of the neighborhood. We had been struggling to cover our rent and living expenses on a single modest salary for over a year, but now the fight was, finally, over.

Oddly, I felt a kind of relief. I was done running.

Love and Heuristics

It had often been pointed out to Jonah that he failed to do the things that were expected of a man in love. Gawkily adhering to reason and pragmatism, he left girlfriends unmet at airports ("Why would I take a taxi to a place you're leaving?"), he never gave flowers ("They rot so quickly it's a pointless extinction"), he stayed dry eyed during the giddy finales of romantic comedies ("The genre presupposes a happy ending"), and one inglorious year, he bought steeply discounted chocolates on February 15, thinking that his girlfriend, Maeve, would admire his frugality, only to watch in confusion as she tossed the satiny, heart-shaped box into the trash.

"Why did you—oh, right," he said, nodding. "Peanuts." He pulled the unopened box out of the trash. "In fact, only a couple of these have peanuts in them. The rest are safe. There's a chart that shows . . . Here, let me get the cellophane off . . ."

"Don't bother."

"Hang on, almost got it," he said, wedging his trimmed thumbnail beneath the shrink-wrap. "I'll select the peanut-free chocolates and isolate them in a dish."

"I said *don't.*"

Ripping the box out of his hands, she flung it across the living room. The cardboard came apart in the air. Chocolates skittered toward the wall like mice.

"Why did you do that?" Jonah said.

"Because we're done."

"Done . . . celebrating?"

She laughed.

For a moment, Jonah thought things might turn around. She was laughing, after all. But then Maeve crossed her arms in front of her chest and her mouth grew pinched, gestures he had observed before, in other girlfriends, which signaled a critical degree of frustration.

"I've put a lot of thought into this," she said, "and you and me, we just don't . . . *fit.*"

They were standing in his apartment, a basement sublet in Astoria with the fluorescent-lit absenteeism of a discount shoe store. Outside, in the brick courtyard, children hollered as they chased each other around a fountain, their legs flashing past the high, inset windows. "I thought we were getting serious," Jonah said.

"So you give me chocolate from Duane Reade with the fifty-percent-off sticker *still on it*?"

"I've been saving to move into the city and I thought it only made sense to . . ."

"Overlook me? On Valentine's Day?"

"It's an invented holiday," he said, only to realize, as Maeve stormed out of the living room, that this too was a mistake. He followed her angry black hair into the bedroom.

"They're *all* made up. That's not the point," Maeve said, yanking open the top dresser drawer, where he had, a month earlier, after prolonged hesitation, combined his socks and underwear to accommodate her overnight clothing.

"I was just trying to be practical," Jonah said. "Next time I'll get you a more expensive box. Since price matters."

"I don't care about the price!"

"So . . . your grievance is exclusively about the belatedness?"

"My *grievance*?" She paused in crumpling a delicate violet-colored bra. "You really want to know my *grievance*?"

He didn't know whether to answer. As questions went, it seemed both rhetorical and menacing.

"Jonah, a gift *represents* something. It's a stand-in for feelings. Not that you have any."

"Of course I do."

"Well you don't show it. You don't do the things you're supposed to do, or say the things you're supposed to say, or else you do and say them in messed-up ways."

"I'll try to do better," he said. He smiled endearingly, enlisting an ideal smile that exposed his central and lateral upper incisors, along with his canines. He had practiced in front of the mirror to perfect it, particularly the nuanced lip curl that rendered some visibility of the upper premolars without revealing more than two millimeters of gum above the teeth, as the latter would lead to a "gummy" look. Perhaps it was time to brush up on the technique, Jonah thought, since Maeve simply turned her back on him. She kneeled beside the bed and extended one arm underneath in search of something.

"It's . . . too . . . late," she said, her voice straining with effort. She got on her side and dipped her shoulder lower. Abruptly, a look of excitement flashed across her face—or, more likely, satisfaction, Jonah amended—since she now stood with her slim blue slippers pressed together in one hand.

"Look, I don't think you're a bad guy," she said. "But at twenty-nine years old, I can't be explaining to my boyfriend that things mean other things. It's just unacceptable."

Jonah began to speak but then caught himself. There was no use in protesting. He had been here before. This was an irreversible process, the way water molecules altered their crystalline structure when adhering to sand to form cement.

"I'm sorry," he said.

"It's okay." She shrugged. "I don't blame you."

"Why would you blame me?"

"And that," she said, wiping a speck of dust from her eyelash, "is why we can't be together."

After Maeve left, Jonah learned not to underestimate the significance of holidays—particularly ones decorated with hearts—but the sentimental expectations of relationships continued to elude him. He missed romantic cues, he misspoke on dates, he failed subtle tests of devotion. Contrary to the claims of his exasperated exes, Jonah regretted their loss; each dismissal further hurt and humiliated him. As much as he required a certain amount of solitude each day, he also desired companionship and affection, a desire that only intensified with each passing year. By the time he met Cleo, Jonah was well into his thirties, and his few friends, all of them now married and distracted with the responsibilities of parenthood, had stopped setting him up with available partners. Left to generate his own introductions, Jonah's frequency of meeting new women plummeted to a discouraging rate—had it been a sound, it would have resembled the sixty-cycle hum in a tube-type stereo amplifier. It was only by accident that one afternoon the hostess seated him across from Cleo at the Dry Dock, a midtown seafood restaurant that instituted table sharing during lunchtime. When he spotted the book she was reading, the fifth in a seven-title fantasy cycle that had gained mainstream popularity after being adapted into a successful movie franchise, he struck up a conversation comparing the books with the film adaptations. To his surprise, Cleo was earnestly critical of the films. Like him, she disapproved of how they had simplified and reduced the books. For nearly an hour they discussed the story lines lost, the characters conjoined, the actions softened. "They cut out all the complexity," Cleo declared, her eyes flashing with delighted indignation. "Sir Hortus doesn't even burn down the village!" After the check arrived, Cleo handed him her number. Jonah took it with bewilderment, astonished that a gleefully shared condemnation would have led to his first date in a year.

Unlike her predecessors, Cleo seemed unfazed by Jonah's eccentricities. She was only in her mid-twenties, which helped—Jonah had observed a bell-shaped curve to tolerance and agreeability, low at twenty-one, peaking at twenty-five, and plunging again after the thirties arrived. In addition, he was careful to remain on his best behavior whenever he was around Cleo. Worried that this might be his final chance, he had sworn not to make any mistakes.

It was a vow quickly broken. One night after they had begun sleeping together, Cleo asked if he would recognize her body naked.

"Recognize you where?"

They were lying in her bed. She sat up against the pillow, pushing away the comforter with her muscular legs. She had been a high school tennis sensation and a promising college player before a shoulder injury sidelined her, and though her daily exercise now was rarely more arduous than climbing four flights of stairs to her apartment, the years of intensive training and competition had sculpted her body into its persistently vigorous form.

"In a picture," she said. "But you can't see my face."

"Why not? Are you wearing a mask?"

"A mask?"

"Like Batman."

"No, not like Batman."

"Sorry. Batgirl."

"No masks at all. Just . . ." She edged closer beside him. "The photo would be cropped so you couldn't see my face. Here." She ran her finger across his throat.

"Yes, I'd recognize you," he said.

"What if it wasn't just me?"

"What do you mean?"

"There are pictures of other girls too. You'd have to pick out my body from all these other pictures."

"How similar are they?"

"Similar enough."

"Enough doesn't mean anything. Which biometric identifiers would I be working with?"

"You mean . . ."

"Skin color? Hair? Weight? Muscle tone?"

"I don't know—all of them. The girls look like me. That's the whole idea."

"And how many are there?"

"Maybe . . . a hundred?"

"A hundred!" He whistled through his teeth. "No way."

She jerked back her head. "Are you serious?"

"If it were out of ten—possibly. Fifteen if I got lucky."

"You seriously wouldn't recognize me."

"A hundred is a lot, Cleo."

"Thanks!" She hopped off the bed, landing on the floor with a heel-heavy impact. He watched in confusion as she ripped the sheet from him and wrapped it around her body.

"Where are you going?"

"What do you care?"

"Are you upset?"

"Of course I'm upset! You just told me I'm totally forgettable."

"I never said that."

"You said you wouldn't recognize me!"

"But nobody would," he explained, stunned by how quickly they had moved from comfort to conflict. Without warning, reason, or fault, he found himself pleading to an emptying bed. "It's an impossible challenge. Identifying one person among a hundred near-identical doubles—"

"*I* would recognize you," Cleo said.

"What should I do?" Jonah asked after the hostess had seated the two men in the crowded brasserie. It was the first time Jonah had pursued a one-on-one social interaction with his coworker, and he was too anxious and intimidated to bother with preliminary civil exchanges. Powerfully built, with a pronounced eyebrow ridge, brutish lips, and noonday five o'clock shadow, Hardy looked like the kind of man who would resolve a problem by hurling it out the nearest window. Yet around the office, Hardy's success with women was notorious, his tales of conquest as widely distributed as the link to a video of a baby monkey riding a piglet, and so Jonah had lured him out with the promise of a free lunch, intending to enlist Hardy's romantic expertise to save his relationship with Cleo.

"Tell me what happened again. I stopped listening," Hardy said. As Jonah repeated his story, Hardy removed the silverware bound inside the black cloth napkin on his plate. His nail beds were the soft whitish-pink of ham fat. "OK, I got it," he said, wagging the knife to silence Jonah. "This is an easy fix."

"It is?" Jonah said.

Hardy ordered a strip steak, rare, with a side of spinach, then turned to face Jonah. "Next time you see her, tell her you can't even imagine another woman's body. Tell her she's ruined you, she's burned herself into your mind—she could line up a thousand women and it wouldn't matter, she's the only one you'd see."

"But that's not true."

"It doesn't have to be. She's not asking for facts, she's asking for assurance. A compliment. Women are as competitive as men," Hardy said. "It's your job to make her feel special."

"Isn't the fact of our dating implicit evidence that I consider her special? It's practically a tautology."

Hardy laughed and shook his head. "It's like talking to a Rubik's Cube."

"That's a silent toy."

Jonah flinched slightly as Hardy reached across the table, but his big hands stopped short and settled on the bread basket. He tore a hunk of warm bread and pressed it between his thick lips. "Right now, in this restaurant," he said, chewing, "there's half a dozen women you could fall in love with, marry, have a nice life together. In the city? Maybe five thousand." His rolled-up sleeves bunched tightly against his forearms as he ripped himself a second piece of bread. "And to each of them, you'd be required to say, 'Honey, you are the only one this could happen with.' If you didn't say that—

even though you both know it's untrue—you wouldn't stand a chance. It's just the way things are. This first basic lie is the price of admission."

Jonah unwrapped his dark bundle of silverware. He ran his finger along the spine of the knife. At the private high school he had attended on scholarship, his financial aid agreement had required him to work biweekly shifts in the kitchen. Too scrawny to carry heavy stacks of plates or bins of food, Jonah was assigned, instead, to stand beside the trash cans where students returned their trays of food and to retrieve any silverware that was carelessly tossed inside. Cringing, he would reach into the deep cylinders and pry the metal instruments from where they clung to powerful magnets glued inside. After the soiled silverware had been fed into the giant automatic dishwasher, it was returned to the stacks. Though the cast-off silverware looked the same, it was different from the other pieces. It had picked up a magnetic charge while in the trash, and when you tapped the end of a charged knife against a fork, the two clung together, letting you drag them across the tabletop. That was how you knew the knife had been discarded.

"If it helps," Hardy said, "don't think of it as lying. Think of it as exaggerating."

Jonah sipped his soda water. It wasn't the first time that he had been given this kind of advice, about the necessity of dissembling, playing along.

"You gave her flowers, right?" Hardy said.

"They just die," Jonah said.

"Not before getting the job done. Give the girl flowers," he said and leaned back in his seat to make room for the arrival of his entrée. As the waiter seasoned the steak with an obscenely long wooden pepper mill, Hardy showed Jonah a picture on his phone of the latest girl he had picked up, a jewelry vendor at a street festival. She was staring into the lens, her arms crossed against her bare chest. Her lips were pursed flirtatiously. A navel ring glinted halfway along her curved, generic body.

"She's very pretty," Jonah said.

"She's *filthy.*" Hardy motioned for the waiter to leave, picked up Jonah's fork, and began to eat.

That night, Jonah bought a parcel of little-necked purple flowers from the corner deli and went to Cleo's apartment. He knocked twice on her door and then stood out in the hallway nervously snapping the rubber band that bound the wet stems. Despite Hardy's confidence in the suggestion, bringing flowers to an angry girlfriend seemed a gesture so clichéd as to be meaningless at best, insulting at worst. Jonah was astonished, then, to be greeted not with a dismissive sneer but an earnest, soft-eyed smile and, after an embrace, Cleo's slightly erotic, approving bite on his lower lip.

Just like that, he was forgiven. It was so simple, so obvious, so unprecedentedly easy that he spent the next week trying to figure out exactly what had happened. At first, it worried him that a woman of Cleo's intelligence would be won over by such a predictable move. Had he misjudged her? Overestimated her? Yet Cleo, for all her vulnerability when it came to traditional romantic gestures, possessed an otherwise discerning mind, and Jonah was soon faced with an even more disturbing hypothesis: Maeve had been right. Love (or its countless approximations) depended on rituals of affection and singularity, and all of the things that he had once dismissed as schmaltzy and fake—champagne with strawberries, couples' holiday cards, pet names—all of these things could *also* signify what they were intended to: adulation. Throughout his years of coming up short, Jonah had never truly entertained the idea that his way of doing things had been wrong. But opting out, as he had for so long, now seemed to him nothing more than petulance, deserving of neither approval nor sympathy. Sympathy for what? For thinking he knew better? When woman after woman had told him—first patiently, then irritably, then icily—otherwise? Abruptly, he was forced to acknowledge the suggested superiority in his unsentimental refusals. Now he understood that it had been his arrogance, as much as his clumsiness, that had caused such damage in the past.

It was Hardy who helped Jonah remake himself in the image of a romantic. Over the next few weeks, he returned to his coworker again and again for advice, soliciting his input for everything from the timing of his text replies to the derivation of a pet name to optimal postcoital phrasing. It was early enough in their relationship that Cleo didn't know him very well, Jonah reasoned, and she would think that this seemingly casual romantic charm was his natural behavior.

But about this, too, he was wrong, he discovered one Sunday morning when he overheard Cleo, on the phone, refer to him as her "sweet little robot."

He sat on the couch in mute astonishment. A cold sensation crept over him, inching along his skin, as if his happiness had been a wet suit, now punctured, into which icy disappointment were slowly leaking.

A moment later, Cleo clicked off the call and came striding out of her bedroom. With a contented smile, she lay beside him on the sunlit couch and folded her thick legs together, gesturing for the paper. Bagels, coffee, and the *Times* crossword puzzle were her Sunday morning ritual, a once-ironic affectation that had since become sincere. Jonah dutifully handed her that section of the paper.

He watched Cleo hopscotch around the grid, having unhurried conversations about the clues. Ordinarily it took great effort not to snatch the pen away and answer the puzzle in proper order, but he was too troubled by her comment to concern himself with correct progressions. While she struggled with a clue, Jonah snuck onto his phone and texted Hardy for help.

Busy, Hardy replied.

Please, Jonah texted. *She told her friend I'm a robot.*

Your cover's blown—time to terminate the human

"Techie's drawing," Cleo said. "Starts with an *S-C,* nine letters."

"Schematic," Jonah replied, unlocking his phone again.

I really need your help, Jonah texted.

Just do something unpredictable, Hardy replied.

Like what?

Be spontaneous

Like what?

Kiss her

Now? It's 10:24 a.m.

Yes NOW that's the point — be spontaneous

OK

Do it until you get her attention then break off and walk away

Thank you. I'm in your debt.

After the robot uprising, I get Australia

"Guard dog's greeting?" Cleo asked. "Five letters, starts with an *S*."

"Snarl," Jonah said and kissed her.

Riding the N train home that afternoon, Jonah came to the unhappy conclusion that the strategy he'd been using to win over Cleo was flawed. Hardy's guidance, though valuable, was too irregular, and in moments of crisis it was reckless to rely on him. What if Hardy wasn't getting Jonah's messages? Or he lost his phone? Equally problematic was Jonah's tendency to respond to trouble, rather than to anticipate it. He needed to learn how to *prevent* Cleo's disappointment, not just soothe her afterward.

Spontaneity was the key issue. He reflected on it all evening and much of the next day, and then on Monday evening he stayed up late modifying a birthday-reminders application for his phone. Once completed, it would randomly send Jonah romantic suggestions between the hours of 6 a.m. and midnight. The application drew from a database of romantic initiatives that Jonah created. He appealed to Hardy for the content in the beginning, but after a dozen ideas, Hardy lost interest, and Jonah was left to source the remaining romantic prompts.

He scoured the Web for ideas, going to dating sites and blogs, surprised by how much effort had been put into the pursuit of endearing oneself to the opposite sex. The pages of romantic guidance and encouragement seemed endless. If this level of industry had been applied to interstellar exploration, Jonah thought, half of the planet would already be living on Mars.

As work-arounds go, the modified app was inelegant but effective: many an awkward lull with Cleo was saved by the sudden appearance of a message on Jonah's phone prompting him to *compliment her shoes* or *ask about her friend(s)*. True, the prompts could be repetitive or, at times, irrelevant. Many websites targeted troubled married couples, and occasionally Jonah would find himself struggling to revise a suggestion like *Give mom a break and take the kids out for pizza tonight!* into something more closely approximating a romantic excursion.

Still, two months passed without incident, and it was just after Jonah had classified his strategy a definitive success when a sudden coolness overcame Cleo. At first, he wondered if he weren't imagining it, but when she canceled dinner twice in a row on him, he knew something had gone wrong. One day, at the office, unable to concentrate, he switched on his phone application and manually selected a prompt.

Surprise her at work with tulips!

He waited until lunchtime and then rode the subway down to Twenty-Third Street. The deli on the corner of Fifth Avenue had an enormous selection of fresh cut flowers but, inexplicably, no tulips, and Jonah deliberated for ten minutes, unable to choose a replacement, before asking the short Hispanic woman behind the counter which flowers she preferred. She pointed to a black plastic cylinder full of sunflowers and then put a tiny piece of carrot cake in her mouth.

In her office, Cleo took the flowers from him with a tired smile and kissed him on the cheek. She worked for her mother, curating art purchases for large corporations; she'd once taken him on a citywide tour of skyscraper lobbies to show him a series of bulky indecipherable sculptures. Jonah suggested they get lunch but she told him she had too much to do.

"We could eat quickly," he said. "Eating itself doesn't take very much time."

"Sorry, it's just too crazy today. But I'll walk you back to the subway." She lifted a sweater from her chair and accompanied him downstairs. They walked along Twenty-Fifth Street until they came to Madison Square Park. Men and women were strolling along the curving pathways beneath the trees, admiring the vibrant eruptions of leaves overhead. It was mid-November, when the entire city makes one final desperate lunge for beauty before surrendering to the cold dark months ahead.

"Thank you for the flowers," she told Jonah at the top of the stairs to the N train.

"Unexpected, right?"

She nodded, and then did something unfamiliar with her eyes that he couldn't quite interpret but he thought might be admiration. Proud of his ability to please her, he boasted, "I improvised the sunflowers. I was supposed to get tulips but the deli had run out of them."

"Supposed to?"

"Tulips were the original suggestion. I modified it—on the fly, no less."

"Suggestion from who?"

A man wearing headphones bumped into Jonah's arm, spilling soda onto the cuff of his shearling coat.

"No!" Jonah spun around but the offender was already gone. The city was in a state of perpetual replacement. "My coat is ruined," he said, shaking the wet cuff with disbelief. "Soda won't come out of sheepskin."

"Jonah, who told you to bring me flowers?"

"No one told me," he said, hopelessly blotting at his sleeve with a tissue. "It was a suggestion."

"By who?"

"By me."

"Tell me the truth."

"I *am* telling you the truth. I created a database of suggestions and the app sends them to me at random times." He carefully tucked the soiled tissue back into its plastic wrapper.

"You created a database for me?"

He smiled, realizing only now how romantic it sounded. Why had he been so insistent on hiding it from her? He was like a poet writing his lover a sonnet.

"What's in the database?" Cleo said.

"Everything. Flowers. Observations. Compliments." He squinted as the sunlight cut below a maple bough to blind him.

"You can't automate romance."

"Oh, it's not like that. It's like . . . how you suggest art for companies to buy."

He reached out and tucked a few wild strands of hair behind her ear.

"It's a nice thing," he said. "I'm not describing it right."

Cleo broke up with him on Sunday. From her apologetic explanation—he was reliable and sincere but predictable—she might have been describing a toaster oven. Jonah argued with her decision, citing numerous instances of spontaneity, and out of sheer persistent pleading, he managed to extract the promise of one final dinner together the following Saturday. Though he hadn't presented it as an audition, that was obviously its purpose, and on Monday morning he rushed into Hardy's office, desperate for his assistance.

But Hardy was unwilling to help.

"This is an emergency," Jonah begged.

Hardy ignored him and continued typing. Wedged into the narrow slot beneath his desk, with just his oversized torso visible, he looked like a gorilla in Brooks Brothers.

"I just need to know what to *say.* If I can make it to dessert without saying the wrong thing, then I can give her her highly romantic early Christmas present—"

Hardy grunted and slapped at the keyboard.

"—then for New Year's we go to Paris, the most romantic city in the world—if mid- and late-nineties romantic comedies are to be trusted—"

"Wait, what?" Hardy looked up from his monitor. "You're taking her to Paris?"

"That's her Christmas present."

"You can't take Cleo to Paris."

"Why? What's wrong with Paris?" Jonah worried. "I could switch to London, I suppose. Or is exotic better? I looked into Fiji, it was very pricey—"

"No, no," Hardy said, shaking his head. "No Paris, no London, no Fiji—no trips. They're not going to help. It's over. Save your money." He reached for the mouse and woke it with his index finger. "Now get out. I have a model to finish."

Jonah peeked over the desk at Hardy's second screen. Hardy was a slow and inelegant financial-model builder. For Jonah, who proudly never touched a mouse while working with Excel, it was painful to watch someone click away at a menu bar.

"You can't automatically resculpt debt payment in a cash flow transaction model," Jonah said.

"I'm not."

"Yes, you are," Jonah said, pointing at F-27. "Right here. It masks the credit quality of the transaction. And it's a circular argument." He took out his phone and opened a note-taking application. "What do I say to Cleo at the start of dinner? That's where I most need your help. Do I address the split or just act like it never happened? If you could put together ten possible conversational openings—"

Hardy scowled and rose up out of his seat. His body seemed to expand in the space between them like a deadly gas.

"Five conversational openings?" Jonah said. "Get the fuck out."

"Okay," Jonah said, backing away from the desk. "You can email me your suggestions later."

Hardy's unwillingness to help was frustrating but not entirely surprising to Jonah. He had watched enough sentimental movies with Cleo—*prompt: Rent a film with the word "sister," "best friend," and/or "petticoats" in the title!*—to be familiar with the complaint of women abandoning their friends for men. Whereas months earlier Jonah had spoken with Hardy almost every day to solicit advice, a week might now pass without a word between them. Surely Hardy resented Jonah for his inconstancy. In fact, Jonah realized belatedly, *that* was why Hardy had seemed so uncomfortable at Cleo's Halloween party, when Jonah had introduced them.

He gave Hardy the workweek to recover from his perceived slight and then, on Saturday, he set off for Hardy's apartment. It was a simple plan. He would mend their friendship by taking Hardy out for lunch at a popular gastropub he had discovered while Googling "male upper east side fun activities heterosexual." Over duck-fat confit sliders, Hardy would provide Jonah with persuasive and charming talking points for that evening's dinner with Cleo.

Exiting the subway station on East Eighty-Sixth Street, he called to ensure that Cleo was on schedule to meet him at the southeast corner of Central Park at 6 p.m. He had designed an evening of overwhelming romance by running a regression analysis on the data from forty-six "best dates" articles.

"I don't think this a good idea," Cleo said.

He stepped back from the edge of the curb as a cyclist whipped past. They had been multiplying throughout the city like metallic wasps, ferocious and oblivious.

"But everything's set up," he said. "I have a whole night planned."

"I don't want a whole night, Jonah."

"You'll really like it. I guarantee it."

"I think it's better to leave things as they are."

"Wait, no, wait." He scrambled to think. "Just . . . give me ten minutes. After ten minutes, if you're having a nice time, then you can choose to stay another ten minutes. And when those ten minutes are up, you can decide if you want to stay for the next ten. If you don't, that's the end of it, I won't say another word or bother you again. But don't I deserve ten minutes?"

Cleo sighed. "Fine. Ten minutes."

"Excellent! I'll meet you at the park. And wear a scarf, it's gotten very chilly—" but she had already hung up.

He slipped his phone into the front left pocket of his jeans, where he always kept it—a faded rectangle had been worn into the distressed material—and hunching his shoulders against the wind, he set off for Second Avenue and Eighty-Eighth Street. He'd never been to Hardy's apartment, but the work directory included employee residences. The building was a four story prewar walk-up situated between a Russian cobbler and a slender coffee shop with windows misted up from the breath of its elderly patrons. Steps led to a heavy glass door that had been propped open half an inch by a free weekly newspaper.

Jonah went inside. At the end of the third floor, he located Hardy's apartment. He could hear a television playing behind the door. A stocky man in his late twenties answered Jonah's knock. He had a pressed-up nose that gave him a slightly piggish appearance.

"Yeah?" he said.

"Is this Hardy's apartment?"

"I'm his roommate," the man said. He scratched at his ear. Jonah noticed what looked like shaving cream on his ear lobe. "Hardy's not home."

"Will he be back soon?"

"Who are you?"

"Jonah." When the roommate failed to react, Jonah added, "A friend from work." In the living room, the television announced the release of a luxury car that claimed to be both excitingly different from and reassuringly familiar to all of the other models that had preceded it.

"He was out all night," Hardy's roommate said. "He'll probably be rolling home soon. Just text him."

"I want to surprise him. I've become a much more spontaneous person," Jonah said. "I'll do some Christmas shopping and come back in an hour. There's a store nearby, Eighty-Fourth and Madison, that sells fancy women's hats."

"That's cool. I always forget to get my mom a Christmas present."

"Oh, it's not for my mom," Jonah said with surprise. "It's for my girlfriend. Well, technically ex-girlfriend—"

"All right, good luck," the roommate said, and began to shut the door.

"Wait!" John stuck his foot in to keep the door from closing. "Is a hat an unromantic gift?"

Hardy's roommate eyed him through the gap. "What?"

"Obviously context has to be considered. This hat is from the BBC adaptation of Jane Austen's *Emma.*" He took out his phone to share the screenshot he'd taken of the sassy-yet-sensitive heroine whose wardrobe Cleo had expressed admiration for while they'd watched. "I'm recreating the entire outfit for her. What do you think? Romantic?"

"I'm . . . sure she'll like it."

"It has to be *perfect.* She can't just like it. She has to swoon. I've only got one chance to win her back. So, with that in mind . . . do you think she'll be amazed?"

Hardy's roommate puffed out his cheeks, exhaling slowly. "Dude," he said, "I don't know you. And I don't really know the situation, all the details or whatever, but I do know that you don't win a girl back with a hat." He shrugged. "Maybe try jewelry?"

Jonah thanked him for the advice and left. He wondered if he should have continued with the Paris getaway plan after all. A week in Paris had scored highest in his best-date analysis, but out of respect for Hardy's real-world expertise, he'd canceled the tickets.

He crossed over to Madison Avenue and walked southward among the boutiques. Almost every block housed a jewelry store and, meticulously, Jonah entered each one. The expense of the beauty on display was tremendous; the contract between devotion and sacrifice had never seemed so explicit. At the ninth shop, a boutique specializing in vintage jewelry, a reedy salesgirl resembling an exclamation point persuaded him to buy a twenty-carat pendant with black onyx in sterling silver. "This would make any woman happy," she said as she took Jonah's credit card.

With his hands tucked into his overcoat pockets for warmth, Jonah headed back toward Hardy's apartment. He had placed the small box in the inside pocket of his coat, and every few steps he would free his right hand and lightly pat his chest to confirm the pendant's presence. On the southeast corner of Eighty-Eighth Street, while Jonah was comfortingly tapping his chest again, a taxi pulled up outside of Hardy's building. It paused midway between the avenues, its red hazard lights flashing. Hardy climbed out. He was cool and unhurried, his cheeks unshaven, his eyes concealed behind sunglasses. He looked like a man who wore cologne and drank scotch and punched people in the stomach for slighting his favorite sports team. He strode up the steps and wrenched open the heavy glass door as if it were constructed of a material as flimsy as paper, as weightless as hope.

Jonah waited at the corner for the taxi to finish clearing Eighty-Eighth Street before crossing. Southbound traffic was moderate, and the driver had slowed to a crawl while attempting to merge. Jonah stared impatiently at the taxi driver as he crept along, inch by inch. He noticed the passenger only at the last moment, when the driver veered right and darted past him into a gap.

In the back seat was Cleo, sitting with her head on her hand, lost in thought.

Jonah ran after the cab, turning down Second Avenue to follow it, but within a few strides the taxi was out of sight. It had slipped into the mass of cars hurrying downtown, now indistinguishable, one of dozens, hundreds, thousands of identical yellow cabs.

How could he be sure he had seen Cleo? It had happened so quickly. Jonah had caught only a glimpse of a woman's profile, obscured in part by her hand, while the vehicle was turning away from him. This was the defense that Hardy presented when Jonah, surging past the startled roommate, confronted his friend in the kitchen. Hardy's calm and reasonable denials almost convinced Jonah. It made sense. The chances of a false identification far outstripped this unlikely coincidence. But from the sickening cramp in his stomach, Jonah knew that the woman in the back of the cab had been Cleo.

"Stop lying to me," Jonah said. "Just admit it."

"I'm not lying." Hardy shrugged out of his coat and threw it onto the table. "That was another girl."

"It was her."

"Dude, I'm telling you—"

"I know what I saw," Jonah said.

"Listen, I'm tired. Why don't you go home and cool off and when your head's straight—"

"Why?" Jonah said. "Why would you do that? You could have any girl. Why Cleo?"

With a yawn, Hardy unlaced his black shoes and kicked them aside. Even in bare feet he stood a good four inches above Jonah. He turned his back on Jonah and poured himself a glass of tap water.

"You don't even deserve her," Jonah said. "That's the worst part. It's like when zebra finches mate. The females choose males with symmetrically colored leg bands for no reason. It's just stupid instinct."

"Don't call me stupid."

"Symmetrical facial features, a pronounced forehead and jaw, and an inverted V-shaped torso—that's the extent of your contribution to the human race."

Hardy put down his glass and stepped toward Jonah. "You better stop before you say something you regret."

"I regret everything already. I regret ever talking to you. Introducing her to you. You poisoned her. Why couldn't you just leave her alone? Why did you have to pick the girl I love?"

Hardy laughed. "Love?"

Jonah was almost as surprised to have said the word. His impersonation of a romantic had originally been intended to persuade Cleo, not himself, but slowly, unexpectedly, almost inexplicably, love had overtaken him. Bit by bit, the performance had changed him. The sentimental demonstrations had lined themselves up, one after another, like a series of electrons spinning in the same magnetized direction, all of them oriented toward Cleo.

"Yes," Jonah said. "I love her."

Hardy's fat-lipped mouth split into a smile. "Come on, Jonah. We both know you're not capable of love."

It was the smile that confirmed it, that primal act of aggression co-opted by humans and perverted into a simulation of amusement and camaraderie. Until seeing it on Hardy's face, a part of Jonah had been hoping he was wrong. He felt his breath leave him, as if he were a child again, and one of the kids in PE had kicked a soccer ball into his stomach. Dizzy, he looked away, trying to find something to focus on, to stabilize himself. Everything was slipping. He stepped toward the window, where a spider had built a web between the glass and the screen, and leaned against the kitchen counter with both hands.

"Hey," Hardy said. "You all right?"

"I'm fine," Jonah said and staggered out of the apartment. He reeled down the steps, taking short hard breaths. He felt humiliated and naive and unforgivably foolish. He swore that he would never have anything to do with Cleo again. But the thought failed to comfort him. Indeed, it had the opposite effect: the moment he considered that he might never again see Cleo enter a room and turn to find him, or feel the sleepy burrow of her head alongside his neck, his desire for her exploded. He missed her with a desperation that was as formidable as it was uncooperative.

The December sky was already darkening. Jonah walked to Lexington and boarded a downtown train. The seats were taken. He stood in the center of the subway car leaning against the chilly metal bar. He didn't understand why the advent of love had been followed so closely, and cruelly, by pain. Why the merciless pairing? As it shuttled into a tunnel, the vehicle gave off a series of cheerful shrieks. A woman with chin-length red hair glanced up from her paperback. She returned her attention to her book but, a moment later, after turning the page, looked up again. She adjusted her glasses and smiled at him. It was a small, tentative gesture, retracted when he failed to respond. She was a lovely woman, but he didn't care about her. Nor did he care about the five thousand or five hundred thousand or five million women in the world with whom he could statistically be happy. He did not want to be with any of them, did not want any of their possible happiness, all he wanted was the impossible unhappiness of Cleo.

He disembarked at Fifty-Ninth Street and walked west until he reached the corner of Central Park, where tourists had come from all around the world to marvel over Christmas decorations. The air was thick with the grassy smell of horses and the bitterness of roasting nuts. He was an hour early to meet Cleo—if she was coming. Jonah pushed the uncertainty away. She would come. She had to.

He found an empty seat on one of the bolted benches that faced the horse-drawn carriages. Hand-painted wooden signs tacked to the carriages stated the prices and duration. The rides were expensive, and fleeting, but that didn't prevent the long line of couples waiting for a turn. Twisting together in the cold, the lovers rubbed their shoulders and blew onto their hands and stamped their boots. It was growing darker, night was coming, but still they refused to give up.

They didn't want to miss the fun.

I'll Be Your Fever

It was getting harder and harder to bring Stella to weddings. With each ceremony, she had grown wilder, and once-mischievous behavior had advanced to recklessness, unruliness, and outright vandalism. Three weeks ago, at the Penn-Watson wedding, Ted had caught her scrawling her name on the side of the wedding cake with her fingernail, and only by chance had he been able to sneak her out of the room and smooth out the fondant without anyone noticing.

"What were you doing?" he demanded, while she leaned sullenly against the banister of the rented Mission Revival house, the toe of her golden shoe driving into the clay tile floor.

"I was bored," Stella replied, pushing off the banister with her palms. She used the momentum to turn a lazy pirouette.

"I asked you to wait for me for ten minutes, fifteen tops, and then I'd—" He stopped short as she completed a second pirouette, the bright California sunlight slicing through the banister to slash her back with criminal stripes. "Your dress! What did you do to it?"

"I was on the hill," Stella said, smoothing down the lattice hem with both hands.

"It's covered in grass stains. The whole back is—I don't even know if a dry cleaner can get this out."

Stella raised her chin and gazed at him, her pale eyes luminous with defiance.

"They don't need to."

"Stella . . ."

Her petite nostrils flared. "I like it like this."

It was true. Stella didn't believe in perfection. Nor restraint. Nor precaution, vigilance, and certainly not afterthought or regret. Stella believed in Stella, first and foremost, and it was for this reason that, on the morning of the Hayden-Waddell wedding, Ted intended to leave without informing her of his true destination. He had stashed his suit in the car the night before while she was asleep, and dressed in jeans and a tee shirt, he waved casually from the front door while Stella sat in the living room a few feet away, watching television and eating cereal with a pink plastic spoon.

"Kiss!" Stella demanded.

Dutifully, Ted lowered his head over the side of the couch. She encircled his head with her arms and crushed their faces together, breathing him in. He wiped the sugary milk-smear from his nose.

"Great. All set. If you, uh, need anything—" He motioned toward Juliza, who was sorting the laundry into color-coded piles in the hallway.

"You shaved," Stella said.

"What?"

"You shaved," she repeated. "You never shave on Saturdays."

"What? That doesn't—I shave whenever I feel like it," Ted said and reflexively touched his smooth cheek with the back of his hand, begrudging its betrayal.

"You shave for weddings. Are you working today?"

"No, no, not . . . I have errands. Business errands. It's not really work." He shuffled backward to the door while she studied him, his hands raised high as if to demonstrate that he was unarmed. "Just watch your shows and I'll see you in the afternoon."

The moment he was outside, he heard Stella scramble around the L-shaped body of the couch. He ran to the car, searching his pocket for the keys and unlocking it in midstride. He hadn't wanted to leave his camera, lenses, and gear overnight in a vehicle parked on the street, they were too valuable, but now he regretted his caution. He couldn't photograph the wedding without his equipment, but if he ventured into the house to retrieve his bags, discreetly stashed in the coat closet just outside the living room, he would run into Stella.

He sat in the front seat, unsure of what to do. Maybe he could call a neighbor and ask him to pick up his bags and bring them out to his car. It was a simple enough request—

And then he saw her. She was skulking along the edge of the concrete pathway in bare feet and pajamas, her shoulders low, her head craned forward. From this angle, she looked tiny and slight, almost kittenish, nothing like the formidable adversary that shared his home.

Fighting back his guilt, he switched on the ignition, pressed his foot to the accelerator, and sped away. In the rearview mirror, he saw Stella's head pop up. She held a hand to her eyes and squinted across the lawn of the apartment complex and out toward the road, searching for him, her darling, her beloved, her captive, her father.

Three blocks from the apartment, Ted pulled over and, cradling the phone in his palm, texted Juliza.

Please take Stella to the park now. I forgot my bags and need to get them from the closet.

A moment passed and then his phone sounded its joyful two-tone chime.

Y do u need yor bags?

For work.

I thot u wernt wurking!!! U sed u wernt wurking!!!

"Damn it," Ted muttered, pressing his face into his hand and squeezing his temples with his thumb and ring finger. Somehow Stella had gotten hold of Juliza's phone.

Y dint u tel me yor going!!! she texted.

It's not a big deal, he wrote. *I'm just helping Byron*

I want to com!

I won't have time to watch you there

Juleeza can com 2!

People can't just go to weddings they have to be invited. I'm only going be-

cause I was hired

Not troo u want to go widout me
Don't be
COM BAK AN GET ME
ridiculous
U DONT LUV ME
please understand
YOR THE WURST DADDY EVER

Ted dropped the phone onto the passenger-side seat to stop himself from replying. Stella's anger had spilled over into a tantrum and no response, however reasonable, would bring it to an end. Only indifference was capable of quelling her indignation.

But first, it inflamed it. Every second, the chime sounded and another message appeared on his phone. For minutes, the screen remained floodlit as little blue dialogue boxes succeeded each other in hasty outrage and appeal, accumulating like pages of a manifesto.

When, at last, the outpouring had concluded, Ted retrieved the phone and scrolled through the messages. There were at least a hundred of them, exhausting in their repetition but inspired, he had to admit, in the variety of their emotional distortion. Stella also showed considerable imagination in her use of punctuation. While she clearly had no idea what a semicolon was for, it didn't prevent her from stringing seven of them together, followed by a trio of fussy brackets and one desperate tilde.

He had waited so long to respond that the air in the car had grown warm and stale. Unrolling his window to let in a breeze, he heard a violent knocking sound coming from down the street. He peered through the windshield and saw a woman slamming the nose of a plastic stroller against the bottom step of a flight of stairs. She had taken her baby out of the seat and was balancing him with difficulty on her hip as she shoved the handlebar with her free hand. The rough, fitful motion caused the diaper bag to slide down from her shoulder and against the neck of her child, whose small face darkened like a peeled apple.

Ted unrolled his window and called out to her. "There's a button on the underside!"

The woman continued to shove the handle as she rammed the stroller against the stair.

Ted unhooked his seat belt and leaned out the window. "Try the green button."

When the mother didn't respond, Ted got out of the car and walked over to her. She was older than he'd first thought, thirty-five, maybe forty, and her bitten fingernails were as ragged as movie ticket stubs. Sensing her uneasiness, and remembering that he was a stranger to her, he drew back a step.

"You have to press the green button," Ted said.

"I already tried that," she said.

"You have to do it while you rotate the handle. Press and then twist. Do you want me to?"

"No thanks," she said, grimacing as she strained with the handle.

"Crank it like you're revving a motorcycle."

With an abrupt swoop, the stroller collapsed into itself, the handle tipping forward and folding into the back. The woman nearly fell over from the suddenness of the motion.

"Oh," she said. "Thanks."

"Sure. I had the same stroller when my daughter was a baby," Ted said. "The big basket underneath is great for groceries, but it's a drag to get the thing shut."

She smiled, her dark eyes crinkling at the corners. It was nothing like the frustrated glare he'd received when he'd approached. But then the baby let out a mewling, fussy cry, and the woman's mouth tightened. She seemed to be reminded, in that moment, of her wariness, reminded of those fearful, suspicious shards that embed themselves in a parent's heart when a child is born.

He returned to the car and drove home for his equipment. An apologetic Juliza confronted him in the kitchen. "I sorry. I have no idea she take it!" Juliza was the fill-in babysitter while Stella's regular babysitter was away on holiday. A short, plump Guatemalan in her fifties, Juliza worked during the week as the housekeeper for a married couple whose anniversary portrait Ted had shot. For the past few Saturdays, she had come to Ted's, where she spent most of the time doing laundry, mopping floors, and otherwise ignoring Stella. Ted had a soft spot for Juliza because she reminded him of his mother, a tiny Greek immigrant with equally broken English and a knack for disappearing into housework.

Waving away her apology, he slipped the straps of the backpack over his shoulders and bunched the handles of the duffel bag in his fist. Then he yanked the duffel into the air and, supporting it on the palm of his other hand, carried it out to the car. After carefully arranging both bags in the trunk, he circled to the passenger side, where Stella was sitting in a white dress, her hands folded in her lap.

"I'm coming with you," she said.

"Stella . . ."

"I put on my dress."

"I'm not supposed to bring anyone. Byron doesn't want—"

"You can't leave me! I don't want to be alone all day."

"You're not going to be," he said. "Juliza will be there with you."

"That's a kind of alone."

"Life is a kind of alone."

She turned her head, gazing up at him. The wide black seat belt looked like a strip of highway ripped up and laid against her chest.

"I'm sorry," he said. "That's not true."

He did not know if she believed him. She was seven years old, and what she thought of the world was a mystery to him.

"Fine," he said, reaching across to close her door. "You can come with me. So long as you behave."

*

Ted had been an involved father from the moment of Stella's birth. He was one of the new generation of men who regularly feed, dress, and bathe their babies, changing diapers and mixing formula with the same ease and confidence with which their fathers had changed tires and mixed martinis. When Stella was a year and a half, he and Stella's mother, Emily, broke up, and an era of allocated parenting ensued. For Ted, this reduced, individualized version of parenthood would have once seemed ideal. What better scenario for a man who had spent his life fleeing romantic relationships because of the ceaseless emotional and temporal demands that accompanied them? Neediness had always panicked Ted, and much of Emily's allure had arisen from her lack of interest in marriage. She had gotten married once before, in her late twenties, to an emotionally abusive film editor, and a decade later what she wanted from a man, she assured Ted, was not commitment but kindness, as her ex-husband's dedication had turned out to be more disastrous than desertion.

The timing of their coming together couldn't have been more fortuitous. They were both nearing forty, with its cresting insularity: forty, when the once great comfort of friendship has been steadily diminished, year after year, by the formation of families. The friends who previously offered vital sympathy, understanding, and support were now little more than familiar strangers posting online photographs of those unfamiliar replacements, their children. Facing this, Ted and Emily moved from introductions to pregnancy within three months, displaying an alacrity to start a family that stunned and worried everyone who knew Ted's history of abandoning relationships. They were right to be concerned. But it was Emily, not Ted, who, only days after Stella's first birthday, announced that she wanted him to think about moving out.

"I don't understand," Ted said. This was, historically, a lie with which he had shielded himself during difficult conversations with girlfriends, but in this instance it was true. He didn't understand what was wrong. They got along well, they were respectful and considerate, they enjoyed raising their daughter together. Except for a handful of times during the first few months when the new parents were short-tempered from sleeplessness, they had never fought. "We don't have a single problem," he told her.

Emily reached for the bottle of red wine beside the stack of BPA-free plastic dishes. It was a habit she had taken to lately, Ted had noticed, drinking wine while he went through the long nightly routine of putting Stella to bed. She refilled her glass and smiled sadly. "You don't want me."

"What? That's—of course I want you."

"As a mother. Okay." She shrugged. "But not as . . . the rest of it."

"We have a kid together. We're a family."

"I know we have a child," she snapped. "You don't have to remind me. You do not have to—I know why we're together. Okay? I don't forget."

She swallowed and then held the wine glass against her neck, tucked in tight just above her collarbone like a shot put. Ted watched her in silence, hoping, like the desperate men before him ambushed by an unpromising conversation, that it would miraculously conclude without blood being drawn.

"It's my fault," she said. "I knew what this was when we started. Friendship. And that's nice. It is." Emily exhaled. "But so is being loved."

"I do love you," he said.

"Not like I need you to. And it isn't just sex," she said, as he began to unfurl his standard apologies—fatigue, overwork, stress. "It's just paying attention." She poured herself more wine. "I overcorrected, I guess."

"If I've been . . . unappreciative," Ted said gingerly, "I'm sorry. I'll do better. We're still getting the hang of things."

"We're strangers. We never even talk."

"Of course we do. We talk all the time."

"About Stella," she said, sighing. "Every conversation we have is about her. It's either nap times or diapers, feeding schedules or play times, which toys are we cycling out, are her teeth crooked—"

"Raising a kid is demanding," Ted interrupted. "We're not the only parents who struggle with finding time."

"But it's all we do together. Parent. And you know it. You know it. I would shut up right now, I would never say a word about this again if just once in my life you looked at me with the same crazed affection as when . . ." She trailed off, starting to cry.

There followed four months of couples counseling and Thursday "date nights" and a prescribed, strained weekend to Palm Springs, and still Ted would not concede. Then one morning, while he was making breakfast for Stella, he ducked into the bedroom to print out a recipe for sticky buns. Emily had used his laptop before leaving for her business trip the day before, and she had forgotten to log out of her email account on the browser. Ted didn't recognize the new name, but when he clicked on Cameron Taite, all of Emily's troubled supposition and abstract dissatisfaction fell away. Ted closed the laptop and returned to the kitchen. Stella was standing on her tiered wooden chair, waving her spoon in a symphonic demand for more cornflakes. The air smelled thick and bitter. On the stovetop, the bacon had gone black in the pan.

Even the discovery of an interloper, though it initially stoked Ted's indignation, didn't persuade him to unstitch their family. In his life, Ted had ruined at least a dozen relationships by blindly reaching out for adulation elsewhere. For the sake of Stella, Ted assured Emily that this was something that they could overcome. But it was precisely his thoughtfulness and understanding, his compassion and his forbearance, that infuriated her. They were the final proof of the mildness of his feelings for her. He could stay in the apartment with Stella, Emily told him, because she was moving out.

That she would choose a man, any man, over her child was inconceivable to Ted, for whom romance had provided two decades of lingering dissatisfaction, and parenthood a year of ascendant devotion. Hadn't they both been disappointed enough by passion, Ted reasoned, not to trust in it? Wasn't that what had first drawn them together, this shared fatigue, and the prospect of something calmer, saner, and gentler? Sure, their family life was dull at times, but what had she exchanged it for? To spend half her days without their daughter in the hopes that a stranger's preliminary interest would continue, along with her own—that novelty would find a way to defy its fate, miraculously providing gratification without end? They were just beginning to teach Stella about Santa Claus, and the notion of a bearded fatso flying around the world invading homes with toys seemed no less absurd, to Ted, than Emily's conception of an all-consuming romantic love.

And so, rather than relish his sudden freedom, Ted resented it. As exhausting as Stella could be already, at less than two years old, he missed waking up to her every morning, missed her high-pitched voice and her grammarless, effusive chatter. He longed for the drumming of her small, serious feet as she hurried from room to room, searching for him, and the way she would tap on the opaque glass door with the nose of her stuffed tiger while he showered. He felt deprived, deserted, and punished, and though on occasion his bitterness toward Emily rose to a level that was as heated and impassioned as she had once wished his love to be, he never gave up the hope that they would one day reconcile and reform their family.

It was a day that would not come. A year after they separated, while driving home alone from a party in the Pacific Palisades, Emily veered off the road and into a utility pole. It was hours past midnight, but the fatal collision was loud enough to wake the neighbors, who, rushing outside to investigate, called 911. On their way to the crash site, paramedics raced along the same cliffside strip of the Pacific Coast Highway that Ted and Emily had once driven in an attempt to lull their restless new baby to sleep. The ride would soothe Stella, Emily had insisted, with its calming, graduated turns, its rhythmic rise and fall. "Just look at her," she had told Ted minutes later, in triumph, as they sped homeward through the black, moonless night. "I was right."

*

With a bag in each hand and Stella riding his shoulders, Ted trampled toward the main house, a big white Colonial with twin dormer windows peeking out of the center of the roof like cat ears. He could feel Stella's weight shift as she swiveled her head to take in all of the property, the acres of avocado trees, the enormous green lawn, the flagstone path leading from the house to the garden, at the center of which fat-necked flowers bullied a stone birdbath. When he reached the cul-de-sac by the front door, Ted crouched and motioned for Stella to hop down.

"You said you'd carry me."

"Just to the house."

"No. All day."

"Stella."

"That's what you sa-id."

"I never said that."

"Well you didn't say you wouldn't."

"Please, help me out, okay? I'm here to work." He shrugged her off his back, flinching when the puffy white tulle of her dress jerked his head to the side.

"Ow! Your dress is caught on my face."

Stella pulled her dress free. "Sor-ry," she said with exaggeration.

Straightening his tie, Ted glanced from the portico to the brick veranda to a cluster of jacaranda trees. Location scouting was as habitual to him as, before fatherhood, smoking had been, and he was considering how the light fell at the foot of the softly explosive jacarandas when Byron emerged from around the side of the house. Sunlight reflected with a buttery shine off his cleanly shaven head.

"Hey," Ted said, striding over to him. "I know we're tight on time. I'll go introduce myself and take the groom party getting ready. Unless you want help with the bride first . . ."

"You said you weren't bringing her," Byron said.

"Yeah, but things got—don't worry, she won't get in the way."

Byron leaned forward and whispered, "Have you seen this place? This isn't the fucking police academy rock garden at twenty-five a head. They're not paying what they're paying to have a photographer's kid crash the big day."

"No one will even know she's here," Ted said. "She'll sit off to the side somewhere."

"I'm serious. I only offered you today because you promised me you'd come solo. I can't have—" He broke off. "Jesus, she's already at it."

Ted spun around. Stella was tugging on a yellow tulip, coaxing it into decapitation.

"Sweetheart," Ted called out. "Please leave the flowers alone."

"It was already loose," Stella replied innocently, holding up the severed tulip by the stem.

"This is your last chance," Byron said. "I'm serious. If she ruins today's shoot, you don't get paid."

Ted carried his bags into the house and, after setting up Stella with his iPhone on a nearby couch, began to photograph the groom and his groomsmen. Ted was a graceful and accomplished photographer, and he didn't know what was more demoralizing: that he was working as a second shooter for Byron, who had the perspectival ignorance of a pre-Renaissance painter, or that he was terrified he would lose the job. His photography career had always been a matter of vigorous tension as he balanced financial necessity with creative fulfillment, but after Emily died and he became the sole provider for Stella, he took on whatever assignment came his way. With rent and utilities to pay, diapers and food and clothing to buy, and preschool tuition and babysitting fees to cover, concern about the trajectory or integrity of his career had become an unaffordable luxury. Actor headshots, high school senior yearbook portraits, second shooter gigs for weddings and bar mitzvahs, pet birthdays . . . so long as it paid decent money, Ted shot it.

There was better, more remunerative work out there, but Ted needed infusions of cash quickly and often, and he could not, like Byron, spend years patiently building a referral network by offering deeply discounted shoots to targeted high-end clients. He couldn't patiently do anything anymore. Ted did everything in haste now, even worry, and within a few minutes he had pushed aside his distress at the prospect of losing his fee—a tenth of what Byron would be receiving—and was arranging a tableau of uncooperative young men in tuxedos.

After a burst of awkward shots, Ted encouraged the men to interact more casually. He brought in a distressed metal bucket packed with ice and beers, and taking their cues from the best man, they lounged around the sitting room drinking and feigning indifference toward the camera. Whether it was the alcohol diffusing into their bloodstream or, as the catering staff bustled around in noisy preparation outside, the realization that they were almost incidental to the day's pageantry, they gradually relaxed, and Ted began to gather his first usable shots. He tried not to reposition himself too much, for fear of reminding the men of his presence, which was why he didn't notice Stella had left the room until almost twenty-five minutes had gone by.

"Hey guys?" Ted said. "I'll be right back. I need to check on my . . . flash batteries."

He slipped out of the sitting room and hurried through the enormous house in search of Stella. He searched the atrium, the kitchen, the TV room, both living rooms, the laundry room, the three bathrooms and six bedrooms—even, to be thorough, the master bedroom, quickly ducking out before Byron noticed him (he was busily shooting the bride and her bridesmaids, tapping at his Nikon D800 with the zeal of a laboratory mouse depressing the lever of a food-pellet dispenser). With the creeping fingers of parental anxiety tightening around his throat, Ted ran out onto the grounds. Short men in black long-sleeve shirts were sweating under the noonday California sun while arranging rows of folding chairs. Ted rushed over to one of the catering staff and asked if she had seen a seven-year-old girl anywhere. The woman tucked her blond, blunt-cut hair behind her ear, exposing a Band-Aid on her earlobe.

"Did you try the arbor? I feel like maybe I saw a kid walking that way a while ago."

"Where is it?"

She pointed down the hill. He ran across the lawn and down a series of gentle slopes until he came to the arbor. It was a sheltered woody enclosure, populated by shaggy trees and a trellis across which grapevines stitched in and out. He scanned the empty space for Stella, urging himself to remain calm. It was an enclosed property. She had to be here somewhere. Unless someone had taken her . . . He pushed away the thought, regrouped. Where hadn't he looked? He'd checked the house, the main lawn, the garden, and now the arbor. Maybe she had wandered back to their car?

He noticed Stella's shoes as he was leaving the arbor. They lay beneath the seat of the two-person swing, the left shoe upside down, the right one atop it, as if they had been kicked aside in struggle. He went over and picked them up, moving with the dull, watery slowness of disbelief. Tiny and dotted with gold sequins, they looked like they belonged on a doll. He felt dread pierce his chest.

"Stella!" he shouted. "Stella!" Why had he waited this long to call out for her? What if, in his discretion, he had squandered his only chance to find her? How could he have let himself be silenced by work in the face of a loss that obliterated meaning? He flung aside the swing in fear and anger. The suspension chain cracked against the trunk of the adjacent mulberry tree as he screamed his daughter's name again.

"Daddy?"

He froze. "Stella! Where are you?" He brought his hand up to his ear, straining to hear above the clanging metallic contractions of the swing's recovery.

"I'm right here."

He followed her small bright voice to the mulberry tree. She was sitting fifteen feet above him, suspended in a tangle of branches and green leaves.

"What are you doing up there!"

"I was bored."

"That doesn't mean you can just . . . You need to . . . " He exhaled with relief. He felt like he was about to cry, and pushed the feeling aside with discipline. "You can't leave without telling me where you're going."

"You said not to interrupt you if you're working."

He understood then that it had been a ploy of sorts, but his emotions, heated and overpowering, were on a ten-second lag behind his intellect, and he was still experiencing the relief from finding her unharmed. Light-headed with gratitude, he promised her that next weekend he would take her wherever she wanted.

"You mean it?"

"Yes," he laughed, generosity spilling out of him. "Now come down. Oh God, I was so worried."

Leaves flurried toward the ground as Stella hurtled from branch to branch, descending with such speed that within seconds she was standing on the grass in front of him, barefoot and out of breath.

"School camping trip!" she screamed.

"Wait . . ." Ted said, but it was too late. Already Stella was pulling him by the hand, up the hill toward the house, where young men waited for him to document the time when their lives had been lived beautifully, easily, and happily, without trouble or compromise.

Ted noticed Maria Russell the moment they entered the campground. She was standing beside the western wall of the main office, her eyes shut against the shower of steady April sunlight. Although her long red hair was distinctive, what made her immediately recognizable among the dozens of anonymous parents from Stella's school was the cigarette in her hand. Parenting was a world of reformed and closet smokers, and Maria's refusal to hide was almost unimaginable.

"What's that smell?" Stella asked, as Ted pulled the car into the visitor lot. Her nose twitched at the cigarette smoke.

"Gasoline."

"What kind of gasoline?" She spoke without looking at him, transfixed by the game on his phone. He didn't mind her distractedness as it made it easier to lie to her.

"Lawn mower gasoline," he said and rolled up the windows.

"Smart bombs! Here we go," she said, rapidly tapping at the screen.

"I'll be right back," Ted said. "I need to check us in."

Stella shifted her hips in the passenger seat, scowling at the events on screen. She stomped her bare feet against the dashboard but then, abruptly, smiled. "Yeah! Ha ha! Do you guys like to get killed? Because I like killing you."

Ted closed the car door behind him and followed the gravel path up toward the main office. To avoid legal issues, the camping trip was classified as an unofficial school event, but it had the attendance of an official one, and families from Stella's school nearly took over the three-hundred-acre campground for the weekend. Ted nodded at a familiar-looking middle-aged couple as they exited the main office, and then he stood in line behind a man wearing a biking helmet large enough to protect the skull of a bull elephant. The office had either been a stylish hunting cabin once, or been renovated to resemble one; it was unclear whether the upscale resort had originated in luxury or been upgraded to appeal to wealthy Southern California campers who demanded smartly furnished cabins, a heated swimming pool, and a mini-market with organic produce. Ted handed over his credit card with the usual trepidation. He could not afford this weekend, but the thought of disappointing Stella—who had missed the previous two annual trips—had convinced him to follow through on his promise. Though she was only seven years old, she had already remarked upon the difference between her life and those of her classmates, children who did not need to win a district lottery to attend the charter school because their parents could afford the grand mortgages in their affluent neighborhoods. Stella had made discreet comments, curious rather than critical, observations about swimming pools and backyard trampolines, horse-riding lessons and people hired to walk dogs. While Ted didn't get the sense that his daughter felt any real deprivation, he knew that her disappointment was on the horizon, five or six years off, when the choices a parent has made become evident, and all that was once in the background, the blurry world of adulthood, sharpens into the foreground.

On his way back to the car he came across Maria again. She had stepped off the path and was crouched above a pile of leaves, pointing her phone at it. She moved the device with exactitude, as if slotting it into an opening. From the inelegant splay of her hips as she straddled her subject, he understood that she thought she was alone. It was a temptation, this discovery of privacy, and whereas years ago he would have watched as long as permitted, now he gently scuffed the gravel with his shoe. Maria didn't change position—she expressed no noticeable recognition of having heard him—but a subtle change came over her, as if the light had shifted in a room. She remained where she was but they both knew. It was a performance now.

"What area did you get assigned?" she said, standing up and sliding her phone into the back pocket of her jeans.

"I'm not sure." He unfolded the photocopied map given to him, along with a parking pass and the key, and searched for the highlighted swatch. "P."

"P? There's a P?"

"Here," he said, and held out the map.

She took it. Her hands were elegant, with slim ringless fingers and prominent white moons on the nail beds. She ran her index finger along the edge of the map. "That's the . . . yurt section?"

"I reserved last minute," Ted said apologetically, though the assignment had less to do with belatedness than with expense. Yurts cost half what the cabins did.

"I've always wondered about them. There's only a few and no one ever tries them." She surrendered the map. "I'm Maria, by the way."

"Ted. We met before actually."

"I wasn't sure if you remembered. There's a lot of parents."

"You're the smoker," he said.

She smiled. "Just the way a girl wants to be remembered."

"Better than being the yurt guy."

A second before the collision he heard the whirring thrum of corduroy pant legs rubbing together, but the familiar sound was so out of place as to be unrecognizable, and as a consequence Ted failed to heed the warning. Stella slammed into him with her arms outflung and her head tucked to the side. Ted staggered forward, almost falling into Maria.

"You left me in the car!"

"Stella!" he shouted, reaching down to break her grip. He turned and hoisted her into the air by the armpits, as if she were a cat. She swung her hips forward and hooked her heels around his back, pulling him toward her.

"I looked up and you were gone!"

"I told you I was checking us in," he said.

"No you didn't!"

"You must not have heard me because you were playing your game."

"You should have taken me with you!"

"Stella, honey, it was for five minutes. I could see the car the whole time."

This seemed to calm her. She went limp in his arms, and he set her down on the ground. She rested the side of her head against his hip and glared up at Maria.

"Are you the gardener?"

"I'm Allison's mom," Maria said. "Do you know Allison? She's in third grade, in Mrs. Dickinson's class."

Stella shook her head.

"She's at the play structure with some of her friends from school. They're having a lot of fun. It's section D. Do you want me to show you on the map where that is?"

"No," Stella replied.

Maria laughed. "I should head back anyway. See you guys at dinner."

As he drove through the resort, Ted honked before every turn, scattering startled children to the sides of the road. Outside of the cabins, families unloaded their cars. Mothers carried pillows and blankets and backpacks, while fathers unhitched bicycles and requisitioned neighbors to help them with the heavy coolers, lifting them in pairs like pallbearers. Beyond the cabins was a brief meadow, and then the yurts appeared, conical and white, arranged on alternating sides of a garrulous brook.

"A teepee!" Stella screamed. He winced at her shriek—a dull headache had set in halfway through the drive—but he was grateful for her enthusiasm. Inside the yurt, while Ted unpacked, Stella ran her hands back and forth along the canvas walls like a harpist. "Let's go to the river!" she shouted.

"Why don't you head down to the playground instead," Ted said. He removed his laptop from its sleeve and plugged the cord into an outlet, then lay with his computer on the firm, tobacco-colored bed. It was a small but beautiful space, with the endearing simplicity of a woman walking naked into the kitchen at night to get a glass of water.

"But the river's so close," Stella said. "It's right outside."

"Honey, I have work to do." He had planned on photoshopping a series of overdue headshots while Stella was running around with friends.

"It'll be fun," Stella said. "We can be pirates."

"All of your friends are here."

"But I want to play with you."

"We came here so you could spend time with your friends, not with me."

"Please? Just for a little bit? Just fifteen minutes."

"I have work—"

"Fifteen minutes and then I'll leave you alone. I won't bother you again."

"I can't just—"

"Ten minutes."

"It's important that I get this work done."

"I'm important too."

"Yeah, but—"

"Five minutes. Okay? What's five minutes?"

He hesitated. It was only for a moment, but a single second of indecisiveness was all it took with Stella. She rushed over and flung herself into his arms. Laughing with triumph, she burrowed her forehead happily into his right eye socket. He put his hands up, shielding himself from the frizzy spurs of her hair as she howled with excitement. Her pleasure was overwhelming, rampant, irresistible; it had the potency of righteousness, the conviction of success.

Half an hour later, while following Stella in a complex hopscotch sequence across the brook, Ted slipped on a stone. He spun and fell on his side with a thud, his shin crashing into a rotted log. He lay in the brook, stunned, as the cold water ran over his body. From the shell of the split log, a column of black ants streamed toward the bank.

He dragged himself out of the water and staggered back toward their yurt to change into dry clothes. Stella walked a few feet behind him, apologizing. "It's not your fault," he told her. He was angry with himself, both for his clumsiness and his relentless capitulation, and it kept him from issuing a convincing reassurance. How had he ended up here?

They arrived early for dinner, overestimating how long the walk to the picnic site would take. The sun was going down. A few parents were drinking wine out of coffee mugs while the caterers set up the buffet. Ted's headache had worsened. The pain from his bruised shin and hip seemed to be radiating outward throughout his body: his back, his shoulders, even his throat had begun to hurt. He huddled on the edge of a picnic table bench, watching Stella play in the nearby clearing with her friends. Their games were continuous, elastic, unvictoried. When a man rang a bell to announce that the buffet was ready, the children looked over but didn't stop what they were doing.

He ran into Maria at the dessert table. She was wearing glasses with a prominent curve at the top outer edge. She held a plastic plate with chocolate chip cookies in each hand and was balancing a third plate on her forearm like a waitress. The smell of cigarette smoke clung to her, a bitter yet pleasant odor that made him think of midnight and youth and redeemable mistakes.

"It's for the table," she said. "They're not all for me."

"Didn't see a thing."

"I like your enabling," she said. "Come hang out with us. Unless you're still eating?"

He joined her table, seating himself between Maria and a lean brunette pouring red wine into cups. It was a small, rowdy group, marked by the happy unruliness of parents getting drunk with their children safely nearby. Jeff and Paul, whose adopted son was in Stella's class, talked about how their son had once required his babysitter to watch him go to the bathroom.

"It was the only way he'd poop," Jeff said.

"I mean the only way," Paul said.

"And so I tell him, 'You need to get over it,'" Jeff said. "'Because this habit's going to get a lot more expensive when you're thirty-five.'"

They drank and told stories of the absurd indignations, negotiations, and humiliations of parenthood. Their own childhoods had been ruled by decree, and now that it was their reign, they had forsworn autocracies, choosing instead to govern sassy republics rife with lobbying and strikes. The sleeves of Maria's sweater had a hole for her thumbs, and when she laughed, she brought her hands up to her mouth, resting her exposed thumbs under her chin. The lean brunette poured Ted more wine. He was enjoying himself, despite the ache spreading throughout his body, and when the bonfire was lit and everyone left the table to toast s'mores, he followed Maria to the edge of the woods. She lit a cigarette and tilted her head back slightly before exhaling upward into the night.

"Do you want one?" she said, reaching into her purse.

Ted hesitated. "No," he said.

She kept her hand where it was. "Are you sure? Because that's the yessiest no I've ever heard."

"Just one," he said.

He leaned into her cupped hands as she lit the cigarette for him. He hadn't smoked since Stella was a toddler, and the easy, familiar flush of pleasure inspired alternating waves of comfort and guilt.

It was dark on the border of the clearing, and the trees further shadowed their bodies. To the children swarming around the bonfire, he was almost invisible. Ted craned his head forward, squinting out toward the distant fire, then retreated a step.

"I can't tell if you're hiding or trying to get caught," Maria said.

Ted shrugged. "Stella just . . . likes to know where I am."

Maria drew on her cigarette. She held it on the right side of her mouth, as if she were kissing the corner of someone's lips.

"So where are you?" she said.

He woke in the middle of the night in panic. He threw off the blanket and lurched out of the yurt. He was drenched in sweat. His thighs shook. He made it three steps toward the communal toilet before his stomach cramped and dragged him to the ground. On his hands and knees, he vomited red wine in a burst of explosive hot splashes. Then he felt hard dirt on his left cheek. He understood that he was lying down. The fact seemed irrelevant, as if it were happening to a stranger. It was cold, and dark, and he remained where he was, unwilling to move, until he heard Stella's scared voice calling for him from inside the yurt.

Forcing himself upright, he staggered back to the entrance. "I'm right here," he mumbled. He pulled the flap shut behind him and swayed across the floor toward the bed. He tried to strip the sweat-soaked sheets but his fingers kept slipping on the elastic. It was an impossible effort. He gave up, passing out on the half-exposed mattress.

When he woke again, he was shivering uncontrollably. A terrible cold had seized him. His entire body rattled in response, as if he were being shaken in a giant fist. Through the domed skylight, the sun blazed impotently down on him. He reached for the blanket and pulled it across his chest. The simple movement exhausted him. Whatever had claimed him in the middle of the night had redoubled its attack.

Stella padded across the floor. He couldn't see her, but he could hear her beside him, shifting her weight from one foot to the other.

He didn't realize he had fallen asleep again until he reopened his eyes to dimness. The sun had shifted position in the sky, and the light now entering was dull from the touch of clouds. Despite this, his body was inflamed. Sweat slicked his skin. His tee shirt was soaked. He struggled to kick aside the blanket and the knotted sheets, feebly cycling his legs. The air felt mercifully cool on his bare feet and shins.

He sat up slowly. Stella lay curled at the foot of the bed with his phone.

"You should get some breakfast," he croaked.

"It's too late," Stella said.

"What time is it?"

"One thirty-seven."

Ted struggled to inhale. His breathing felt woolen and labored, as if strands of yarn, rather than air, were being pulled through his lungs. He knew that his illness had nothing to do with last night, but with his child neglected all day, he couldn't help but feel ashamed of his pursuit of pleasure.

"They serve lunch until two," he said.

Stella didn't answer.

"It's just down the path." He coughed, grimacing. "Same place as last night."

"I'm not hungry."

"You need to eat."

"I don't want to go."

"Please," he croaked. "You need to eat."

"I want to stay here with you."

She crawled up the bed and nosed against him, rubbing her forehead against the side of his neck and along his clammy cheek. He tried to turn away but she pursued him, burrowing into his eye socket. He raised his hand and weakly pushed at her chin.

"Don't. You'll get sick."

"I don't care."

"Stella," he said, "I have a fever."

She smiled. "I'll be your fever."

The heat of her body against his was oppressive. Bunching the disheveled sheets around her like the petals of a flower, she gazed affectionately down at him.

He was trapped. She was everything he had tried to avoid in love, he understood in dismay, every woman he had spent his adult life bewildering, disappointing, and then fleeing; all of the possessiveness and covetousness, the neediness and stubbornness had been incarnated in his tiny, demanding daughter. Only Stella was inescapable. He was fettered to her. She was the one lover he could not evade.

It was his fault, he thought, as she fussily tucked a pillow behind their backs. He had made her like this. He had loved grandly and attentively, while covertly reserving a small part of himself for dissent. It was this secret section where his unhappiness and resentment resided, where he fantasized of freedom, a life that once again belonged only to himself, that she had learned to detect.

Or perhaps she had known of it all along. From the moment that his daughter could speak, what had she been saying except *Wait for me, stay with me, don't go.* Alone except for her father, she was even more attuned to his silent longings for escape than the women who had preceded her.

A flock of noisy sparrows glided above the skylight. Both father and daughter turned their heads to watch their swift passing. Then the birds were gone.

"I'm sorry," Ted said.

"It's okay. You can't help that you got sick."

"Not about that. Stella, if you ever thought I wanted to leave you—it's not true."

She wound a strip of the blanket around her hand. "It would be easier for you," she said quietly.

"You shouldn't think that. It's not true."

"Yes, it is. I'm a holy handful."

He laughed, surprised by the phrase—where had she heard that?—but then, seconds later, he found himself crying. "I love you so much, Stella. I *do* want to be with you. OK? I want us to be together always. I can't imagine life without—" A ragged coughing fit took hold of him before he could finish.

Stella unwound the blanket and flattened it along the bed while he struggled to catch his breath. She kneaded the fabric in silence. He tried to decipher the emotion behind her scrunched-up nose and tiny pursed lips, but then a second, more severe spasm gripped him, curtailing whatever assurance or investigation might have come next. He felt his strength ebb, flowing away from him with a tender, yielding menace.

He woke in darkness, blinking up at the skylight. Night had fallen.

"Stella?" he whispered. "You okay?"

A woman switched on the bedside lamp. Out of the periphery of his dull gaze, he recognized the curve of Maria's glasses. She sat along the side of the bed, a half-peeled orange in her palm. The fragrance of the citrus rind clung to her, binding with the scent of tobacco.

"Stella's out getting dinner with Allison and some other kids," Maria said. "Jeff and Paul are keeping an eye on her."

"How did you . . . Is this a dream?"

"If it were a dream, I'd be skinnier." She pressed her hand to his forehead. "Stella came and found me."

Maria set down the half-peeled orange and retrieved her purse. She removed a travel-sized packet of acetaminophen and tore it open with her teeth.

"Thanks," he murmured, as she offered him two white tablets. He swallowed them with water from a bottle that she held against his lips.

"You could have let someone know what was going on."

"No cell phone service." He coughed as one of the tablets caught in his throat.

"Because that's really what held you back," she said.

He laughed weakly. His body still ached—his skull, his back, his chest, his limbs, even his skin somehow hurt—but after a few minutes, the medicine began to take effect, and a slight yet hopeful restlessness returned to him. He sat up in bed, his back propped against the pillows, while Maria prepared him a plate of saltines and orange segments.

He was chewing with quiet deliberation when Stella pushed open the door, followed by a young girl with a dark ponytail.

"Look who's up," Ted said.

Stella ran over to the bed, knocking the plate onto his lap as she mashed herself against him. "Someone brought fireworks," she told him in a rush. "They weren't supposed to but they brought them anyway and the ranger came and he drove a truck with a siren and he had a dog with him. No one went to jail," she concluded with disappointment.

The girl with the ponytail tugged on Stella's arm.

"Dad?" Stella said. "Can I get a glow-in-the-dark necklace from the candy store? Please? Everyone at the bonfire has them."

"They just charge your cabin," the girl said. She glanced at the single, wraparound canvas wall. "Or . . . teepee."

Ted nodded.

"Thank you! Thank you!" Stella kissed her father on the cheek and raced out of the yurt, knocking over a chair in her haste.

"I'll get that," Ted said, but Maria dismissed him with a wave.

"Don't push it," she said, righting the chair. "It's still early."

She prepared him another plate of food, refilled his water bottle, and left a pile of white medicine packets on the bedside table. Then she pulled on her sweater.

"Where are you going?" he said, halving an orange segment between his teeth. Its juice stung his cracked lips.

"I should let you rest."

He took another bite. The flesh was pulpy and tart.

"Stay," he said.

Notes

"The Flower of One's Heart" includes quotes from Yamamoto Tsunetomo, *Hagakure: The Book of the Samurai*, translated by William Scott Wilson, ©1979, 2002 by William Scott Wilson. Reprinted by arrangement with The Permissions Company, Inc., on behalf of Shambhala Publications, Inc., Boulder, Colorado, www.shambhala.com.

Acknowledgments

I would like to thank Martha Rhodes and Ryan Murphy from Four Way Books for their editorial passion and vision. I'm lucky to have had the chance to work with such dedicated and astute editors (it comes as no surprise that they're also wonderful poets).

Thank you to friends who encountered early versions of many of these stories: Meredith Skrzypek Arthur, Alexia Brue, Darcy Buck, Kimberly Burns, Benjamin Donner, Tim Fitts, Matthew Freeman, Dr. Greg Henderson, Rita Hsiao, Dan Kessler, Christian Kiefer, John Reed, Will Ryman, Sam Sheridan, Susan Sheridan, and Paul Wernick. Storytelling has become a strangely solitary undertaking since the nights when people huddled around a fire sharing tales, and friendship, as ever, goes a long way toward chasing away the darkness.

My gratitude to Heather Jacobs at *Big Fiction* and Elizabeth McKenzie at *Chicago Quarterly Review* and *Catamaran Literary Reader* for supporting my work, and to my agent, Markus Hoffman, for his patience. Alas, I am not the fastest writer.

Anne-Laure Maison, merci de me permettre d'inclure votre superbe illustration.

Martha Carlson-Bradley, copyeditor extraordinaire, thank you for your perspicacity. As for my love of ellipses, I promise to show more restraint going forward . . .

David Daley deserves his own acknowledgments page. He's a great friend and editor, and publishing the collection was his idea in the first place. I can't thank him enough.

Robin Black, David Gates, Daniel Torday, thank you for taking time away from your own dazzling writing to support mine.

The title "I'll Be Your Fever" came from a song by Villagers so catchy it worked its way into my book. The inspiration for the divine Millicent was lavender-nosed Suky, a dog whose abilities to charm were deservedly legendary.

Thank you to my children, Mathilda, Adele, and Roman, who snuck into these pages as soon as they could speak, animating sentences with every unpredictable phrase.

And finally, thank you to my wife, Molly, who is my first and best reader, among the many superlatives that describe her.

Panio Gianopoulos is the author of the novella *A Familiar Beast*. His writing has appeared in *Big Fiction*, *Brooklyn Rail*, *Catamaran Literary Reader*, *Chicago Quarterly Review*, *Los Angeles Review of Books*, *Northwest Review*, *Rattling Wall*, and *Tin House*.

A recipient of a New York Foundation for the Arts Fellowship, he has been included in the anthologies *The Bastard on the Couch; Cooking and Stealing: The Tin House Nonfiction Reader;* and *The Encyclopedia of Exes*. He lives with his family in New York.

Publication of this book was made possible by grants and donations. We are also grateful to those individuals who participated in our 2016 Build a Book Program. They are:

Anonymous (8), Evan Archer, Sally Ball, Jan Bender-Zanoni, Zeke Berman, Kristina Bicher, Carol Blum, Lee Briccetti, Deirdre Brill, Anthony Cappo, Carla & Steven Carlson, Maxwell Dana, Machi Davis, Monica Ferrell, Martha Webster & Robert Fuentes, Dorothy Goldman, Lauri Grossman, Steven Haas, Mary Heilner, Henry Israeli, Christopher Kempf, David Lee, Jen Levitt, Howard Levy, Owen Lewis, Paul Lisicky, Katie Longofono, Cynthia Lowen, Louise Mathias, Nathan McClain, Gregory McDonald, Britt Melewski, Kamilah Aisha Moon, Carolyn Murdoch, Tracey Orick, Zachary Pace, Gregory Pardlo, Allyson Paty, Marcia & Chris Pelletiere, Eileen Pollack, Barbara Preminger, Kevin Prufer, Peter & Jill Schireson, Roni & Richard Schotter, Soraya Shalforoosh, Peggy Shinner, James Snyder & Krista Fragos, Megan Staffel, Marjorie & Lew Tesser, Susan Walton, Calvin Wei, Abigail Wender, Allison Benis White, and Monica Youn.